SWORD OF BETRAYAL

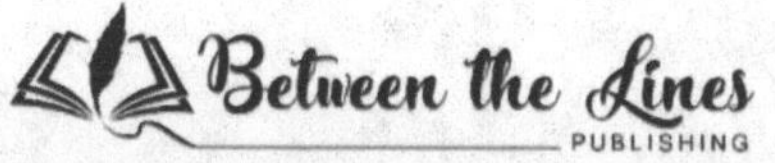
Between the Lines
PUBLISHING

Between the Lines Publishing
1769 Lexington Ave N, Ste 286
Roseville, MN 55113
btwnthelines.com

ISBN: (Paperback) 978-1-950502-05-9

ISBN: (Ebook) 978-1-958901-45-8

SWORD OF BETRAYAL

Robert Evert

PART ONE

One

Edris stalked along the edge of the makeshift boxing ring; bloody fists raised. This was his fifth fight during the autumn festival, but the cheers of the crowd washed away any fatigue he might have felt. It was drawing close to midnight, and people were still streaming into the clearing to see who would win the title.

Brushing the hair from his eyes, Edris gave Cedric an opening. Cedric took it and sprang forward, a fist sailing through the smoky air. Dodging the blow, Edris grabbed Cedric and hoisted the two-hundred-and-fifty-pound man off his feet. Laughing, he slammed him to the ground, shaking the lanterns hanging from the tree branches. The crowd roared.

Slowly, Cedric stood. He wasn't going to stay in the match long at this rate. Edris could see it in the man's blackened eyes. Twenty gold wasn't worth the beating he was taking.

Cedric charged again, throwing a right hook at Edris's dirty but otherwise unmarked face. Edris caught the blow with his left hand, then sent a sharp right jab into Cedric's nose. It wasn't a hard shot, certainly not as hard as Edris could've thrown, but it jolted Cedric's head back. He hit Cedric two more times for good measure, sending him reeling to the ground.

Maybe he'd stay down this time. Nobody would blame him for quitting. He'd gotten in a few good licks and had fought honorably. Besides, Edris hadn't lost a match since he was twelve years old, and everybody knew he wasn't going to lose now.

The referee's count reached seven as Cedric struggled to one knee. He rubbed his puffy face, blood dribbling over his distended bottom lip, his breaths coming in great wheezing gasps. He heaved himself to his feet.

Edris crossed the ring. He dropped his guard slightly.

Cedric's expression brightened as he threw another right hook.

With the crystal clarity he always experienced when he fought, Edris calculated the route the punch would take and then analyzed his best option. He'd block the blow with a sweeping left forearm and then send a right to Cedric's—what? His eye? He'd hate to hurt him too badly. Nose? He needed to finish the fight. He drank five pints of beer before the match and had to get to the privy. Hitting him in the nose might not end it. He'd hit him in the chin, but not so hard that it'd break…

A scowling face in the crowd seized Edris's attention. It was his father, Lord Elros, and he wasn't happy.

Cedric's blow exploded flush against Edris's jaw. For a heart-faltering moment, the onlookers sucked in air, their cheers cut short. They leaned closer. But the punch barely budged his young head.

Lord Elros sneered in disgust.

Cedric cocked his left, but Edris couldn't play around anymore. He had to end the fight, even if it meant hurting his father's captain.

Edris slipped a right jab into Cedric's nose, then came up with a left uppercut. It connected with Cedric's chin, nearly flipping him over as he collapsed to the ground. The crowd erupted.

The referee counted to ten and then raised Edris's blood-spattered hand in triumph. "And our harvest festival champion—"

If he said anything else, Edris couldn't hear it through the shouts and whistles. His muscular shoulders sagged as his father climbed into the ring.

"Sir…" Edris began.

His father slapped him across the face. Edris could've ducked or blocked the blow, but he'd learned long ago it was better to take the beating than to anger his father even more. Besides, the slaps never really hurt.

Lord Elros grabbed Edris's ear as though he were a little boy. If anybody in the now-silent clearing thought it was funny, they didn't dare laugh. Nobody wanted to anger the Lord of Bend, not if they valued their lives.

"Come with me." He pulled Edris through the crowd. "Now!"

He led Edris into the woods. Edris didn't know why. It wasn't as though they were alone. People were strolling by as they headed home, and his father wasn't exactly the type to talk in hushed tones.

Lord Elros rounded on his son. "What the hell was that?"

Edris hesitated. If he answered and the question was meant to be rhetorical, he'd get another slap, or worse. Yet if he didn't answer quickly enough—

"I won," he said, immediately wishing he had kept his mouth shut.

"Won?" the lord repeated. "Is that what you call it? Because I call it a fucking *farce*. Picking him up and spinning him? And don't tell me you weren't carrying the worthless pile of shit. You could've knocked him senseless within two minutes."

Edris bowed his head. "Yes, sir."

"The most powerful weapon you will ever have is your reputation. It'll serve you well with your friends and it'll serve you well against your enemies."

"Yes, sir."

"By the gods!" Lord Elros cried, not caring whether the passing villagers could overhear him. "Look at you!" He reached up and pounded on his son's bulging chest. "The gods made you a mountain for a reason. You're going to be the best knight to ever walk these god-damned lands, understand? They're going to be talking about you a hundred years from now. If they aren't—" The lord paused, his anger growing.

Edris knew what he was about to say. He'd heard it a thousand times.

"And *if* they aren't," the lord said, "you aren't my son. Do you understand? You lose. And you don't come home. You aren't the best; you don't use my name. You're nothing to me. Understand?"

"Yes, sir."

The lord pointed to the clearing. Boys were shimmying up the trees, retrieving the brass lanterns. Workers had taken the boxing ring apart and were carting it away. "What you did back there was a disgrace."

"Sorry, sir."

He considered his son, towering nearly a foot above him. "You think this is a game? Is that it? Do you think it's going to be a game when you begin serving the god-damned king?"

Edris had heard these rants before as well. His father's clashes with his brother-in-law, King Michael, were legendary. Everybody knew they hated each other. But saying *god-damned king* was blood-chillingly close to treason. He tried to calm him, but his father wouldn't let a word in edgewise.

"Listen to me," Lord Elros ordered. "The next match you have, you hurt the son of a bitch. Make him bleed. Break his bones. Cripple him. Do you understand? You make him hurt every single damn day he wakes up. You make him limp for the rest of his life."

"But…" Edris sputtered. "What about the Code? It isn't honorable to—"

"You and your damned Code. Let me tell you something, boy, there is no honor in the real world. There are no rules. You get into a fight, and you use every trick you can in order to win. That's the only way you'll survive. Nobody is going to show you mercy, so you can't show them any. Understand?"

"Yes, sir."

"If you show people what you can do in the ring, your foes will think twice about challenging you outside of it. And your friends will know they can count on you to do what needs to be done."

Lord Elros got even closer to his son's face. Edris's eyes watered from the wine on his breath.

"I want you to kill the next man you fight. You kill him and strike fear into everybody who ever crosses your god-damned path. Are you listening to me? The next man you fight, you kill. Snap his neck."

Edris nodded, not sure if he could live with himself if he actually killed somebody. The fights were games. All of this was supposed to be for fun. But fighting dirty and killing somebody? That wasn't the type of person he wanted to be.

"Look," Lord Elros said. "You're starting your service to the king next year. The job of a kingsman is to kill. That's what you're being trained for. You're a warrior. Warriors kill. Get used to it. The king points, and you kill the man, woman, or child on the other end of his prissy little finger. You can't be the best if you're soft."

Edris didn't say anything. The tirade was nearly over, and he didn't want to inflame his father's wrath by saying something wrong.

"Be the best," his father finished, "or you aren't my son. Got it?"

"Yes, sir."

Lord Elros regarded the villagers streaming past. Few met his gaze.

"When you enter the king's service, you won't be the biggest, strongest man anymore. And you'll be my son. That won't help you in some people's eyes. So, you'll need fear on your side. You need to be able to strike terror into people's hearts. You need to be able to snap their necks and not lose a moment's sleep over it. Understand?"

"Yes, sir."

Lord Elros dragged the back of his hand across his dry mouth. Edris could tell he was craving a drink.

"I'm only doing this for your own good," his father said. "I'm trying to toughen you up, so you'll be the best. I'm helping you."

"Yes, sir."

Lord Elros seemed to search for something else to say. "How are you getting home? Your horse was in the stables when I left."

Hands jammed in his pockets, Edris shrugged. "I was thinking about having a beer or two and then coming home in the morning." Knowing what his father wanted to hear, he added, "The run would strengthen my legs."

"Good. I'm glad you're finally taking your preparation seriously. Though I want you home by dawn. Have your drink, if you believe you deserve one. But I want you home before sunup."

The lord's country estate was twelve miles away. That wasn't too far. But it was located in the foothills of the mountains and, after fighting all day, running up the rocky slopes was going to be a challenge.

"Yes, sir," Edris said.

"All right, then." Lord Elros pulled on his riding gloves and straightened his weskit. "I'll see you at dawn."

Edris watched his father shove his way through the dispersing crowd. He smiled when a little girl flipped the Lord of Bend the middle finger. Good thing the lord didn't see it. Edris knew firsthand his father had no qualms about beating a child.

Cedric limped toward him. "Ed."

"Hey, Cedric. How are you feeling? You look like you could go another couple rounds."

Cedric snorted, holding a bloody rag to the gash over his left eye. He handed Edris a small pouch. "Thanks for taking it easy on me."

Edris checked the pouch. It was his twenty gold for winning the tournament. "I didn't take it easy on you. You fought well. Better than last time."

"You're a rotten liar. You'll need to work on that before you become a kingsman."

"I didn't realize being a good liar was part of the job."

"Trust me. It's the most important part. That and being able to look the other way."

Edris didn't know what that meant, so he surveyed the townsfolk leaving the clearing and waited for Cedric to say whatever was on his mind.

"I overheard your father," Cedric said eventually.

"I'm sorry. He gets that way. If he really thought you were a pile of shit, you wouldn't be captain of his guards. He's not going to sack you."

"In all honesty, I wouldn't care a wit if he did. I'm sure every other lord in the kingdom would hire me at twice the pay, if only to hear me tell stories about your father."

That was probably true. The number of people who valued the Lord of Bend's company was rapidly dwindling.

"No...I meant," Cedric continued, "what he said about being a kingsman."

"He's rather prone to exaggerate. You should hear him talk about his own exploits when he was my age."

"He *does* exaggerate, I'll give you that—but not this time. Look, Ed. You know how highly I think of you. And my face is a testament to your fighting prowess. But your father is right. When you go serve His Majesty, you need to be prepared. Like he said, you won't be the biggest and strongest anymore. And you'll be with men who are seasoned warriors."

Edris wished he had something to drink, then worried he was becoming like his father.

"I mean it, Ed. You're good. Very, very good. But you won't be the best in the company. Not at first, at any rate."

"If I'm not the best..." Edris muttered.

"Don't worry about that. Not right away, at least."

"Easy for you to say."

"I sympathize with your position. However, you need to understand, you'll be starting at the bottom. You'll be what the officers call a dreg. You're a piece of shit. And that's how they'll treat you. They'll push you. They'll push you hard, waiting for you to lose your cool. Especially the nobles. Every lordling and bastard of a duke will challenge you, knowing you can't lift a finger against them."

Attempting to lighten the mood, Edris chuckled. "Hey, those bastards and lordlings are my cousins!"

"They may be family," Cedric replied, "but they won't treat you like it. They won't do you any favors—trust me. Then there's the fact you're Elros's son..."

An inebriated man shouted his congratulations as he passed. Edris waved in gratitude.

He sighed. "Right."

"You'll have to play things smart. You ain't one to follow orders. You tend to go your own way. And that won't cut it in the king's service. If they have you stand all day in the hot sun guarding a pile of reeking horse manure, you do it without saying a word."

Cedric must've caught something in Edris's expression, a hint of the anxiety that had been building in his gut ever since his father announced he had enlisted his youngest son in the military.

"You can do it. Try to treat everybody like you treat your father. Eyes forward. Nod when appropriate. Lots of 'yes, sirs.' You'll do fine."

Edris shook his head, droplets of drying sweat tumbling from his scraggly hair. "I don't think I can, Ced."

"You'll be fine. Keep your mouth shut and realize that once you put on the king's tabard, you aren't noble anymore. You're a stinking, lousy dreg."

Cedric glanced past Edris. Evidently, somebody was coming up the path behind him.

"Thanks again for not beating me senseless," he said as he limped away.

But Edris was too deep in thought to answer.

A moment later, somebody put a tender hand on his arm. Turning, Edris found Beatrice smiling up at him.

"You okay?" she asked, concerned.

Edris touched the purple lump on the side of his chin. "It's nothing. Believe me. By the time he hit me, he was too tired to do much damage. Hey, Brago!" He inclined his head toward the much smaller boy standing behind Beatrice.

"Ed," Brago said in his quiet, almost menacing tone. "Good fight."

"Thanks. Make any money off it?"

"Regrettably not. Nobody was willing to wager against you."

Edris laughed. "Sorry about that. Wait a minute." He felt in his pocket and pulled out the pouch Cedric had given him. He handed the disheveled boy a gold coin. "Here. Get something good to eat."

A greedy gleam flickered behind Brago's cold eyes.

"Hold on." Edris dropped another couple coin into the boy's hand. "Get some decent boots, too. It'll be winter soon."

Brago struggled to speak. "Thanks, Ed. That's remarkably kind of you."

"I don't need it. By the way, did you find a job yet?"

Brago's dark expression returned. "I'm afraid people are a bit leery of hiring thieves."

"You're not a thief," Edris said, knowing full well that he was. "Tell you what—come by the manor sometime. I'll see if we can find something for you to do. The dogs always need tending. Or the horses."

"What about your father?"

"I'll take care of him. Besides, you'll be cheaper to hire than anybody else. He'll work you hard, but you'll make a few coins."

"I appreciate that. Thank you."

Edris turned to Beatrice, admiring her long leg exposed by the slit in her skirt.

She arched an eyebrow, knowing exactly what he was thinking. Edris blushed.

Next to them, Brago fidgeted uncomfortably. He gestured toward town. "I'll be on my way then." His fingers tightened around the coins as he snuck a glance at Beatrice staring lovingly up at Edris. "I'm in your debt, Ed." He gave a slight bow. "Thank you yet again."

"Stop by the manor," Edris called to him. "The one in the country, not the one in town."

"Indeed, I will."

Edris watched the diminutive Brago disappear among the departing crowd, then pulled Beatrice to him. She tried to protest, but not much.

"By the gods, Bea," he said. "You look inviting." He kissed her neck.

"Not *too* inviting, I should hope." She giggled, slapping his bare chest. "Please! Not here. People will think I'm a whore."

"If anybody calls you that, I'll kill them."

Beatrice extracted herself from Edris's powerful arms. "Which brings me back to what I was asking. Are you okay? And I don't mean your various bumps and bruises and cuts. Though, the gods know, I worry about them as well."

"What do you mean?"

"Your father!" she said pointedly. "Everybody heard what he was telling you." Her expression turned concerned again. "You okay?"

Edris shrugged. "You know him. Only the best will do."

"Are you really going to kill the next man you fight?"

"Of course not. To tell you the truth, I wouldn't mind losing the next match to spite him."

"He'd disown you!"

"I don't care. Honestly. I could put all of this behind me and find a job on a farm or in a logging camp."

"Or as a poet?" Beatrice suggested.

He hushed her, shooting furtive glances at the people walking by.

"What?" she asked. "I think your poems are sweet."

"Yeah, well, let's keep them just between you and me."

She rolled her eyes. "Men."

Edris grabbed her tiny waist and pulled her close once more, feeling himself melt into her arms. It was strange how holding her made him feel safe. Wasn't it supposed to be the other way around?

She stroked his shoulder. "What's wrong?"

He tried to think of something clever to say, but the truth slipped out of him. "I don't want to serve the king."

"Don't you have to?"

Edris frowned. "I suppose."

"I don't understand. You've always wanted to be a knight. It's all you've talked about since you were a boy."

"There's a lot of crap to wade through in order to become a knight."

"So? There's nothing you can't handle. By the gods, Ed. Nobody can beat you with blade, bow, or fist."

Edris dithered. "Nobody here, you mean."

"Or in Lower Angle. Or Bend. You've won every contest you've ever entered."

Edris didn't answer. He held Beatrice to his sweaty chest.

"What's wrong?" she asked again.

"Nothing. Oh, here." He handed her the pouch with the rest of his winnings.

Beatrice pushed it away. "I'm not—"

"Bea," Edris said, "I like taking care of you."

She beamed.

They both knew she could use the extra money. Although she wasn't a street urchin like Brago, Beatrice and her parents weren't far from being homeless, and a fistful of gold coins would go a long way.

"Thank you," she said begrudgingly.

She kissed him.

He bounced his eyebrows. "If you truly want to thank me…"

"Oh! So that's your plan, is it? I heard your father. You have to be home by dawn."

"I have a few minutes."

"Edris, son of Elros," Beatrice chided him playfully. "If you ever give me only a few minutes in that way, you'll never see me again!"

He laughed. "Fair enough. I have more than a few minutes."

They kissed.

"You better get going," she said. "It's a long walk."

"I can run and get there well before dawn."

"Even so, get going. I'm tired and have to work in the morning. See you soon?"

"On my honor."

They kissed again.

"Ed?"

"My lady?"

"You can tell me anything. You do know that, right? Anything you're thinking or feeling."

"I'm fine. But…" He grimaced. "It's going to be a long five years with the king."

"For me as well."

Two

For the first couple of miles, Edris ran. The night air was cool, and the earthy smells of the dark forest pleased him. But soon, his legs grew heavy and he slowed to a jog, then to a leisurely walk. He reminded himself that he'd fought all day. But his fatigue troubled him. When he served the king, he'd have to go on long marches while wearing a full pack and chainmail.

He had to be the best…

He was only half kidding when he had told Beatrice he wanted to be a farmer. He liked being outside where he could do whatever he wanted, and although he'd never admit it to anybody—he liked plants and flowers. Seeing things grow made him feel…well, different. The time or two he'd helped the servants in the fields were probably the most peaceful moments in his life.

Being a farmer, however, was out of the question. He'd never met a wealthy man who worked the soil. And having money had its advantages, especially when you ate as much as he did. He couldn't live if he were poor. Not like Beatrice or Brago. How they managed, Edris could only guess. He liked sleeping outside, but Brago slept on the streets or in the woods every night, even in the winter. Poor half-starved kid…

No. If he was going to defy his father, he'd have to be able to support himself, and farming wouldn't do that. Neither would gardening or being a logger. Or a poet.

He thought about serving as a kingsman. His stomach sank.

He could tolerate his father's tantrums mainly because he could always go ride, or fell a tree, or fight. While in the king's service, he wouldn't have such luxuries. He couldn't merely walk away from his commanding officers. Every moment of every day was going to be lived to please the king—a king who hated his family.

His mind slipped back to Beatrice again. Oh, how he longed to spend the night with her. Even if they didn't do anything other than hold each other, being with her made everything seem okay. Someday, maybe…

No, he was too young to think about marriage. Besides, getting married to a peasant girl would only add to his growing list of problems.

Edris trudged up an incline. Through the thinning trees, he could see the eastern horizon turning amber. Dawn couldn't be far off.

"Bollocks!"

He broke into a jog, then pushed himself into a run.

Climbing the last hill, he peered down onto his father's estate. The east guardhouse was a mile away, but the main house was another mile beyond that.

Did he have to be inside the house to be home on time? Or was being on the grounds close enough?

He knew the answer. His father would most likely be waiting for him at the manor door, watching the sky. If he didn't cross the threshold by the time the sun was up…

Edris bounded down the hill, tired feet pounding the stone road. Reaching the bottom, he put on a burst of speed. Up ahead, a guard with a black dog appeared behind the closed iron gates.

"Malcom," Edris called, out of breath.

The guard opened a gate, the dog waiting obediently by his side. "Morning, Master Edris. Out early? Or in late?"

"In late." Edris peered at the eastern hills. A sliver of the yellow sun peeked above the forested ridge. "Could you do me a favor?"

"Name it, sir."

"If asked, can you tell my father I got here before sunup and that we stood at the gate chatting a while?"

"Due back by dawn, I take it…"

"Exactly."

"I don't particularly like lying to his lordship, but if you return the favor, I'd be much obliged."

"Name your price."

The guard offered Edris an envelope with King Michael's royal insignia—a green dragon coiled around a tall, lopsided hill. The seal had been broken.

"It wasn't me!" Malcom said defensively. "The messenger delivered it like that. When I told him to go to the lord and explain himself, he rode off, leaving me with an open letter from the king! Can you imagine?"

Edris took the envelope. "I'll give it to my father and explain what happened."

"You're most kind, sir. I've been worrying all night what His Lordship was going to do me when I gave it to him."

"I'll take care of it. Before dawn, right?"

"Absolutely. If I recall correctly, the sky had yet to turn when you came running up."

"Thanks, Malcom."

"Thank you, sir!"

Edris pet the dog, then followed the road of crushed red stone to the manor house.

Passing the elegantly manicured lawns and bushes trimmed to resemble woodland creatures, Edris inspected the envelope.

It was from the king, all right. The handwriting was all too familiar.

Didn't His Majesty have a secretary or somebody to write his correspondence?

Edris's stride slowed.

The letter must be pretty important if His Highness wrote it himself.

What could it say?

Maybe it was about his service to the king.

His gaze drifted to the windows looming above him. Yellow light streamed through the curtains in the servants' rooms, but the rest were still dark.

Edris regarded the envelope again.

"Oh, hell."

He peeked inside.

The top sheet read simply: "Elros. Announce the beginning of the month. Yours, M."

Then Edris read the proclamation underneath.

Three

Edris placed the king's letter on his father's imposing desk, atop a scattered pile of papers and unanswered correspondences, then sat in the corner.

Would his father be displeased he'd read the letter? It wasn't as though it said anything confidential. Then again, his father only had two emotions—angry and oblivious. Edris had survived largely by keeping his father unaware of his actions. He'd gone weeks without his father speaking to him. When he was a child, Edris was convinced his father didn't remember his name. The lord simply addressed him as "Boy." Unfortunately, now that Edris was going to be serving the king, Lord Elros was paying more and more attention to his youngest son—and it would only get worse as his enlistment date drew closer.

Edris rubbed his tired face.

He needed to blow off some steam. He needed to have a little fun before his life as a free man came to a miserable end. He had to get away from his father before they came to blows.

Edris stared at the royal envelope. Its flap was creased; it had obviously been opened.

Yes, his father was going to be displeased.

Another beating…

Perhaps if he smoothed it out somehow—

The familiar stomping footfalls echoed along the corridor. Edris jerked his hand from the letter and sat up straight. The door to the study flew open.

Lord Elros took several steps toward his cluttered desk before realizing he wasn't alone.

"Edris," he said, surprised. He checked the window. The sun had been up for nearly an hour. "Did you get home by dawn as I asked?"

"Yes, sir."

The lord sat in his chair, apparently no longer interested in the conversation. "Fine. I'll check with the guards."

"Yes, sir."

Lord Elros searched through piles of papers, extracted one, and reached for a quill. He looked at Edris. "Anything else?"

"No, sir." Edris got to his feet, but then thought it would be best to address the state of the king's letter. "That is, yes, sir."

Lord Elros slapped the quill onto the desk. "Well, which is it? Yes or no? Honestly, I realize you aren't as intelligent as your brothers, but you should have some inkling as to whether there is anything else."

"Yes, sir." Edris gestured to the ruffled envelope. "A messenger from the king arrived early this morning. The letter he delivered was open. I didn't want you to think that any of the servants read it."

Lord Elros slid a contemptuous glance at the letter, then returned to the paper in front of him. He scribbled on it, the scratching of his quill breaking the painful silence.

Lord Elros paused, then lifted an eyebrow. "I suppose there is something else."

Edris fought the urge to say *No, sir.*

"I was wondering…" he said slowly.

"Oh, by the gods, spit it out. You are the stupidest son anybody could have. If Edran had your body, he'd be a god."

I was wondering if the letter had anything to do with my service…to the king, that is."

"King," grumbled Lord Elros. Aggravated, he threw the letter at Edris. "You remember how to read, don't you?"

"Yes, sir."

Edris eagerly opened the envelope, trying desperately to maintain his charade. His father watched him read the note, and then the second page. Edris took his time, making sure his eyes drifted across each line he'd read earlier that morning.

"Well?" Lord Elros demanded. "What does our illustrious *king* have to say? I'm sure he has many thoughtful insights on how I can improve my rule."

Edris's eyes reached the end of the announcement, letting the disappointment show on his face.

"It's nothing to do with me, sir." He gave the letter to his father. "It's an announcement about the next Kings' Quest."

"As I thought." Lord Elros returned to his writing.

"Yes, sir." Edris made for the door as though puzzling over a rather challenging problem. He stopped, holding the silver doorknob.

His father slammed the quill again. "What is it now? Forget how to open a damned door?"

"Sir…" Edris said, trying not to overplay his hand. If he said things correctly, he might be able to get away from his father for a bit and have some fun before enlisting. "The reward for this quest is a thousand gold pieces."

Sighing, Lord Elros scanned the royal proclamation. "It appears you are able to read after all. I am so very glad all that money I spent on tutors didn't go to waste."

"Yes, sir."

"Out with it, boy. What is it you want to say?"

"What if I undertook the quest?" Before his father could answer, Edris pushed his idea. "It would be great training before I go to Upper Angle.

I've been getting rather lazy here, with servants cooking for me and tending to my every need. So, I believe I should challenge myself more."

A wave of anger washed over the lord's face. "You'd lose."

"Maybe."

"Maybe?" Lord Elros's anger gave way, replaced, perhaps, by pride at his son's bravado. "Trust me. You'd lose. Is that what you want—to be known as a loser?"

"No, sir. But nobody has to know I'm competing. Anybody would assume I was spending my last year before serving the king exploring and having a good time. They'd only know I'm competing if I win."

"*If* you win?" Any pride in Lord Elros's expression quickly changed to sarcasm. "What do you know about adventuring? What do you know about—?" He checked the royal proclamation. "The Sword of Betrayal? Do you know anything about who it belonged to?"

"It belonged to Prince Raaf," Edris said, praying he was right.

"And what do you know about him?"

"I know the legends."

His father grunted. "Think! If the legends were true, there wouldn't be any need for a quest, would there? Everybody would know where his sword was."

Lord Elros reclined in his leather chair, irritated. However, something in his calculating, slightly hungover stare suggested he was mulling the matter over. Edris attempted to sweeten the pot.

"Markus will undoubtedly be competing," he added. "At the very least, I might be able to get in his way a bit. You know, slow him down. Maybe tell other adventurers what he's up to so he doesn't win."

Lord Elros looked sharply at him. "Be careful, boy." But Edris could tell his father wouldn't mind if the king's son lost the competition. "Don't underestimate Markus. You might have a few inches on him, but he's smart and ruthless. As are all of the king's brats."

"Perhaps, he should be taken down a peg or two."

Lord Elros chuckled. "Think you could do that?"

"I'm not saying we're going to brawl in the streets. But if he and I are both in the same place, I might be able to keep an eye on him and get in his way, like I said."

"You don't get in the way of a charging bull." Lord Elros stared out the window, thinking.

"And also," Edris said, attempting to tip the scales, "I can start the quest before it's actually announced."

"Moron! Don't you think Michael has already told his son what the next quest is? Why do you think the envelope was open? I'd bet a hundred gold that the messenger allowed some adventurer to look inside. Half the adventurers throughout the realms have probably started the quest. Idiot."

Edris opened his mouth, but then decided not to say anything.

"If you get found out…" Lord Elros began.

"I won't. Nobody will—"

"Don't interrupt!"

Lord Elros peered out the window again. Bright sunlight flooded the untidy room.

"You realize you're talking about interfering with the king's flesh and blood," he said.

"Yes, sir. Again, I only mean to spy on him and maybe pass information to his competitors. Perhaps distract him a bit or give him false information. That sort of thing."

Lord Elros drummed his fingers on the desk. A faint smile trickled across his lips. "I'd love to see Markus lose this one."

"Yes, sir."

"You know what will happen if you get caught?"

"Yes, sir."

"Do you?" Lord Elros turned more fully toward him. "I'm the Lord of Bend. How do you think it'd look if my son was found sabotaging the king's son? Do you know what I'd have to do to you?"

Edris swallowed. "You'd have to disown me."

"Precisely. And the king will undoubtedly do worse to you. At the very least, you'd see the inside of a prison." The lord regarded him. "Still wish to proceed?"

There was only one answer Edris could give. Even if he wanted to change his mind, he wouldn't dare. He'd never hear the end of how he chickened out. His father would probably disown him right then and there.

He nodded. "Yes, sir."

Lord Elros leaned back in his chair, appearing almost proud. "Very well. Go talk to Edros. He has a head for these sorts of things. He can get you started."

"Started, sir?"

"Yes, boy. If you don't know anything about adventuring, how are you going to stop Markus from winning? You'll need to be able to anticipate his moves before he makes them. And you can't do that if you don't have a clue what's transpiring."

"Thank you, sir." Edris opened the office door, wondering what he'd gotten himself into.

"Edris."

"Yes, sir?"

"I know nothing about this. I have given you permission to spend the rest of your time before you enlist traveling and training. Nothing more. Do you understand?"

Edris bowed. "Yes, sir. I'm on my own."

"Exactly so."

Four

"Father agreed to this?" asked Edros.

He and Edris sat in Edros's musty study in their mansion at Bend, a town a few hours' ride from Lord Elros's preferred country estate. Edros was Edris's second brother. Edran, the oldest, was the lord-in-waiting and undisputedly Lord Elros's favorite. But Edros also commanded some of the lord's respect due to his ability to master various languages and memorize nearly everything he read. At twenty-two, he was a cleric and was rising quickly up his order's ranks—though this might have been assisted by his father's many gifts and donations.

"He's agreed in his fashion." Seeing his brother's confusion, Edris added grudgingly, "Initially, I had proposed to undertake the quest as a means of getting in better shape."

"And getting away from Father."

"Precisely."

"Then he twisted it into something he wanted?"

"More or less."

Edros stroked his beard. "I don't understand. You have no chance of winning. Maybe after you get some experience. But a boy your age—" Edris bristled. "Forgive me. I mean, *young man*. What I'm attempting to say is, allowing one of his sons to fail isn't within our father's nature. What does he really want you to do?"

"He wants me to make sure Markus doesn't win."

Edros's eyes lit up. "Oh! Yes, I see. That would be more consistent with our dear father's magnanimous character." He studied Edris sitting across from him, wringing his calloused hands. "What are you going to do?"

Edris shrugged.

"Look," Edros said, "if you want my advice, you should forget about Markus and go off and enjoy yourself. Serving the king isn't going to be particularly pleasant."

"Wonderful. Five years of hell."

"I don't know about hell, but you might as well have fun while you can."

Edris clenched and then unclenched his fists. "What about Father? He seemed keen on the idea of Markus losing."

"He's always like that. He'll get excited about something until something else comes along. Trust me, meddling with a king's son never ends well." He gestured to the packed shelves around them. "Read any history book or faerie tale."

"That's my life," Edris muttered sarcastically, "a faerie tale."

"It isn't that bad, is it? Other people have it a lot worse."

"I suppose."

"Just stay clear of Markus. Being around him will only lead to trouble."

"You know how Markus and I get along. He'll pat my head like a damned dog and call me Fatty Eddie. Believe me, I'd rather stay clear of him."

"Fatty Eddie!" Edros laughed. "I'd forgotten about that."

Edris grumbled.

"Oh, don't worry," Edros said. "You're far from fat nowadays. And besides, he'd need a ladder to reach your head!"

"Speaking of ladders, I should've left him stuck in that tree when we were kids. It would've served him right to be trapped up there all night."

"Yes, well, who knows how things would've turned out for either of you had you acted differently. Every action has a corresponding consequence." He watched his younger brother absentmindedly massage his palms. "What's wrong, Ed? This can't be about Markus or running all over the countryside until you enlist."

Again, Edris shrugged his muscular shoulders. "I…"

"You what?"

"I don't know what I want." He gave his brother a meaningful look. "But I know what I don't want."

"Ed, we've been through this before. You have no choice. You're going to be a kingsman. It's your lot in life."

Edris cursed under his breath.

"What exactly are you worried about?" Edros asked. "I would've thought you'd love to serve in the military. You've talked about nothing else since you were four."

"I talked about being a knight."

"And serving as a kingsman for a few years will get you one step closer to earning a knighthood. What's the problem?"

"I don't deal particularly well with being pushed around."

"True. Oh, don't take it that way. You know what I mean. You manage father's invectives well enough."

"I can escape from him. His belittling and snide comments only last a few moments of the day. Then he sends me off running or sparring or what have you. But when I go into the service, I belong to the king. I'm his to do what he will with." He glared at Edros. "I won't be owned."

"Everybody is owned in one way or another."

"Not me."

"His Majesty isn't all that bad. You've met him. He's always treated you civilly. So out with it. What's really going on?"

"I'm not exactly the type who takes orders well."

"You'll learn."

"I don't want to learn!" Edris cried. "I don't want to be trapped for five fucking years doing somebody else's bidding."

"Which returns us to what you really want to do."

"I want to…I don't know. I want to ride and explore and fight and wench and…mostly wench." They laughed, despite Edris's growing anxiety. "I want to be my own man."

"Then you're going into the wrong profession."

"I know!" Edris got up and strode about the tiny room. The smell of dusty books and aged parchment gave him a headache. "But other than farming, I'm not sure what else I could do."

"Farming?"

"You know, physical labor. I'm good at that kind of thing."

"I'm sorry, Ed. There are only three occupations suitable for a lord's son—lord-in-waiting, cleric, and the military. Nobility don't do physical labor. That's how it is."

"I know."

"And besides, you're built for fighting. If you were a cleric, you'd scare all the sinners away!"

Edris raked his fingers nervously through his brown hair.

"You're going to be a terrific knight someday," his brother said. "But first, you have to show the king your worth. That's how things work. Five years of toil and labor for a lifetime of being a drunken, womanizing knight. It's a pretty good deal, if you think about it."

"Perhaps."

"It'll go by fast. Trust me. In the meanwhile, enjoy your freedom while you can."

Five

Edris buried the ax head eight inches into the tree trunk, chunks of wood flying. He jerked it free and swung again. The pine tree quivered. Another blow and it'd bow before him like a defeated foe.

He swung again and, as he predicted, the tree listed to one side. Then, with the cracking of splintering wood, it crashed to the ground. It was the third tree he'd felled since returning from Bend. Not that speaking with Edros had actually helped. He was more confused and conflicted than ever.

Edris wiped the sweat from his brow and inhaled deeply.

He loved this kind of thing. Chopping down trees always relaxed him. There was something about being outside in the sun, stripped to the waist, and swinging a weapon until life's aggravations left him. There was also something calming about the smell of freshly cut wood. Why couldn't a lord's son get a job in a lumber camp? That he could do without complaint.

Edris hefted his ax, preparing to chop the toppled tree into more manageable sections.

A dark dot rode toward him, cutting across the rolling green fields.

Planting his ax in the dirt, Edris grabbed his shirt and toweled away the rivers of sweat cascading down his chest. He strode to meet the rider halfway.

"Father," he called when Lord Elros got within earshot. "Is everything all right?"

The Lord of Bend reined his black stallion to a halt in front of Edris. "What are you doing here? You were told to go meet with Edros and discuss your next steps."

"I met with him earlier this morning."

"And?"

Edris prepared himself for the lord's fury. "Edros didn't believe I should undertake the mission."

"Oh, didn't he, now? What did the learned scholar have to say?"

"He seemed to believe that I should find a better way of spending my last year before serving the king."

The lord's lips tightened, then twitched. "Better way?"

"Yes, sir. He suggested I stay clear of Markus and travel instead."

"And did you tell him my thoughts on the matter?"

"Yes, sir."

"Bollocks!" Cracking his reins, the Lord of Bend kicked his horse into a gallop—not toward the manor house, but toward town.

When Edris entered his quarters later that evening, he found his brother sitting patiently by the fireplace.

"It seems," Edros said evenly, "our father wants you to learn about the Kings' Quests."

Six

"So, what do you know about adventuring?" Edros asked as Edris entered the parlor.

Still stripped to the waist, and covered in dirt and wood chips, Edris collapsed into a chair across from his brother.

"The one who finds the quest item wins," he said with the weariness of a lumberjack who'd felled half a forest.

Edros shook his head. "No. The one who gives the quest item to their king wins. The person who finds it rarely keeps it."

"The other adventurers can steal it?" Edris wiped his shirt across his red face, then threw it into the corner. "I thought that was against the rules."

"There are no rules." Edros's smile turned grim. "Beginning to see what you've stumbled into? Adventurers often die under unusual circumstances. If you're going to do this, you need to watch yourself."

"Don't worry. I will." Edris pulled off a muddy boot and tossed it next to the shirt. He leaned forward, interested. "Maybe we should start from the beginning."

"Fine." Edros crinkled his nose. "But don't get too close. You stink."

Lifting an arm, Edris sniffed. "What? This is what adventurers are supposed to smell like!"

"Maybe one who's been dead a week. Next time visit the bathhouse before coming home."

Edris pulled off his other boot and let his tired feet breathe. "In your line of work, the only ones who sweat are the poor souls begging for forgiveness. But go on. And try not to inhale."

"As I was saying, the kings take turns selecting relics that have been lost throughout the ages or have been alluded to in tales. These can be anything from worthless trinkets to golden statues to ancient artifacts."

"Why would the kings want worthless trinkets?"

"To prevent other kings from getting their covetous little hands on them." Edros took a sip of wine and returned the goblet to the end table next to him. "Ed, kings don't need rusty armor or ruby rings. These quests have nothing to do with the items themselves. The kings are playing a game against each other. They're sending their adventurers out to compete. It's all about honor. And to kings—"

"Honor is everything."

"Precisely. There's nothing more important to kings than their honor. And when you win, you win more than gold. You win favor…and power."

Reclining in his chair, Edris considered this. He was seeing the allure of questing.

"Tell me about the Sword of Betrayal," he said. "If I'm going to interfere with Markus, I'll need to know where he might think it is."

"Ah! Now comes the fun part. Before you can find a long-lost object, you need to understand its history. What do you know about Raaf?"

"He was the eldest child of King Rolf of Hillshire. He was supposed to become king but was killed." Edris lifted a helpless hand. "That's it, I suppose."

"Do you know who killed him?"

"Legend had it that it was his younger brother, Renier. But—" Edris shot Edros a wicked grin, "who would kill their own flesh and blood?"

Edros laughed. "Ever wonder why Edran and I don't get along? If he dies, I'm lord-in-waiting."

"Oh, he knows you'd never—"

"Of course, I wouldn't. But to become king? Let me put it to you this way. How many sons of kings have died mysteriously? Think about that. They have a remarkably high mortality rate. That's why royal families always have a spare to the heir."

Edris chuckled. That's what they used to call Edros when he was a child—*Spare.*

"All right," Edros said, trying to refocus the conversation, "so let's assume for the moment the legends are true. Renier killed his older brother in order to become king. Do you know the circumstances of Raaf's death?"

"Not really."

"This is the crucial part, so pay attention." Edros leaned forward, took a sniff, and then—irritated—pushed his chair further away from his filthy brother. "In a nutshell, Raaf went riding and never returned. When the royal guards looked for him, they found the trail they believed he'd taken drenched in blood."

"They assumed it was his blood."

"Correct."

"But they didn't know, right? I mean, he could've still been alive."

"Maybe. They never found his body. After a couple weeks searching, they declared him dead."

"Weeks? Seems like a rush to judgment, if you ask me. I hope you'd wait longer than that to seize the lordship from Edran."

"I'd wait a full month."

"That's big of you."

"I prefer the life of a cleric to that of a lord."

"Sure you do," Edris said. "What about Raaf's guards? Did the idiot ride off on his own?"

"He had two bodyguards with him. Both dear and close friends, it is said. They were never found either."

"Dear and close friends, my ass. I bet you anything they were in on the murder."

"Possibly."

"So, what happened to his sword?"

Edros took another sip of wine. "Nobody knows."

"Obviously Renier wouldn't keep the sword," Edris said. "It would be a clear indication he killed his brother."

"Right. Hence the name—Sword of Betrayal. That, and the fact people who wielded it in battle rarely won, though that was most likely because Raaf's ancestors weren't particularly skilled at fighting."

Edris thought for a moment, trying to make sense of everything he'd been told.

"So, what do you think happened to it?" he asked. "Take a guess."

"I have no idea. But you can eliminate several possibilities."

"Like what?"

"Well, as you deduced, Renier couldn't keep the sword. And he wouldn't throw it away. It was an heirloom and a symbol of their house. It was close to six centuries old. He wouldn't let anybody else have it."

"I bet he'd bury it with the body."

"So, the rumor goes."

An excitement crept into the pit of Edris's stomach. This was a riddle. And he liked unraveling riddles.

"Where was the blood found?" he asked.

"Nobody knows anymore. Remember, this was over two hundred years ago."

"What path was Raaf riding when he was attacked?"

"Again, nobody knows."

"But he was out for a day ride?"

"Correct."

"That means he had to be relatively close to the castle. How hard would it be to find a grave within a few hours' ride of a given starting point?"

"Keep in mind, dear brother, people have been attempting to solve this mystery for a long time. Everything you've said here has been considered by scores of other adventurers. What you need is a piece of information nobody else has."

"Like what?"

"I don't know. But adventurers have an expression: *All quests begin in the library.*"

"Library, eh?" Edris put his hands behind his head and leaned back. He immediately regretted it. He really did stink. "Tomorrow, I'll ask Father if I can look through his books."

"No. As extensive as our library is, it is mainly filled with copies. You need to go to original sources, diaries and letters, things that were written when Raaf disappeared. You need to find something nobody else has read. Some missing piece of the puzzle."

"Missing piece of the puzzle…"

"There's another axiom adventurers have: *never trust what one source tells you.* If you have something pointing you in a direction that is contrary to everything else, it's probably wrong. Too many adventurers fall for red herrings."

Edris pondered all of this, ideas pummeling his brain. For the first time in a long while, he felt motivated to do something.

"If I were you," Edros said, "I'd go to Upper Angle and visit the king's personal library."

"The king?"

"Absolutely. Kings collect many kinds of historical documents. And King Michael is said to have an exceptional library. Who knows what answers are hidden in those tomes of his?"

"How the hell am I going to get in there?"

"That, you'll have to figure out for yourself."

Seven

Edris approached his father's receiving hall with trepidation. From a hundred strides away, he could hear the Lord of Bend berating somebody for failing to pay their taxes. The stained-glass windows shook with his wrath. As he reached for the doors, they swung open. An elderly farmer emerged, sobbing.

"Next!" Lord Elros shouted.

Edris poked his head inside. His father sat at a wide table, reviewing various reports and papers. Around him stood an army of his advisors, secretaries, and tax collectors. They all appeared as shaken as the farmer.

"Have a moment?" Edris asked.

"Is it important? I'm busy."

Edris shifted his gaze to the men standing by his father. "It concerns the matter we discussed yesterday."

Lord Elros took his meaning. "Give me a few minutes with the boy."

Bowing, the men filed out of the room.

When they were alone, Lord Elros eyed his son. "You aren't quitting, are you?"

"No, sir. I'm actually eager to get started. But I want to get your input on something."

"Since when have you ever asked for my *input* on anything?"

"I haven't done anything this important before."

This appeared to be the correct answer. The lord's annoyance ebbed. "What is it?"

"Edros has been educating me about adventurers. He suggested I go to Upper Angle and snoop around the king's personal library."

"Michael's library? Why?" Then the lord seemed to understand. "That's where Markus will be, trying to figure out where the sword may be hidden."

The thought that Markus might also be utilizing the king's library hadn't occurred to Edris; but seeing his father's pleasure, he played along. "Yes, sir."

"Good!" Lord Elros stood and strolled about the room. "You could say you wanted to research military traditions or stratagems—preparing for your induction."

"That was my intent, sir."

"Splendid." He placed his hand on Edris's shoulder. "Get close to your enemy. Get real close."

Unnerved by his father's enthusiasm, Edris nodded. "Yes, sir."

"This is an opportunity, Ed. You need to study Markus very closely. Note his habits and his routine. Get to know him. Then—make sure he never wins another quest again!"

Never wins another quest again…

What was his father implying? Things were getting out of control.

"Yes, sir," Edris said uneasily. "I'll do my best."

"See that you do." Lord Elros returned to his seat. "I'll write a letter for you to bring to Michael. I'll explain you want to get a head start on your military training and request permission to have access to his personal library. He's very proud of his books. Use that against him. Stroke the bastard's ego. He's the type of man who falls for flattery."

"Yes, sir."

"Send me word as events progress. But be mindful of what you write. No letters are safe. Refer to your mission as 'your preparation.'"

"Yes, sir."

"Finally, a chance to put Michael in his place!" Lord Elros gloated. "He's always so smug about Markus. He thinks he's going to be the next Sir Drake. Truthfully speaking, I can't imagine how he's managed to win as many quests as he has."

"Perhaps His Majesty has used his influence," Edris said, knowing that bad-mouthing the king was a surefire way to get on his father's good side.

"Yes, undoubtedly. Now get ready. I want you in Upper Angle by the day after tomorrow. Markus is almost certainly preparing for the quest. It'll be announced by the end of next week."

Eight

Edris drained his beer in one long pull, then thumped his tankard on the table with satisfaction. Across from him, Beatrice simpered.

"What?" he asked, wiping his mouth.

"I think you're trying to impress me."

"By drinking a beer?"

"Oh, you know." She leaned closer, her hazel eyes glinting in the lantern light. Around them, the tavern's patrons laughed and chatted. "You men are always showing off."

Edris grew serious. "And have any men been showing off for you lately?"

"Why? Would that make you jealous?"

"Horribly."

"Then why are you leaving so soon?"

She asked the question playfully, but Edris could tell the news of his departure in the morning bothered her.

"I'm sorry, Bea," he said. "I have to. Father's orders."

"He isn't trying to keep us apart—is he? I mean..."

"No." He stroked her hand. He was always amazed at the roughness of her skin. She had more calluses than he did. "It's nothing like that. I doubt he knows about you. No offense."

"None taken." Their fingers intertwined. "Your father not knowing about me is safer for both of us."

The conversation was straying into perilous waters and they both knew it.

"Oh!" Beatrice said, abruptly changing the topic. "I have something for you." Reaching into a pocket, she produced a small book.

Taking it, Edris read the cover. *"Ode to My Starflower."*

"It's by Balen the Bard. They're sonnets he wrote for his daughter. They're absolutely marvelous."

"Thanks, Bea. I've never seen this one before."

Edris casually scanned the surrounding patrons as he tucked the book under his belt behind his back. Around them, the din of conversation continued unabated.

Beatrice rolled her eyes. "Afraid people might find out you like poetry?"

"Shhh!"

"What are you afraid of? Who cares that you like to read?"

"Bea!" He hushed her again.

"Well, I think it's endearing." She took his enormous hand again. "And I want you to think about me when you read it."

Edris's expression softened. "I will. I'll read a verse every night before I go to bed and imagine I'm reading it to you."

Across the packed tavern, somebody started singing. Soon a dozen other drunken voices joined in.

"When are you returning?" Beatrice asked sadly.

"I don't know."

"But you're only going to Upper Angle, right? You aren't doing anything dangerous?"

Edris waved for the serving girl to bring him another beer. "I don't know. I'm headed to Upper Angle first. But I may have to go elsewhere. It all depends on how things unfold."

"You'll be safe?"

"Of course." He kissed her knuckles. "Oh, don't look at me like that. I'm getting in a bit of training before I enlist. That's it."

"Why can't you do that here?"

Edris paused; he was painting himself into a corner. "Look," he said as reassuringly as he could, "I can't tell you what I'm doing." She frowned at her glass of wine. "But I can tell you that I will miss you and I'll be thinking about you each and every day."

Her smile reappeared. "Are you going to write me?"

"As often as I can. And if you need anything, you can send a note to Upper Angle. I'll make sure the king's staff knows where I am."

She frowned again.

He stroked the side of her cheek. "What's wrong?"

"I'm afraid. I know I sound crazy, but I think something bad is going to happen to you."

"I'll be fine. Trust me."

"Your father isn't asking you to go kill somebody, is he? You're only training, right?"

The serving girl brought Edris another beer. He thanked her and gave her a couple coins. The serving girl winked at him.

"You know me, Bea," he said once the serving girl had gone. He took a long drink. "I'd never do something like that."

"But your father told you—"

"Don't worry about him." A patron patted Edris on the shoulder as he staggered by. Edris waited for him to get out of earshot before whispering, "I'm not like him."

"I know, but..."

"I'm never going to be like him. Okay? There's a right way to live your life and a wrong way." He made her look at him. "I'm not going to kill somebody in order to please my father. I want to live with honor."

"I just want you to be happy."

"I'm with you and I have a book of poetry." He kissed her. "How can I *not* be happy?"

Nine

Edris stood in the crowded corridor outside the throne room. He had introduced himself to one of the royal door wardens and presented his father's letter. Now he had to wait with the hundred other people petitioning to see the king.

As he strolled about, pretending to study the busts of some long-forgotten nobles, the gilded double doors opened. Then King Michael of The Angle issued forth, followed closely by two bodyguards in brightly polished plate mail. The king scanned the throng scrambling to kneel before him. His gaze fell upon Edris, passed Edris by, and then returned to him. The king's brows furrowed.

"Eddie?" Before Edris could answer, the king hurried to him, hand extended. "By the gods, look at you!"

Bowing, Edris shook the king's hand. "Your Highness."

The king retreated a step, marveling at Edris's immense size. "Last time I saw you, you hardly came up to my waist."

"Yes, sir. It's been a while."

"Indeed! Too long." To everybody's astonishment, the king threw his arms around Edris and hugged him.

The king wasn't a short man by any means. In fact, he was taller than most, with a tightly knit build still firm with muscles. But as he hugged Edris, His Majesty's head barely reached his nephew's chin.

The king stepped back again. "By the gods!"

Edris never knew what to say to these sorts of comments. He'd been big his entire life; though, granted, when he was younger, he was a tad on the chunky side. So, he stood, saying nothing, as His Majesty inspected him.

"I understand you're here to study before enlisting," the king said.

"Yes, sir. If you'd allow me the honor of having access to your library."

"Of course! I have an extensive array of books and treatises on military matters that will interest you. You know, there's no better weapon a man can wield than a sharp mind."

"Yes, sir," Edris replied, still standing at attention. "My father says the same thing."

"Splendid! Come with me." The king strode through the passageway, heedless of the many bows and curtsies given to him. "I want to introduce you to some of our men. I believe you'll enjoy their comradeship while you're here. They can also help get you ready for your service."

Edris followed the king, painfully aware of the two guards behind them, their plate mail and weapons clanking as they marched.

"How's your father?" the king asked. "Come beside me. No need for court formality."

Quickening his pace, Edris walked alongside the king. "My father is…" He struggled to find a proper response. He wanted to say "bitter" or "spiteful," but neither was appropriate.

His Majesty chuckled. "I know what you're trying to say. Don't worry about misleading me."

They turned down another corridor, its grey stone walls covered with bejeweled tapestries of red and gold.

"Your father is a good man," the king went on. "I know things haven't been easy for him since my sister passed."

Edris had never known his mother. She'd died giving birth to him. And the topic often brought swells of guilt and pain stabbing deep within him.

"Yes, sir."

"I wish your father and I were closer. But perhaps your being here will provide the kindling our relationship needs. I tell you; it'll be wonderful to see you around these halls again."

"Yes, sir." Then, thinking he needed to ask something of the king, Edris added quickly, "How are Merrick, Morris, Markus, and Mariam?"

"Merrick is in Hillshire, courting the Lady Louisa."

"Hillshire?" Edris found himself saying. Raaf was from Hillshire. He wondered if that was a coincidence.

"Indeed. It'll be a good match if they can learn to live with each other. I've long wanted to reinforce the bonds between our two realms since we share a common border. And Lady Louisa is appealing enough."

If his boasts were true, Edris's eldest brother, Edran, had slept with Lady Louisa on multiple occasions.

"Yes, sir," Edris said. "I hope they'll be very happy together. And the others?"

"Morris is studying the law codes in Eryn Mas, though I daresay he's most likely drinking and whoring more than studying. I wish he had your dedication to learning."

"I've done my share of such things as well."

The king chortled. "Haven't we all? What's the point of being noble?" He sighed. "At least Markus is making something of himself. However, I hardly get to see him these days. He's always off adventuring."

"Yes, please congratulate him on his last win. The Necklace of Peneli, I believe. You must be proud."

The king lit up with delight. "I am! Ask him about it when you see him. He narrowly survived, by all accounts."

"When I see him?" Edris asked, trying to be subtle. "So, he's in Upper Angle?"

"Yes, he's here. Though he's liable to disappear at a moment's notice, I'm afraid."

"And Mariam?" Edris asked, considering what the king had said about Markus. "She's still living with you? Is she well?"

They went through a doorway and entered a large courtyard, bright with the afternoon sun. Across the way, a company of men wearing the king's tabard stood outside the stables, whooping and cheering.

"Oh, you know young women," the king said, heading toward the commotion.

"Not as well as I'd like, sir."

The king laughed. Many of the men in the courtyard snapped to attention.

"I know the feeling!" he replied. "So, you're still single?"

"I am."

"Wise," the king told him, approaching the shouting men. "Best to focus on career and fortune before turning your thoughts to love."

"Yes, sir."

Before them, in the stable yard encircled by brawny kingsmen, a shirtless man was being propelled forward as though he were a wheelbarrow, while others shoveled great heaps of horse manure on him. The guard holding his feet sped up, driving the wheelbarrow man's head into a reeking pile of dung. The onlookers who hadn't seen the king hooted and jeered. Some threw feces.

"Kriton," the king called.

Leaning against a fence railing, the Captain of the Guard turned. Seeing who approached, he stood erect and saluted—as did the rest of his men, even the one being used as a wheelbarrow. Through the smears of horse manure, Edris could see his face. He was Douglas, the fourth son of Lord Denton.

"I would like you to meet Edris," the king said. "He'll be joining your company in the spring. Eddie, this is Captain Kriton."

Kriton shook Edris's hand. "Edris?" Kriton's polite smile broadened into something more mischievous. "Lord Elros's son? I've heard of you. You're supposed to be a hell of a fighter." His hand tightened around Edris's.

"I can hold my own," Edris said, ignoring the captain's crushing grip.

"Can you?"

Edris held Kriton's gaze. "Absolutely."

Kriton squeezed Edris's hand harder. "Excellent!" He let go. "We're always looking for men of worth to mold."

"Yes," the king said. "Eddie will undoubtedly be an asset to your company."

"I'm sure he'll be very entertaining," Kriton said.

Several men snickered.

"To demonstrate his enthusiasm for his chosen profession," the king went on, evidently heedless of the hungry glances slipped in Edris's direction, "he's decided to come here early and study a bit, military strategy and so forth. Are there any books you'd recommend he delve into?"

"Books?" Kriton repeated, surprised. "No, Your Highness. I believe we can teach the lord's son everything he needs to know. Work hard—and do whatever he's told."

Manure dripped from Douglas's face. Judging from his swollen eyes, he'd been beaten.

"Yes, well," the king said, "there's that, isn't there? However, if you think of anything that might be useful, please let Eddie know. He'll be staying in the guest house."

"Sounds comfortable," Kriton said, staring at Edris.

"I'm sure it is," Edris replied, returning the glare.

"Very good. Thank you for your time." The king gestured to a many-windowed tower across the courtyard. "Let me show you the library, Eddie. It's right this way."

Edris shook the captain's hand again.

"Pleasure meeting you," he said, squeezing.

Kriton winced in pain, then scowled. "The pleasure will be mine—Eddie."

Ten

Edris sat at the long wooden table where the elderly scholar told him to wait. Moaning, he put his head in his hands. What was he was supposed to do now? He loved to read. He might even enjoy reading about military strategy. But his real mission wasn't to sit around a stuffy library. He had to figure out how to "deal with" Markus—whatever that meant.

Markus…

How do you stop an adventurer from winning any more quests?

Maybe he should forget about his father's vendetta and focus on preparing to be a kingsman.

Kingsman…

Clearly, things hadn't gone well with Captain Kriton. Edris should've been politer. Maybe he could buy him a drink or two. That usually helped. Kingsmen always drank like fish. After a few pitchers, they'd be laughing about what had happened.

Then he recalled Douglas's face.

Why did he allow himself to be used as a wheelbarrow? And the piles of shit? He was noble. Where was his dignity?

Edris thought about the king. He'd treated him with more than courtly courtesy. In fact, he'd gone out of his way to make him feel like long-lost family. Still, he couldn't have been blind to what was happening to Douglas. He let a fellow noble be used as a damned wheelbarrow and didn't say a word.

What would Edris have done if he were Douglas? Would he go along and pretend it was all fun and games?

He pictured Douglas spitting and wiping manure from his mouth.

No. He wouldn't go along. If anybody piled shit on him, he'd break their nose. There were some lines he wouldn't let people cross. He was Edris, son of Lord Elros. That should mean something.

Of course, if he got disowned…

His thoughts returned to Markus. He had to figure out a way to make his father happy.

Edris fidgeted in his chair, wondering where the hell the librarian had gone off to. He glanced about.

The library was situated in the castle's southernmost tower. Rows of tall shelves lined the stone walls, all crammed with hundreds of tomes. Between each row, faint afternoon light seeped through windows of thick glass. In the center of the dimly lit room, a narrow circular stairway connected each floor.

Heavy footfalls echoed as somebody bounded down the stairs. Boots appeared, then thick legs and a muscular chest. The man's face came into view. Edris stood.

"Markus."

Markus eyed Edris. "You shouldn't be here," he said sternly. "This is the king's private library."

"Yes, I know. He brought me here." Then Edris added because he thought he should, "It's good to see you again."

Stepping off the stairs, Markus drew closer, perplexed. "Who…?"

"It's Edris. Lord Elros's youngest son."

Markus gaped. "Fatty Eddie?"

Edris fought to hide a grimace. "That's me."

"By the gods!" Markus threw his arms around Edris and lifted him off the ground. "Fatty Eddie!" He dropped Edris and patted his head like a dog. "I can't believe it! By the gods!"

Edris ran his fingers through his hair, trying to fix the mess Markus had created. "I've grown a bit since we last met."

"I'll say. Great gods! How old are you now? Twenty? Twenty-one?"

"I'm fifteen."

Fifteen! Shit. If you grow any more, you won't fit through doorways! What are you doing here?"

"I'm enlisting next spring. I'm going to be a kingsman."

"A kingsman," Markus said, impressed. "Still dreaming about becoming a knight, eh?"

"Something like that. Congratulations on your last quest, by the way. Your father's very proud."

"Is he? It's hard to tell sometimes. You know how it is. If you aren't the heir or the spare, you're an afterthought. But thank you. What are you doing in the library? I would think you'd be bedding all the lucky women of Bend."

"My father thought it would be a good idea for me to study military strategy before I begin my service. And—" He lifted his hands helplessly. "—here I am. How about you? What are you doing here? Bedded all the women in Upper Angle already? Nobody else to sleep with?"

Markus laughed. "I believe there are a few peasant girls living on the nearby farms who have yet to make my acquaintance. But actually, I was upstairs, reading a few things. I got up to stretch my legs." He surveyed Edris. "You're a damn giant!"

"I'm only a few inches taller than you."

"A few inches? I barely come up to your nose!" Markus stood on his tiptoes, hand sliding from the top of his head to the bridge of Edris's nose. "See! And how did you get so muscular?" He thumped his fist against Edris's bulging chest. "I don't recall any of your brothers being so blasted big."

"My father makes me work in the fields—felling trees, moving boulders, digging out stumps. It's exhausting, but it's definitely made me stronger."

Markus nodded, as though he wouldn't mind trying the same things. "Well, it's amazing. Honestly, I think we'll have a devil of a time finding armor that'll fit you. How long will you be in the city?"

"To tell you the truth," Edris replied, not sure how he should proceed, "I don't know. My father is rather insistent I make something of myself, and he says he doesn't appreciate me taking up space in the manor."

Markus's expression grew somber. "How is he—your father? Are things well with him?"

"I'm sure he hasn't changed since you last saw him."

"No, I'm sure he hasn't." Markus's tone brightened. "Which reminds me, I've heard about your many exploits! It seems nobody in Bend can best you in a fair fight. Your father must be pleased about that."

"According to my father, I haven't fought anybody worthy of my sweat."

"Ah. Well, he's like that, isn't he? Say, do you want me to set up some matches here? You could expand your reputation."

"Perhaps it would be best if I kept a low profile. Some of the men I'd fight might be serving in my company next year. I'd hate to cause any animosity."

"Oh, please. The men are professionals. They beat on each other all the time. Let me see what I can do. I'm sure my father would love to see you compete."

There was no use arguing. Every time Markus or his siblings wanted to have things their way, they'd say it'd please their father. It was how they indicated the matter was closed.

Edris bowed. "As you wish."

"Wonderful!"

Bells in the tower rang the dinner hour.

"Have you eaten?" Markus asked.

"Not yet."

"Then you must have dinner with the family. Merrick is off trying to find a woman who'd be willing to marry him. Morris is the-gods-know-where. But Mariam's here. I'm sure she'd love to see you."

"I'd like that."

"Splendid!" Markus guided him to the stairway. "So tell me about your brothers. How is Edran? He's still single, isn't he?"

"He is. I'll tell you all about his failures with the fairer sex during dinner." Edris motioned to the aisle where the librarian had disappeared. "I'll catch up with you. An elderly gentleman went off to fetch me some books. I'd hate to disappear on him."

"Jarred? You may have to wait. He's a good man, but he's getting slow ascending the stairs. We tried hiring a young scribe to help him, but he won't hear of it."

"If he doesn't return soon, I'll leave him a message."

"Do that. Tell him to leave the books here and you'll get them later. I have an entire table littered with things upstairs. Nobody will touch them." At this, Edris's ears pricked. "Hey, I have to go to the privy. Meet you in the dining hall in a few minutes?"

"I'll be there."

Markus beheld Edris again. Shaking his head, he laughed. "By the gods. It's good to see you, Fatty."

"It's good to be seen."

"At your size, how can you not? Come to dinner. I mean it. Everybody will want to see you."

"I'm looking forward to it."

Markus descended the circular stairs with the urgency of a man whose bladder was threatening to burst. When he'd gone, Edris rushed up the stairs to the next floor. There, by one of the west windows, he found a table laden with piles of books, scrolls, and maps. He riffled through them.

The maps were of Hillshire and the surrounding countryside. The books were about Prince Raaf and his family. Edris picked up an old journal with a tattered leather cover. Flipping through its brown pages, he quickly realized it was a diary—Raaf's personal diary.

The librarian called for him. "Young man?"

Edris shoved the diary behind his cloak and hurried down the circular steps. "I'm right here!"

Eleven

The royal dining hall erupted with laughter.

"I can't tell you," the king said, still chuckling, "how wonderful it is to have you here, Eddie. Or should I say Edris? You're definitely no longer the little Eddie who used to run around these halls waving my sword and attacking the cat."

"The cat had it coming," Edris said, eating.

"Lord Blacknose?" Across from him, the king's daughter, Mariam, pouted playfully. "He was a delight."

"He bit!" Edris and Markus cried together.

"Only men!" Mariam replied, peering at Edris over the rim of her goblet. "Some men deserve a good biting."

"And some cats deserve to be chased with a sword and taught how to obey," Edris replied.

"Oh, *obey*, is it?" She winked at him. "Cats of reputable breeding don't obey. They rule."

Was she flirting with him? Or was this one of her jokes?

Growing up, Mariam always went to great lengths to make Edris feel uncomfortable. Once, he received a note to come to her quarters. When he entered, the shapely teenage girl pretended to be naked and screamed.

Screaming himself, the embarrassed Edris sprinted from the room, down the corridor, out the castle. He'd run several miles before he realized what had happened.

"Speaking of obeying," Markus interjected pointedly, "how do you think you'll like life as a kingsman, Eddie?" He took a bite of his lamb, relishing more than the tender meat.

"He'll do splendidly," His Majesty said. "Look at the size of him! Why, I bet he'll be the champion of the guards within a year."

"You did grow," the queen said from the other end of the table. "It's remarkable. How old are you now, Eddie? Nineteen?"

"Fifteen, ma'am."

"Fifteen!" she exclaimed. "I bet you still have a couple more inches left in you."

"I hope not," Edris replied. "My father refuses to buy me any more clothes, and the mail I have scarcely fits me as it is."

Markus snorted. "I bet!"

"How is your dear father?" the queen asked. "We haven't seen him in ages. You really should have him come for a visit, Michael."

"I've offered," the king said, tearing a piece of bread and dabbing it in the gravy. "But short of an order, I doubt he'd make the trip."

An uncomfortable silence settled around the dining hall as people ate.

"He's been busy," Edris found himself saying.

"I'm sure," the king said pleasantly. "His fiefdom is one of the most prosperous in the realm. I should probably send him a commendation."

"That's a fabulous idea," the queen said. "When are you returning to Bend, Eddie? Perhaps you can deliver it to him."

"I'm not sure, ma'am. To be honest, I'd like to do as much as I can before I enlist. I'm looking forward to traveling."

"You should go with Markus to Hillshire," the queen said, cutting her meat. Both the king and Markus stiffened. They shared a glance. "He could use the company."

"Why are you going to Hillshire?" Edris asked Markus as casually as he could.

Markus slowly drained his goblet, perhaps to buy himself time to think. "I'm going to visit Merrick. He's there trying to find a woman who'll love him."

"Oh, stop!" the queen said. "Lady Louisa is a perfectly pleasant girl. You make it sound like Merrick is scraping the bottom of the barrel!"

Markus began to make a retort, but Edris cut him off, not wanting the topic to slip away. "Well, if you're willing to have me, I'd love to tag along. I haven't seen Merrick in years, and I've never been to Hillshire."

A panicked expression flashed across Markus's face, but it was swiftly replaced by an affable smile. "Of course! I'd enjoy having you. Though I don't know how long I'll be away or where I might head after seeing Merrick."

"Not to worry. You don't have to mind me. I can find my way home."

"Feel free to take a few of my books with you," the king said to Edris. "You can return them when you begin your training."

"Oh, you men!" said Mariam. "Books and traveling and training! Let's talk about things that actually matter." She sipped her wine. "So, Eddie, have you gone skinny dipping lately?"

Twelve

Edris lay on his bed in His Majesty's guesthouse, reading the book of poems Beatrice had given him, sipping a glass of red wine as the warm autumn breeze caressed his bare chest. Perhaps it was the wine, or the faint smell of the beeswax candles lit about the room, but he never felt so relaxed. He could only imagine what his father would say if he walked in. Lying about and reading poetry? He'd be apoplectic. But Edris didn't care. His father was a hundred miles away, and he'd had too pleasant of an evening with the king's family to worry about him.

Somebody hammered on the door.

"Eddie!" Markus shouted.

Edris held his breath, hoping his cousin would go away. He'd spent all evening listening to Markus bragging about his many adventurers. It was nice to be rid of him.

He went back to reading.

Markus continued pounding. "Come on, Eddie. Leave the poor whore alone. Open this door."

Edris turned a page.

"I know you're in there. The servants told me."

Groaning, Edris put a scrap of paper marking the sonnet he'd been reading, then tucked the book under his pillow.

"All right! All right!" he hollered.

He stomped down the hall and opened the door with a jerk.

Markus was leaning against the jamb, grinning. "Who is she?" He pushed past him.

"Who?"

"The tart you're plowing."

"I'm alone."

"I bet."

Markus burst into the bedroom. He noted the wine, then the unmade bed, and then the open window.

"Well," he said, delighted, "it looks like this little birdie has flown! I hope you got what you wanted."

"I told you, I was alone."

"Sure you were." Markus flung Edris the shirt he'd been wearing for dinner. "It doesn't matter. Get dressed. We're going to town. I've set up a fight for you."

"Markus…"

"None of that. I'm dying to see the great mountain, Fatty Eddie, do battle. Besides, I'll get you two women if you win."

"There's something to be said about quality over quantity."

"Spoken like somebody in love."

"I'm not in love," Edris replied. "I was merely enjoying myself."

"Doing what?"

"Relaxing."

"You can relax later." Markus held open the door. "Come on. One fight. And if you don't knock him unconscious, you're not coming with me to Hillshire."

Thirteen

Markus led Edris though winding streets descending the lopsided hill upon which Upper Angle was built. They entered the lowest tier of the city, passing seedy taverns, flamboyant brothels, and the ill-kept houses of the lower classes. Turning off a major thoroughfare, they came to a town square crammed with people.

"Who am I fighting?" Edris asked, stretching his arms.

They pushed through the murmuring crowd to where a boxing ring had been erected. Then Edris saw the man waiting for him. It was Captain Kriton.

"Markus…"

"Don't worry, Eddie. You can take him."

Edris pulled Markus aside. "He's going to be my captain."

"Then now is the time to beat the crap out of him. Isn't it?"

"Markus!"

"Don't worry about it. Everybody respects a fair fight."

"What's wrong, Eddie?" Kriton called from the ring. "Need a book?"

"Markus…" Edris said again, pleading.

"You can't renege now."

This was true. Edris had to fight. He'd never live it down if he walked away. The question was: should he let his future captain win?

"Daddy isn't here to save you, Eddie." Kriton announced to the growing crowd, "If you don't know, ladies and gentlemen, this is the famous Edris, son of Lord Elros the drunk. Let's see if he's as good as the rumors make him out to be."

Edris glared at his beaming cousin, then the taunting mob. He repressed the anger rising within him. "Okay," he said, attempting to lighten the situation. "But I want three women if I win."

Markus clapped Edris's shoulder. "That's the spirit!"

Taking off his shirt, Edris ducked under the ropes and stepped into the ring.

"Don't worry, dreg," somebody shouted. "Consider this your initiation to the company."

"Show us what you can do, Fatty Eddie!" Markus cheered.

Edris stretched some more, wondering how to lose tactfully without his father finding out.

Then the referee signaled for the fight to commence.

Better make this look good…

The combatants circled each other, staying near the middle of the ring.

Edris sized up his opponent. Kriton was slightly shorter than he was and didn't have his enormous reach. But the Captain of the Guards was thick and muscled, and he obviously knew how to handle himself.

Kriton charged him, swinging a big right hand at Edris's jaw.

Edris easily slipped under the blow. With Kriton's defenses dropping, he could've countered, but decided against it.

Kriton shot a flurry of jabs at Edris's nose. Weaving to the left, then the right, Edris dodged them all.

Several of the men in the crowd booed.

"Come on!" one of them yelled. "This ain't no dance! Fight!"

Kriton threw another powerful right at Edris's head. Again, Edris dodged the blow. He then slipped a left jab into Kriton's forehead. It wasn't hard and Kriton knew it.

"You laying back?" Kriton hollered, furious. "You think you can lay back with me? I can take anything you got."

He faked a left to Edris's chin, then kneed him in the groin. Edris doubled over, clutching himself. The referee attempted to get in between the two fighters, but Kriton shoved him away. He pummeled Edris's head, then sent uppercuts into his unprotected face.

"How's that, Eddie?" Kriton asked as he battered Edris mercilessly. "Where's your father now? The drunken whore-chaser!"

Enraged, Edris grabbed Kriton's legs, then drove forward with his shoulders lowered. Tackling the captain to the dirt, Edris leapt on him, hitting the prostrate man repeatedly as hard as he could. Kriton's nose snapped, blood gushing everywhere. Then his front teeth broke. Then his jaw.

"Bastard!" Edris struck Kriton in the eye. Kriton tried to defend himself but couldn't. Blow after blow rained down upon him, blood spraying across the dirt. "I was going to carry you. You stupid shit! It didn't have to be like this."

The referee attempted to pull Edris off, but he kept hitting Kriton. A dozen other men leapt into the fray. Several piled onto him.

Edris stood up, throwing them in all directions. He sent one reeling across the ring with a hard right to the mouth, then dropped another with a blow to the stomach.

More people streamed into the ring. Edris batted them away as though they were children. Soon seven men lay at his feet; three weren't moving.

Amidst the chaos, Markus raced forward, waving his arms and screaming. "It's over! It's over! In the king's name, stop the fight!"

Edris sent a guard flying over the ropes, crashing into the spectators.

His face swollen and bloody, Kriton staggered to his feet. Cradling his jaw, he snarled. "This ain't over, Eddie. Come spring, you're mine."

Fourteen

Dripping blood, Edris stomped into the guesthouse in which he was quartered. The fight had only lasted a few minutes, with the ensuing chaos afterward accounting for another quarter of an hour, if that. The night was still young, but all he wanted to do was be alone. His battered head throbbing, he collapsed onto the bed.

Under different circumstances, he would've been pleased. He'd never fought so many people at the same time. Knocking out seven men all at once might have impressed even his father. But it was Kriton's last words—slurred with blood and broken teeth—that gave him reason to cringe.

"This ain't over, Eddie. Come spring, you're mine."

Spring was six months away. Perhaps Kriton would forgive and forget by then.

Now Edris actually did laugh. Men like Kriton didn't forget a beating like that. And he definitely wouldn't forgive it.

Six months…

He couldn't have messed things up worse had he killed Kriton.

Perhaps his father was right. There was something to be said about being feared.

He massaged the purple knots on his forehead, then attempted to make himself more comfortable. Two books poked out from under the mound of pillows. One was the book of poetry. The other was the diary he'd stolen from Markus.

He inspected the diary.

It was stupid of him to have taken it. It was stealing, plain and simple. But then again, his dear cousin did make him fight his future commander.

Asshole.

Turning to the last entry, he immediately forgot about the fight and the coming spring.

The passage read: *"I endeavor to take tomorrow morning for myself and ride in the hills north of town. The fresh air will undoubtedly clear my head."*

The hills north of Hillshire? There couldn't be more than a few trails in that direction. How hard would it be to search them?

Wait…

Something wasn't right. The quest couldn't be that easy.

Flipping through the diary, Edris noted how tidy the penmanship was. Each letter was skillfully crafted, almost drawn, in neat lines extending across the pages.

He flipped through more passages.

There wasn't a single error or cross-out. Not one.

Nobody could write that perfectly.

Nobody but a scribe…

The diary was a copy. It had to be. It might even be a complete fake. The story of Raaf and his lost sword had been a fireside staple for nearly two centuries. Thieves and counterfeiters undoubtedly created such books and sold them to the highest bidder.

Did Markus think it was real?

Probably not. He was rapidly becoming one of the most famous adventurers in the kingdom. He hadn't won so many quests by being gullible.

Edris tossed the diary onto the table next to his bed and picked up the book of poems.

Markus…

He might not be able to stop his cousin from winning another quest, but Edris was going to make him pay for the fight with Kriton.

Fifteen

"Come on, Eddie," Markus said. "The boat's leaving."

Still bleary-eyed from a lack of sleep, Edris followed his cousin's example and led his whinnying horse up the gangplank. Markus had awakened him before dawn, saying if he wanted to go to Hillshire, he had to get ready that instant.

"Couldn't we have caught a later barge?" Edris asked.

"You could've," Markus replied, guiding his sleek grey stallion to one of the stalls. "But I'm leaving on this one, and you said you wanted to go. Besides, after trouncing Kriton like that, I thought you might want to get out of town."

The boat's captain approached.

"All ready, sirs?" the heavy, balding man asked as Markus hitched his horse to the railing.

"We are," Markus said. "How long until we reach Lower Angle?"

"The river is high with all the rains we've had. Should make it in three days, sir."

"Splendid." Markus gave the captain several coins.

"Thank you, sir."

"My pleasure." Markus called to his squire, "Jacob!"

A happy-faced lad appeared from around a corner. He was roughly Edris's age but barely came to his shoulders. "Sir?"

"We'll be in our cabin. Stow the gear. Then tend the horses. Make sure they are fed and watered."

"Yes, sir!"

To Edris's surprise, most of the items on the squire's horse were weapons and armor. A bundle tied to the saddle must have contained fifty arrows. Two-handed swords were strapped to the horse's flanks.

"Expecting a fight?"

"Always." Markus led him along a narrow passageway to a small room with two hammocks stretched from wall to wall. "It isn't spacious. But it's only for a few days. Besides, it beats sleeping in the common room with the riffraff."

Edris closed the door as his cousin flopped onto one of the hammocks.

"You mentioned getting out of town because of Kriton," Edris said.

Markus stretched out, his hands behind his head. "Do you want to run into his men?"

"Do you..." Edris wavered. "Do you think Kriton is the type of man who can forget what happened? Let bygones be bygones?"

"Trust me. He'll be thinking about you for a very long time." Markus laughed. "Honestly, Eddie, I thought you were going to kill him."

"Perhaps it'd make my life easier if I had."

The barge lurched forward as it was pushed into the middle of the swirling Greater Green River.

"Let me ask you this," Markus said seriously. "Are you actually planning on being a kingsman next year?"

Edris sat on the other hammock, trying not to be thrown to the floor. "That's the plan."

"Whose plan? Your father's?" Seeing Edris's reaction, Markus shook his head. "It's time for you to forget about your father. You have to be your own man."

"He'll disown me."

"Oh, no, he won't. Believe me. That's what fathers like ours always say. It's their biggest threat against their lay-about sons. In truth, they wouldn't stand the scandal. Who disowns their sons for not doing what they're told? Think about it. The most they'd do is lower our allowance. Trust me."

"When was the last time you spoke to my father? Ten years ago?"

"Something like that."

They swayed in their hammocks as the barge rocked slightly. Outside, other passengers filed past the closed door.

"Is he really that bad?" Markus asked. "I mean, I've heard—"

"He wants me to kill people. He told me that if I didn't kill the next person I faced in the ring, I shouldn't come home."

Markus started to chuckle, but then caught Edris's sullen expression. "He means it? Literally kill somebody? He didn't mean…"

"He thinks it's better to be feared than loved."

"I suppose there's some truth in that. Doubtless, there are occasions where you'll have to use excessive force."

"Not in the ring!" Edris cried. "It's a game!"

"Well, if it helps, you nearly killed more than a few people last night. I've never seen anybody fight like that."

For a moment, the two men stared at the ceiling. Tree branches scraped by the small, circular window as the barge plodded slowly downstream.

"Am I going to be able to be a kingsman?" Edris asked eventually.

"No, Ed. I'm afraid that ship has sailed, as they say. Some of the other kingsmen will love you for what you did, but Kriton will make your life miserable, if not end it altogether."

Edris groaned. "What am I going to do?"

Markus yawned. "I am of the opinion that people should only deal with problems as they occur. You have—what? Six months before you enlist. Plenty can happen in that time. So, relax. Maybe find a few dozen women to bed. That always makes things seem better. And, above all, try not to beat the crap out of anybody else unless you absolutely have to."

Early in the morning of the fourth day, the barge docked alongside a wharf in Lower Angle. Like Upper Angle, Lower Angle was built upon a stone hill wedged between two diverging rivers. However, rather than being situated in the mountains, Lower Angle was surrounded by rolling plains of knee-high green grass.

From Lower Angle, Edris, Markus, and Jacob rode southeastward into the wooded hills surrounding Hillshire. For the most part, Edris and Markus rode side-by-side, discussing everything from women to the worsening political tensions with the neighboring kingdoms to the trials of being the youngest sons of powerful fathers. However, Markus seemed to be happiest when discussing the quests he'd undertaken.

"And you managed to get the Golden Mace from them?" Edris asked, trying to sound amazed, though he believed little of what his older cousin was saying. "It was five against one!"

"It isn't about the odds," Markus replied as their horses clomped along. "It's about the opportunity. Sometimes you know you'll never have another opportunity like that again, so you have to take it—odds be damned. Besides, fighting five men really isn't any different than fighting one. It isn't as though they're all attacking you at once. It's like life, Eddie. You take one problem at a time." Then he added, "And you do whatever you have to do to win."

"Sir," Jacob said behind them as their horses splashed through a creek trickling across the road. "If our maps are correct, there should be a suitable place to camp not too far to our left."

Markus checked the darkening sky through the overreaching branches. Evening was deepening around them.

"Very well. It's a bit early. But I'm in no hurry. My brother will still be at Hillshire when we get there."

They turned off the path and followed a creek to a small clearing.

"I'll get some firewood," Edris said.

"I can get it," Jacob objected.

"I want to help out. I have to get used to not having servants doing everything for me. Besides, you have to tend the horses."

Edris hiked into the woods, picking up what dry wood he could find. He hadn't been gone more than ten minutes when he heard an outbreak of angry voices coming from camp. Two were unfamiliar. Setting the firewood aside, Edris quietly drew his sword and a dagger. He stalked closer to camp and listened.

"Fate it may be," said a stranger. "Still, I find it exceedingly odd you're heading to Hillshire when the quest was declared only yesterday."

"And I find it equally odd," Markus replied testily, "that you are in these woods as well. As you said, the quest was declared only yesterday."

"I'm from Hillshire!" the stranger shouted. "I have every right to be here. I've been exploring these lands since before you were born."

"This is why I don't think the sons of kings should be allowed to quest," somebody else said. "They're given advantages over real adventurers."

"It wouldn't matter," the first voice replied. "If it wasn't their sons, kings would appoint their bastard offspring."

A sword rang as it slid from its scabbard.

"I am no bastard," Markus said, coldly. "And you'd best mind yourself. You may talk about your king that way, but you dare not speak of mine."

Through the trees, Edris could see Jacob draw his sword as well, though he appeared far from confident about its use.

"I'll speak any way I wish," the first man said. "The third son of a worthless king is no matter to me."

Edris leapt into the clearing behind the newcomers. "He matters to me. And he won't stand alone or at a disadvantage."

Two men, tall and broad of frame, whirled to meet Edris, weapons ready. They were in their mid-thirties, seasoned fighters by the looks of their scars—but Edris's size gave them pause.

"And who are you?" one asked.

"Edris, son of Lord Elros," Edris declared proudly. "Nephew to King Michael and cousin of Markus."

"Another noble," the shorter of the two men said, as though his point had been made.

His partner maneuvered so that he couldn't be flanked by Edris or Markus. "I've heard about your boxing. But can you handle a blade?"

Edris matched the intruder's moves, making sure to keep his footing on the uneven ground. "Let's find out."

The first man jabbed a finger at Markus. "You're cheating. We all know it. You're a worthless, noble fraud." He waved to his companion. "Let's leave these ladies to their affairs."

The second man smiled at Edris. "Boxing isn't fighting, lad. And being big only means you're an easier target. Keep that in mind."

The men withdrew into the woods.

"Friends?" Edris asked when they'd gone.

"Colleagues." Markus sheathed his sword. "I'm glad you came along on this little expedition. I always need trustworthy people watching my back."

"Yes, well," Edris replied, also sheathing his sword. "We're family. We have to stick together."

Sixteen

Edris thrust more sticks into the popping campfire. It wasn't his turn to watch, but he wasn't sleepy, and he didn't want to be taken unaware should Markus's colleagues return in the middle of the night.

"So, who were those men?" he asked Markus.

Orange firelight danced across Markus's tired face. He exhaled resignedly. "The tall fellow with the dark complexion was Sir Emory. The other was Sir Morris."

"Knights?"

"Adventurers. They were knighted a few years ago but have been adventuring for King Louis for ages."

"Why did they say you were cheating?"

Reclining against his pack, Markus stretched his legs out before him. "How much do you know about Raaf?"

Edris faked ignorance. "I've heard the legends. He vanished mysteriously a couple hundred years ago. He was probably killed by his brother. That's about it. Why?"

Markus studied Edris as if trying to resolve some internal debate. "The latest quest is to find his sword."

Edris pretended to put two and two together. "Wasn't Raaf from Hillshire?"

"He was."

"So, when you told me you were going to visit Merrick," Edris said, wondering if his cousin would finally tell him the truth, "that wasn't accurate, was it?"

Markus grimaced. "Not completely. I'm sorry about that, Eddie. As an adventurer, I need to keep certain things to myself. I know I can trust you; but you never know who's listening. But if it helps, we really *are* going to visit Merrick. I wasn't lying about that."

Imitating Markus, Edris reclined against his backpack and stretched his legs. "Why are we going to see your brother if you're on a quest?"

Markus peered around them. The campfire's leaping flames sent shadows scurrying about the surrounding trees. Somewhere in the woods, an owl hooted.

"Merrick has been gathering information for me," he whispered. "He thinks he might know where Raaf is buried."

"You're kidding. Where? People have been searching for his remains for centuries."

"I don't know what he's found. Hopefully, he's found Raaf's diary. I had a copy, but I seem to have misplaced it."

Throughout their time together, Edris had been trying to figure out what he was going to do with the book he'd stolen from the library. Now he thought he saw an opening.

"Diary?" he said, attempting to sound perplexed. "Half a moment." He dug into his pack and produced the tattered journal. "Is this yours?"

"How the devil—?" Markus cried, more overjoyed than angry. "How did you get this?"

"It was on my table with the other books the librarian brought me." As if offering proof, he held up the books the king had told him to read. "I was wondering what a diary had to do with military matters."

Markus laughed. "I can't tell you how relieved I am that you have this! I must've had it in hand when we first met."

"Then set it on the table when you lifted me off the ground," Edris agreed.

"Exactly." Markus examined the diary. "This is a glad tiding!"

"Do you think it will help you with the quest?"

"Maybe!" Markus stared at Edris. For a second, Edris thought Markus had remembered that he hadn't had the diary when they met in the library. "Care to join me?"

"Questing?"

"Absolutely."

"Me?" Edris replied, genuinely surprised. "You don't need me. Like you said, Merrick knows where the sword is."

"Perhaps he does. But even still, it isn't about finding the sword—though that'll undoubtedly be challenging."

"It's about getting it to your father?"

"Precisely. Come on. Join me, Eddie! You said yourself that you have nothing to do. I could really use another blade by my side. And I know you're trustworthy."

Edris didn't answer, a pang of guilt needling his stomach.

"I'll give you the prize money," Markus said eagerly. "That's a thousand gold pieces!"

"First tell me why those men thought you were cheating."

Markus rolled his eyes. "The quest was announced yesterday."

"You knew ahead of time?"

"Oh, everybody knows ahead of time! At least the *real* adventurers do. We all have our sources and spies. Everybody who has a brain knew the Sword of Betrayal was going to be the target this go-round. It isn't like I have an advantage somebody else doesn't have. Why, I bet Morris and Emory have been searching for the sword a month, if not more."

"Then why were they so angry?"

"I've won three out of the last five quests. They're jealous. Come on, Ed. Join me! It'll be fun. Maybe I'll even be able to smooth things over with Kriton."

"You could do that?"

"No. You're screwed there. Kriton is going to make your life miserable."

Edris gave a disgusted laugh. "What am I going to do?"

"Come with me. We'll find the sword. I'll get my seventh win. And you'll get a stack of coins."

"Coins won't help me with Kriton."

"You're missing the point! With that kind of money, you won't have to worry about being disowned by your father."

Edris hadn't thought of that.

"Come on," Markus pleaded. "With the diary and whatever Merrick discovered, we're bound to win. Think about it. One thousand gold! You could go anywhere you want and not be beholden to your father."

One thousand gold would certainly give him freedom. It wouldn't last forever, of course, but it would be a monumental start.

"I'll tell you what," Markus said. "I'll give you five hundred gold simply to journey with me. That's whether we win or lose. I'll even speak to Kriton. I'll promise him a promotion if he lays off you. What do you say?"

"Do you honestly think he'd take it easy on me?"

"If I promise him a cushy job at twice the pay? Maybe. What do you have to lose?"

As far as Edris could see, he didn't have anything to lose.

"Very well," he said. For the first time, he felt he might have a way out of serving as a kingsman. His father wouldn't like it, not by a long shot, but with a thousand gold, he'd have options—and he didn't have to end his cousin's adventuring career. "What do we do now?"

"Now we rest. Tomorrow, we'll get to Hillshire and see what information Merrick uncovered."

Seventeen

Markus, Edris, and Jacob arrived in Hillshire the next evening. Situated around three rolling hills covered in green grass, Edris had expected Hillshire to be a sleepy town of sheepherders, but he was surprised to find that it was a bustling city filled with quaint shops and stately two-story brick buildings.

"Are they anticipating a war?" Edris asked Markus as they passed yet another group of heavily armed men. "Seems like there are a lot of soldiers around."

"Those aren't soldiers," Markus replied. "They're adventurers. Like I said before, I'm not the only one who knew the quest would be in this region."

Several adventurers raised their hands in salute. Markus returned the gesture.

"Now what?" Edris asked.

Markus indicated the castle on top of the middle and largest hill. "First we see what Merrick dug up. Keep all information as close to your vest as possible. You're playing a game that could end our lives. Always remember that."

Pushing through the crowds, they headed up the winding road to King Louis's castle. When they reached its gates, they found that the wardens had been expecting them.

"Master Markus," one of them said, bowing low. "Your brother requested that you seek him out at your earliest convenience."

"Splendid," Markus said, dismounting. "Where shall we find the miscreant?"

"I can take you to him," the gate warden replied. "And I can fetch a boy to stable your horses and bring your possessions to your rooms."

"Wonderful." Markus said to his squire, "Jacob, help with the gear, then come find us."

"Yes, sir."

Markus bowed to their guide. "Please, lead on, my good sir."

The gate warden led Markus and Edris around to the east side of the castle. There they found Merrick sitting with a woman in a colorful garden by a burbling fountain.

"Markus!" he cried, rising to his feet. The brothers embraced, then Merrick introduced the woman standing next to him. "You remember Louisa."

Markus kissed her gloved hand. "Charmed, my lady. It is exquisite to see you again."

"Good to see you, Markus." Her gaze drifted over to Edris, her brown eyes sliding up his towering frame. "And...who is this?"

"Ah!" Markus laughed. "A hundred gold says you can't guess who this is, dear brother."

Merrick extended a hand to Edris, visibly baffled as to who the young fellow was.

"Now, don't ruin my surprise," Markus told Edris. "Let him guess. I'll give him three chances."

"Sir..." Merrick struggled. "Sir Walter?"

"Sir Walter?" Markus chuckled. "He's a fat lout. The gold is good as mine!"

"You're Sir Arthur," Louisa said. "Aren't you? I've heard of your many exploits."

"No, ma'am," Edris said. "I'm not a knight."

"No clues!" Markus cried. "Come on, Merr. You have one more guess. And don't even think about welching, or I'll tell father."

At a loss, Merrick stared at Edris. "I'm not in the mood for your games, Markus. Tell us who your companion is."

"Yes." Louisa smiled at Edris. "Who is the mystery man?"

"This—" Markus made a grand sweeping gesture to Edris, "is little Fatty Eddie."

A wave of confusion washed over Merrick's face, replaced swiftly by disbelief. "Fatty Eddie?"

Edris bristled, then bowed.

"Fatty Eddie!" Merrick attempted to hug Edris but could scarcely get his arms around him. "Great gods! Look at you!"

"Nice to see you, Merrick."

"Great gods!" Merrick said again. He stepped back and examined Edris's bulging muscles. Lady Louisa did as well, but less openly. "Little Fatty Eddie?"

Markus leaned closer to his brother. "If you call him that again, he'll punch your head off. He can do it. I've seen him fight."

"Oh, yes! Of course. Sorry, Eddie." He marveled at his cousin. "But...by the gods! What happened to you? Last I saw you, you were—what? Six? Maybe only seven years old?"

"It's been a long time," Edris admitted.

"*Too* long," Merrick agreed.

"Will you be visiting with us as well?" Lady Louisa asked, her tone more than a touch hopeful. "We'd love to have you."

"I'm not sure, ma'am," Edris replied. "Markus has agreed to entertain me until spring."

"What happens in the spring?"

Markus's grin turned mischievous. "He's enlisting as a kingsman!"

Merrick groaned. "Oh, no."

"Oh, yes! And guess who he fought when he was in Upper Angle."

"You didn't have him fight Kriton, did you?" Merrick gasped. "Markus!"

"He didn't just fight Kriton. He fought practically the entire company. Knocked half of them completely unconscious. You should've been there. I've never seen anything like it. Kriton lost four teeth!"

"I didn't mean to hurt him," Edris said apologetically.

"You didn't mean to hurt him?" Markus exclaimed. "You broke his jaw! He won't be able to chew meat for a year!"

"Honest, Merrick," Edris said, "I didn't mean to! He hit me low and I got a bit angry."

"A bit angry?" Markus laughed. "I'd hate to see you furious!"

"Well, I can see you want to spend time with your family." Lady Louisa touched Merrick's forearm. "I trust you boys won't get in much trouble. No fighting."

"No, of course not." Merrick sized Edris up. Standing on tiptoe, he came up to Edris's clean-shaven chin.

"Are we allowed to drink and whore?" Markus asked politely.

Lady Louisa narrowed her eyes. "Drinking is one thing. Whoring is another."

"We'll see you for dinner, sweetheart." Merrick kissed her cheek.

She offered Edris her hand. He kissed it.

"It's very good to meet you, Eddie. Any family of Merrick's is family of mine—or at least will be."

"Yes, ma'am." Edris bowed. "It's wonderful to finally meet you."

They all watched Lady Louisa walk across the courtyard. Reaching the castle, she wiggled her fingers at them. They waved back. Then she went inside.

"So, what did you find?" Markus asked his brother urgently.

"What? Oh, yes. The quest. I found something useful, by the looks of it. Come with me."

They followed the heir to The Angle's throne through the garden and into the opulent guesthouse.

When they came to his quarters, Merrick locked the door behind them and went to the sofa in the middle of the room. From behind a cushion, he produced a book with a black leather cover.

Markus seized it. "Is it the original?"

"Of course."

Markus flipped through the pages. Over his shoulder, Edris could see it was the same diary he'd stolen from Markus; however, this one was much older. The entries were also written in a sloppy hand, the color of ink slightly different for each entry.

Markus got to the last page and slapped the book. "I knew it!"

"What?" Edris asked.

"The last page in the copy we have isn't in the original."

Disappointed, Markus handed the diary to Edris, who read the last entry. It said nothing about looking forward to going riding in the hills. In fact, it looked as though Raaf hadn't finished it. He'd been talking about feeling ill when the writing abruptly ended.

"What do you want to do now?" Edris asked Markus.

"No idea."

"Judging by how many of your competitors are in town," Merrick said, "it seems everybody believes Raaf's sword is somewhere nearby. Several of King Louis's adventurers have been searching the hills for the better part of a month."

"See!" Markus said to Edris. "It's like I said; they all knew what the quest was before it was announced."

Edris examined the diary, trying to read the faded writing.

Next to him, Markus fell into an armchair. "We're missing something important."

"Isn't this all kind of pointless?" Edris asked. "I mean, how can you find something that others couldn't find for centuries?"

"We have to be smarter than everybody else," Markus said. "This is a game, Ed. Just like boxing. And even more dangerous. You still want to play? My offer stands."

Edris thought for a moment. He enjoyed travelling with Markus, but autumn was slipping away, and sooner or later, spring would come, and he'd have to do his time.

"I don't know how much help I can be. But I'll do what I can."

"If you can watch my back, you'll earn your money and then some. Knowing you're around gives me one less thing to worry about and more time to determine what piece of the puzzle we're missing."

"Perhaps we should concentrate on what we know," Merrick told them.

"But we don't know anything," Edris replied. "Not really."

"Yes, we do," Markus said. "We know the sword isn't in these hills. If it were, it would've been found by now. Moreover, somebody altered the copies of the diary to suggest Raaf was killed nearby."

"So, by default," his brother deduced, "he probably wasn't."

"Right!" Hands behind his head, Markus stared at the frescoed ceiling. "The question is: where was Raaf riding when he died?"

Eighteen

Later that night, Edris sat in his spacious quarters, reading. He started with the book of poems Beatrice had given him, but his concentration kept creeping to the original version of Raaf's diary Merrick found. He'd been reading it for a couple hours when somebody tapped on his door.

"Enter," he called. "It isn't locked."

The door opened, revealing the plain face of Lady Louisa bathed in yellow candlelight. Edris stood.

"May I come in?"

"Please, my lady. Are you looking for Markus or Merrick?" he asked, though he had an unsettling suspicion she wasn't looking for either. "Unfortunately, they are not here at the moment."

A smile creased her thin lips. "I know."

She stepped into the parlor and closed the door quietly behind her. She was wearing a different dress than the one she had on earlier by the fountain. She also had her long hair braided and over one shoulder.

"I have something for you," she said, as if remembering why she'd come. She held out a letter. From across the room, Edris could tell who it was from. The short, choppy script was a dead giveaway. His heart faltered.

"A letter from my father?" He took it. "Here?"

"It arrived a few days ago. It came with a note to my father indicating that you may be stopping by this way. I thought it might be important." She peered up at him. "So, I brought it myself."

Edris examined the envelope.

Half of him hoped that it was some sort of reprieve—a letter saying that he'd only been joking about making sure his cousin never won another quest. But he knew his father too well. He wanted to hurt the king, and the best way to do that was to hurt his famous son.

Edris smelled roses, then realized Lady Louisa was standing unnaturally close to him.

Her smile broadened ever so slightly. Then she noted the book he'd been reading.

"You're adventuring?" she asked, surprised. "I thought you were going to serve as a kingsman in Upper Angle."

"What? Oh..." Edris picked up the diary. "Well, yes and no." He took a self-conscious step away from her. "I'm helping Markus, if helping is what you call it. More like killing time before I report for duty." Something occurred to him. "Wait a second—how'd you know this had something to do with the quest?"

"I understand the games men play." She touched Edris's arm, her finger tracing his bulging bicep. "Women play games of a similar sort."

She drew even closer.

Edris retreated another step. It wasn't that he didn't want to play whatever games Lady Louisa had in mind; however, he was confused and needed to think. This woman was betrothed to his next king. In all probability, he'd be serving Merrick once his father died. Sleeping with his future queen was a deadlier game than hunting quest items.

"Perhaps you're weary from your journey," she said, still smiling at him.

"A little, my lady." Edris bowed, hoping the formality would send the message he couldn't say; however, she seemed to find the gesture titillating.

"And—" He held up the envelope she'd given him, "there's my father's message."

"I understand." She caressed his shoulder. "I'll leave you to your reading." She glanced at the diary. "If you'd like a distraction from your labors—send word. I am across the courtyard."

She left Edris rather dry-mouthed. Perhaps he'd sleep with her just once. After all, she wasn't his queen yet.

No. He was in enough trouble as it was. He couldn't afford to make any more enemies. There was also Beatrice to think about. He wanted to be loyal to her.

He examined his father's letter again.

With a sinking heart, he broke the seal and withdrew the crisply folded piece of paper. It read simply: "Do what needs to be done."

Nineteen

The next morning, Markus led Edris out into the green hills surrounding Hillshire. Without any new information, they had no hope of finding the Sword of Betrayal; however, Markus wished to mislead the adventurers who were watching him. If they saw him searching the countryside, they might believe the sword was near at hand. Then Markus could slip away and determine its actual hiding place.

After receiving his father's letter, Edris was more than happy to get away. He needed to think about his position and hiking always cleared his mind.

"What did you do last night, tucked away all alone in your room?" Markus asked as they trekked along one of the many rolling paths Raaf could've taken for his last ride. "You missed dinner."

Edris was tempted to mention Lady Louisa's advances but thought better of it. Markus wasn't exactly known for his discretion. "I read the diaries," he said with some truth. "I was comparing the original to the one you had obtained at Upper Angle."

"And?"

"You were right. Apart from the last entry, they're the same."

"Added, undoubtedly, to throw off anybody who might be interested in finding his body. Surely it didn't take you all night to determine that."

They plodded up a steep slope, the squire Jacob following at a discreet distance.

"It's interesting reading," Edris said, feeling the need to go on. "It seems Raaf's father, King Rolf, was an overbearing blowhard. His son hated him. Did you know Raaf didn't even want to become king? He wanted his brother to supersede him."

Markus swatted a stick at the waist-high grass. "Well, he got his wish, now, didn't he? Did you learn anything else?"

"Nothing helpful."

They continued along the path, scaling one hill, then another, the early autumn sun beating down upon them. Finally, Markus broke the silence. "If you were going to become a king, but didn't want to…what would you do?"

Edris had been considering a similar question.

"Are you suggesting Raaf didn't actually die? That he disappeared to avoid being what his father wanted him to be?"

Markus frowned at the dirt track as they walked. He exhaled heavily. "I don't know. I can't imagine anybody giving up the noble's life, especially with only the clothes on your back and the horse under you. And people would've undoubtedly recognized him had he stayed in the kingdom. Still, we have to consider all—"

The tall grass to their left rustled as a masked man with a bow leapt to his feet. "Hold!"

Both Edris and Markus drew their swords.

"Give me the letters," the man commanded, "and nobody will get hurt."

Markus eyed the intruder. "I've heard your voice before. And I'm sure I'll hear it again. Are you sure this is how you want to play things?"

Aiming an arrow at Markus's chest, the masked man drew his bowstring to his ear. "Shut up and give me the letters."

"I don't know what you're talking about, friend."

"The letters Lady Louisa gave your brother. Give them to me!"

"Letters?" Markus replied, confused.

"Do you mean this?" Edris rummaged in his pack and held up the letter from his father.

The masked figure's jaw clenched. "Raaf's letters, you simpleton."

"The only thing we have is Raaf's diary." Edris took the copy they'd gotten from Upper Angle and tossed it at the man's feet, hoping he'd bend down to retrieve it. Then he'd rush him. "It's yours if you want it."

"It's worthless. Everybody's read the diary. I want the letters. Give them to me, or I'll stick you in your guts."

"You might get one of us," Edris said, tightening the grip on his sword. "But there's three of us against—"

The arrow slammed in Edris's thigh. He crumpled to the ground, screaming. "Son of a bitch!"

Before Markus or Jacob could react, the archer had another arrow fitted to his bowstring.

"Now there are two of you," the masked figure said. "Give me the letters, or I'll aim higher next time."

"We don't have any letters." Markus jabbed his sword into the ground. "Check for yourself." He gave him his pack. Jacob did the same.

The masked man hunted through their belongings.

"Give me the big fella's."

Markus gave him Edris's pack as he rolled about, clutching his thigh.

The masked man searched through Edris's things, then swore. "Undo your belts. Move your cloaks aside. Show me what you're carrying."

They showed him that they didn't have any letters tucked behind their backs.

The masked man swore again. "Blast it! If I find you've been holding out on me…"

"Trust me," Edris said through gritted teeth, "if I ever find you, you stinking, little…"

Markus stepped forward, hands raised. "He doesn't mean it. He's not one of us. He's merely my young cousin keeping me company. You have nothing to worry about."

"If either of you follow me," the intruder said, withdrawing, "I won't shoot for the leg."

"Understood," Markus said. "Good luck with the quest."

The masked man scowled, then fled into a small grove of elm trees.

"Good luck on the quest?" Edris snarled. "What the hell was that? You should've rushed that bastard."

Markus jerked the arrow from Edris's thigh.

"He's a crack shot. If he wanted to, he could have hit a bone or worse. Best not make enemies when you're at a disadvantage. Remember that, Eddie." He examined the wound. "You'll be fine. Let's get you to town. You're no good to me like this."

Twenty

Later that night, Edris once again found himself in his quarters lying on the sofa, his heavily bandaged leg elevated by a stack of satin pillows.

He picked up his father's letter, read it for the hundredth time, and then flung it on a stack of dirty dishes.

"Do what need be done," he said, disgusted.

Markus had practically carried him back to Hillshire. Could he really betray him?

There was a soft knock on the door. Edris knew instantly who it was.

Reluctantly, he called, "Enter."

Lady Louisa entered bearing a silver tray laden with grapes, white bread, and a slab of pink lamb that filled the entire plate. When she saw the other trays on the table, she laughed. "I suppose you won't be needing any of this."

With the assistance of a cane, Edris fought his way to his feet. His leg throbbed, but the pain was manageable.

"Thank you, my lady. It smells wonderful."

"My, you're being awfully formal." She set the tray next to the others. "Please sit. I know you must be in agony."

Edris sat. The lady moved the cushions upon which his leg had been propped and sat next to him.

"Is there anything I can do?" she asked, rubbing his uninjured thigh. "Anything at all?"

Edris tensed as her hand slid higher.

"I'm sure I can find some way to take your mind off of your discomfort." She leaned closer, her warm lips kissing his neck.

Edris shot to his feet.

"I'm...I'm sorry." He hobbled away, putting a chair between them. "This is inappropriate."

"Why?"

"Because you're betrothed to my cousin!"

"At the moment, I'm not betrothed to anybody."

"But you...you could be my queen someday!"

"And you think queens are all pure as new fallen snow, is that it?"

"Well..."

"Oh, please!" She hooted. "I suppose you think that men in my position are all chaste too?"

"That's different."

"How?" Lady Louisa cried.

"They're men! Men are...you know."

"Womanizing asses?" She folded her legs under her as though she were sitting up all night, chatting with one of her girlfriends. "Eddie, women and men aren't all that different. We enjoy the thrill of the hunt too."

"Thrill of the hunt?"

"Yes!" She shook her head as though seeing him as an adolescent boy, rather than a desirable young man. "Women enjoy being pursued. And we enjoy being the pursuer. And—" She shrugged. "—we enjoy sex just as much as men do."

Edris glanced toward the window, yearning to escape through it.

Lady Louisa huffed in disbelief. "You actually believe we're all delicate little flowers, don't you?"

"I didn't say that!"

"But you thought it! I can tell." She tied her hair into a bun. "I keep forgetting how young you are. You have a great deal to learn about women."

"Tell me about it."

"If you're not interested in me, simply say so. You won't break my fragile female heart. Women might not be as physically strong as men, but we're a lot stronger in other ways. Trust me. We can handle disappointment. If a man doesn't give us what we want, we're perfectly capable of moving on. We're not going to hide in some tower, pining away until old age takes us."

Edris took a deep, uneasy breath. "I'm sorry. It's not that I'm not interested or anything, but...you see, there's a girl back home. And, well...she means a great deal to me."

Lady Louisa smiled fondly at him. "That's really sweet. I hope she knows how lucky she is."

"I hope she is as lucky as she deserves."

A tear tumbled down Lady Louisa's cheek. She brushed it away. "So, help me if you are saying those things so that I'll be more attracted to you!"

"I'm not! Actually, the whole reason I'm helping Markus is to earn enough money so that, if my father disowns me, Bea and I could go off on our own."

"Bea?"

"That's what I call her. Her name is Beatrice."

"She sounds pretty."

"She is. Beautiful, in fact."

"Well," Lady Louisa said, standing up, "I was hoping to have a stimulating evening—but I see you're in love, and I won't get in the way of that. Though, I must say—" She surveyed his muscular body, disappointed.

"—you present a tempting trophy." She curtseyed formally. "I bid you good night, Edris. You'll make a wonderful husband someday."

"Thank you, my lady. Again, I'm sincerely sorry."

"You have nothing to be sorry about. But don't become like other men. You hear me? Men of honor are as rare as quest items. Good night."

Edris called to her before she could leave.

"May I ask you something?"

She stopped.

"What?"

Edris gestured to a book next to the trays of food. "You knew about the diary and its connection to the quest."

"Who do you think got it for Merrick? The games women play, remember?"

"Yes, I understand," Edris said before she could finish closing the door. "One more thing, if you don't mind."

She waited.

"When we were attacked..." Edris tried to recall the exact wording. "...the bowman mentioned you and asked if we had *the letters*. Know what he was talking about?"

Lady Louisa sighed dramatically. "You want them as well?"

"I don't know. Do they have anything to do with the quest?"

"Perhaps. They're from Raaf. One was written the day he disappeared."

"You're kidding me! Can I read them?"

She considered him.

"Oh, very well. I was going to use them to make Merrick do a few special things for me. But I suppose I could let you have them."

"Thank you! Thank you very much! They might be what we need to win this quest."

"Just make sure this Beatrice appreciates the sacrifice I'm making for her happiness."

Twenty-One

"Raaf wasn't even in Hillshire when he died?" Markus asked, shocked.

He, Edris, and Merrick were sitting by a window in Markus's parlor, discussing their next move. They were at a dead end, unable to decide what to do, until Edris showed them the letters Lady Louisa had given him.

"According to what I read; he was in Strombath." Edris searched the pile of papers and found the two he was looking for. "They're dated within five days of his disappearance. One is to his father. The other to his sister, Rachel. But," he added, trying to contain his mounting excitement, "they could be fake."

"Perhaps." Markus examined the letters. "Though the handwriting is similar to what's in the original diary."

"You'd be surprised what forgers could do," Merrick said. "But you're right. They look like they were written by the same person. See how he signs his name? It's almost identical to the diary."

"And there's an entry in the diary saying he was feeling ill," Edris said. "That seems to coincide with what these letters are saying."

"When did he write that?" Markus asked.

Edris flipped through one of the journals. "The fifth-to-last entry of the original states: *The distress in my gut hasn't subsided. The healers have suggested*

I take to the waters." Edris checked the other diary. "The copy from Upper Angle has the same entry, but it is the sixth to last."

"The waters…" Markus repeated.

"Strombath is known for its hot springs," Merrick said. "Even Father has been there."

Markus stroked his chin, thinking. "Other than the last entry, is the copy from Upper Angle identical to what is written in the original?"

"What we assume is the original, you mean," Merrick corrected. "This could all be a wild goose chase. I can't believe nobody has read these letters before."

"Good point."

"I've only begun to read the original, but…" Edris consulted both books. "They appear very similar. There are words in the original that are crossed out and don't appear in the copy, but everything else seems verbatim."

Markus strolled about the polished parquet floor. "Everybody's looking in the wrong place."

"So, it would seem," his brother replied. "But we still don't know where around Strombath Raaf was killed. I've been there many times. It's a small hamlet, but the hills are woven with trails. He could've been killed anywhere."

"And his body could've been buried anywhere."

"Exactly."

"What's our next move?" Edris asked, the exhilaration he'd felt at finding such an important clue dissipating into disappointment.

"We need to get to Strombath and have a look around," Markus said. "The issue is how. The moment we leave here, we'll have half the adventurers on the continent following us. We need a diversion."

"You could head in the opposite direction," Merrick offered. "Then circle around to Strombath from the north."

Markus shook his head. "No. They'll follow me wherever I go."

"Then you need a plausible excuse to leave Hillshire. Something that'll throw them off your trail."

"Yes, but what?"

A company of the king's archers practiced in the courtyard; the *thwap* of their arrows striking targets punctured the heavy silence.

"How did you come across these, by the way?" Merrick asked Edris.

"Yes, how did you find them?" Markus added. "It was the stroke of good fortune we were lacking. You're quickly earning your five hundred gold!"

"They were in the king's library."

He'd hoped that that was a sufficient explanation, but Merrick pushed on. "Yes, but how did you get access to them? You wouldn't believe the things I've had to do to get my hands on Raaf's original diary."

Edris blushed.

"I bet," Markus said, chuckling, "our little cousin had to do many of the same things."

"What?" Merrick cried.

Edris's ears burned red.

"You slept with her?"

"Absolutely not!"

"But you did something other than sleeping, didn't you?" Markus prodded.

"I swear on my mother's life," Edris protested, "I did nothing—"

"I can't believe this!" Merrick said, tossing his hands.

"Oh, come on, Merrick. You knew how she was before you started with her. Besides—" Markus grinned. "At least she's staying within the family."

"That's hardly any consolation!"

"On my honor—" Edris interjected, but nobody was paying any attention.

"Were you really going to marry her?" Markus asked his brother. "Seriously?"

"Maybe!"

"Maybe isn't good enough, Merrick. You know the rules. Anybody without a ring on her finger is fair game."

Merrick slumped in a chair, grumbling.

"Speaking of letters," Markus said to Edris. "What did your father have to say?"

"The same as always," Edris replied, happy for the change in topic. "He basically told me what I needed to do to prepare for the spring."

Merrick gave a bitter grunt. "Come spring, I should tell Kriton to give it to you good. Sleeping with my precious bride-to-be. Who does that?"

"Dammit, I told you," Edris sputtered. "I didn't—"

"You slept with Prince Kendal's wife!" Markus said to Merrick.

Merrick hushed him, shooting an anxious glance at the closed door. "That was completely different. She initiated the affair."

"I didn't sleep with her!" Edris insisted.

"Sure, you didn't."

Edris placed a hand over his heart. "My word to the gods!"

"Yes, well," Merrick said. "I'll forgive you, Eddie. But I should warn you, other men might not be as kind as I. You'd best learn some restraint. Sleeping with another man's woman is a good way to get killed. You have to be discreet."

"You slept with Hamilton's wife as well," Markus stated. "The day after they got married, in fact."

A sly smirk broke over Merrick's lips. "She was still thin then. Got as huge as a whale once she had her first child. Hamilton deserves her."

"For the record, absolutely nothing happened," Edris said defiantly. "We only talked. That's all!"

"I bet, Eddie," Markus said. "But I believe we're drifting off track."

"What were we discussing?" Merrick asked. "Besides not sleeping with your cousin's soon-to-be fiancée?"

"We need a reason to leave Hillshire," Markus said. "Something plausible enough so that the others won't follow us."

"Any ideas?"

Markus shook his head. "Not a one."

"My letter!" Edris exclaimed, pulling it from his pocket.

"What about it?" Markus asked.

"We can say I have to return to Bend. People will know I got mail from my father. I could let slip that he's demanding I stop frolicking around and return home. Anybody who knows him will believe that to be the king's truth."

"And you'd need aid getting there because of your leg," Markus said, mulling it over.

"Exactly."

Markus and Merrick regarded each other.

"That could work," Merrick conceded.

"No, it won't," Markus said. "Nobody's going to believe I'm giving up the hunt this early."

"You don't have to pretend you're giving up the hunt. In fact, you should tell people you're mad as hell you have to leave the trail temporarily to bring your baby cousin home. Besides, what other option do you have?"

"None, seemingly." Markus sighed at Edris. "How's your leg? Can you travel?"

"I can't run on it, but I can ride."

"Hmm." Markus leaned on the windowsill, watching the archers take aim. Another series of *thwacks* filed the courtyard. "Let's put a splint on it. Make it look like it's broken. Hobble around a lot. That might do the trick."

"So, we're headed to Bend?" Edris asked, not looking forward to seeing his father.

"Yes. It'll be a couple weeks out of our way, but if we can throw off any pursuers, it will be time well spent. We'll leave the day after tomorrow."

Twenty-Two

Two days later, Markus and Edris set out for Bend. To confuse would-be followers, they openly took the main road out of Hillshire and rode at an unhurried pace. Markus also sent his squire home to Upper Angle.

"So, tell me," Markus said as their horses trotted along a country lane. "How was she?"

Edris rubbed his injured leg. He could walk with the assistance of a cane, but it throbbed continuously, and the jarring motions of his horse didn't help matters. "What are you talking about?"

"Louisa. Homely girls are always the best in bed. Very willing to please, if you know what I mean!"

"She isn't homely."

"I have horses that are prettier than she is."

"I think she has a bit of a spark to her."

"A spark?" Markus laughed. "You're not sweet on her or anything, are you? Because if you are, you'll need to talk with Merrick."

"What? No. No, not at all. And again, I *didn't* sleep with her."

"Was she noisy?" Markus persisted. "I love noisy women."

"Are there any women you don't like?" Edris asked irritably.

"None that I have yet encountered."

"Let's drop it. Okay?"

"As you wish."

They were still at least a week's ride from Bend, but Edris's spirit fell with each step their horses took toward his father's fiefdom.

"You all right?" Markus asked. "You know I was only kidding about Louisa. If you say you didn't sleep with her, I believe you."

"I'm fine." Then Edris added, begrudgingly, "I'm just in a black mood. My leg hurts and I don't like being a cripple."

"It's a minor wound. You'll be up and chasing women in no time."

The clomping of their horses' hooves echoed hollowly around them as the autumn leaves fluttered from the trees lining the road.

"Okay, out with it," Markus said. "What's bothering you? I can't believe a troll like you is bothered by a scratched leg."

Edris shrugged. Not wanting to talk about his father, he picked a different topic. "I was thinking about what your brother said. About the dangers of sleeping with women who are spoken for."

"You worried about retribution?" Markus made a dismissive sound. "Trust me, her brother Lawrence is terrified of you. He kept saying that you could probably lift a bull over your head. You have nothing to fear from him."

"Perhaps, but he's hardly typical." Then Edris asked to keep the conversation going, "What would you do if you caught somebody with your sister?"

"With Mariam? I'd kill the bastard. I'd cut off his prick and feed it to my dogs. She deserves nothing less than a king. Thank the gods she's as pure as the spring rain."

Edris checked his horse.

Markus did the same. "What's wrong? Hear something?"

Edris did hear something—galloping hooves. While they weren't trying to be secretive, the last thing he wanted was to come across bandits when he could barely stand.

Behind them, two horses came into view. One was a large grey charger, the other a medium red sprinter. Both riders reined their steeds to a sudden stop.

Markus called to them. "Following us, Archie?"

"Not at all!" the armored man on the charger said defensively. "We're simply going the same way as you."

Markus waved for them to approach, then whispered to Edris, "No need to worry. This is Sir Archibald of Elmwood. Not a bad fellow by any means."

"But a competitor, nonetheless."

"Indeed."

Sir Archibald maneuvered his massive horse next to Markus's mare. Leaning out from his saddle, he extended a gloved hand. Markus shook it.

"Good to see you, Markus."

"Good to see you too, Archie. Allow me to introduce my cousin, Ed. He's Lord Elros's third son."

The knight saluted. "Lord Elros?" he said, confused. "I had no idea any of his sons were in the business."

"I'm not an adventurer," Edris told him.

"He was visiting my family when the quest was announced," Markus explained. "Duncan shot him in the leg, so I'm bringing him home to Bend."

"Duncan?" Sir Archibald repeated. "He isn't exactly the egregious type. Get into a scrape over a woman?"

"Nothing so personal," Markus replied. "We were on the hunt when he got the drop on us. You know how he gets when he has a bow in hand."

"So, you say," Sir Archibald said, unconvinced. "Or perhaps Raaf was riding in Bend?"

Markus's horse turned, uprooting a clump of grass by the roadside.

"I'll tell you what." Markus jerked his reins to one side so that he faced his comrade. "Let's have a little wager. Ten gold says my big, young friend here has a fresh wound in his left leg."

"Make it twenty," Edris said. "I don't drop my pants for strange men in the wilderness for anything less."

"You're legitimately off the hunt?" Archie asked. "That's not like you, Markus. Giving up so soon."

"It's only for a couple of weeks. Like I said, I'm bringing him home so he can recuperate."

Sir Archibald eyed Edris's leg skeptically.

"Blast it! I'll give you twenty gold to see the wound. But if you're lying, I want thirty!"

"Fair enough," Markus said. "Show him, Ed."

Gingerly, Edris climbed from the saddle. Steadying himself against his nickering horse, he pushed down his pants far enough to show the ugly black thread crisscrossing the gash in his left thigh.

"Sons of bitches!" Sir Archibald wheeled his horse the way he'd come. "Turnabout, Chancie. Turnabout!" he shouted to his squire. "We've been duped."

"What about our twenty gold?" Markus asked merrily.

Archibald drew a small pouch from his pocket and threw it at Markus. He spurred his horse into a gallop, his squire hot on his heels.

"And tell the others to stop following us!" Markus called, laughing. He tossed the pouch to Edris as he buttoned his pants. "Here. In case your father disowns you. Next time we'll ask for fifty."

Twenty-Three

"Sir," Edris said, entering his father's private office, "you remember Markus?"

Lord Elros stood. "Of course! How are you, Markus? Come in! Come in! Have a seat."

"Thank you, sir," Markus said, entering the cluttered room.

"Please. Call me Elros. After all, we're family!" Lord Elros returned to the chair behind his imposing desk. "It's an honor to have you in our little neck of the woods. You're rapidly becoming one of the best adventurers in the land. Why, I wouldn't be surprised if you surpassed Sir Drake himself someday!"

"You're too kind. Thank you. But I have a long way to go before I match his tally."

Amazed, Edris watched his father. He'd never seen him so attentive and gracious. His dark eyes were practically shining with pleasure.

"I am hardly being kind in the slightest," Lord Elros continued. "I'm simply stating the facts. Won three out of the last four quests, I believe. Very impressive."

"Three out of the last five, I'm afraid," Markus said, taking a seat in front of him.

"Still, three out of five…" The lord marveled. "You're one of the best adventurers we have. Immensely talented, I must say. Not like—" He scowled at Edris limping over to an empty chair in the corner. "—this one. Tell me, boy, how did you injure your leg? Fall down and skin your knee again? Did you cry?"

Edris gingerly lowered himself into his seat.

"He was shot by a bandit," Markus lied. "He fought bravely."

"Did he kill the bandit?" Lord Elros asked, as though he already knew the answer.

"Well, no," Markus replied. "The villain got away."

The disgust on the lord's face was palpable.

"You should've seen your son in the ring!" Markus exclaimed, changing the subject. "He fought the biggest, meanest man I could find and beat him senseless within three minutes. Then a dozen others rushed into the ring, and he knocked them all unconscious. People in Upper Angle are still talking about it!"

Lord Elros crossed his legs and brushed lint from his freshly laundered pants. "People don't discuss the exploits of mere boxers for long. They're the fancy of idle idiots sitting in taverns, drinking the local swill. Within a week, even the drunks forget them."

Flustered, Markus blurted out, "I think your son is exceptional!"

"I think he's a worthless sack of shit who can't do anything but hobble home because he can't catch a common, run-of-the-mill bandit. I wish he had died instead of his mother."

Edris stared out the window at the rose gardens. He'd heard this all before and expected nothing less; however, Markus was beside himself. His mouth repeatedly fell open as he tried to find something—anything—positive to say.

The Lord of Bend reclined in his chair and smiled. "And how is your father, His Royal Highness? Well, I hope."

After dinner, Lord Elros summoned Edris to his office.

"You have some nerve bringing that shit here," he hissed. "To my home? After what I told you to do?" He stomped about the room, his rage building. "I realize you aren't Edros, but I thought you had a brain in that fat head of yours."

"Yes, sir."

"I want him gone. Do you hear me?"

"Yes, sir. We'll be leaving in a couple days. We wanted to throw off—"

"You don't understand!" He glared at Edris, eyes ablaze. "I...want...him...gone. Do you understand me? GONE."

"I'll see if I can get him to agree to leave in the morning."

"That's not what I mean." Lord Elros leaned closer. "I want him dead."

Edris swallowed. "Dead? How? Why?"

"Figure it out." Then Lord Elros whispered, "Make sure his body is never found. Not knowing what happened to his precious son will drive the king crazy."

"Father, I—I couldn't! He's—"

"You'll do as I say...or else!"

Twenty-Four

The next evening, Edris and Markus stayed in Bend. Edris's explanation for the change was that they could set out in the morning a few miles closer to Strombath and that the White Deer had the best beer in the region. The main reason, of course, was that he had to show some sort of semblance of following his father's orders.

As he sat in the darkened corner of the tavern, pretending to listen to Markus's stories, Edris wondered what he was going to do.

Could he kill Markus?

He stared at the tankard of ale sitting in front of his cousin as he went on about his last adventure.

Edris knew the answer.

In his head, he heard his father mocking him.

"How can you possibly be a kingsman if you can't kill?" he'd ask. *"Or a knight, for that matter? What the hell do you think they do for a living? You've been nothing but a disappointment to me. Your entire life is a waste. Why didn't you die instead of your mother?"*

Perhaps his father was right. Perhaps he was soft.

He tried to imagine his father praising him for a job well done. An unfamiliar feeling welled inside.

When was the last time his father had said anything remotely positive?

His first fight came to mind. He remembered seeing the satisfaction in his father's eyes when he'd beaten one of the guards bloody. Edris was twelve at the time and had stood a hair over six feet tall. He smiled. That was a good day.

"Something I said?" Markus asked. "Or daydreaming?"

"Sorry? No. I was thinking."

Markus took a drink and wiped the brown suds from his neatly trimmed mustache. He leaned forward sympathetically. "About your father?"

Edris's fingers tightened around his stein's handle.

"I had no idea things were *that* bad," Markus said. "I've heard stories, of course, but—great gods! How long has he been like that?"

Edris shrugged. "A couple years. Maybe longer. Forever, I suppose." He took a long pull of his beer. "He has a point. I mean, I've never done anything to actually distinguish myself."

"Ed, you're only fifteen! And you've distinguished yourself plenty in the ring—believe me. Have you ever lost a fight?"

Edris shook his head. He'd stopped counting how many fights he'd won because the number never mattered. After demonstrating how easy it was to punch somebody senseless, his father no longer valued the effort.

"Maybe," Markus said softly, "I should have my father talk to him."

"No!" Edris cried, startling the patrons around them. "By the gods, don't. Promise me!"

"All right! All right!" Markus said, conscious of the people watching them. "I was only offering. I don't want to make matters worse."

"Well, that'd do it. Parenting advice from His Majesty would likely get me killed."

Markus studied him from across the table.

"You know..." he said optimistically, "perhaps you'll like being a kingsman. I mean, it'll be a stroll in the park compared to what you're used to."

"Do you really think so?"

"Ed, if you can stand living with that man, you'll be able to tolerate anything Kriton throws at you." He clinked his tankard against Edris's. "Trust me. You'll be great as a kingsman." He took a drink. "And it'll only be for a few years. Then, who knows? Life has a tendency of unraveling problems on its own."

Edros often said the same thing.

Markus lifted his head, his eyes widening. Judging by the gleam in them, an attractive woman had entered the tavern.

Edris peered over his shoulder and found Beatrice approaching their table.

He got to his feet, beaming.

Markus followed suit.

"Bea!" Edris hugged her.

"Ed." Beatrice stood on tiptoe and let Edris kiss her cheek. "I'd heard you were in town…" She noted the black walnut cane perched against the table. "…and that you were injured." She touched his arm affectionately. "You okay?"

"Oh, it's nothing. A scratch." He examined her. She was wearing a sage-green dress he'd given her that summer. "You look beautiful."

She smiled lovingly at him. "Thank you. I missed you."

"I missed you more."

Markus coughed.

"Oh!" Edris said. "I'm terribly sorry. This is my cousin, His Royal Highness Prince Markus from Upper Angle. Markus, this is Beatrice."

Beatrice curtsied. "Your Highness."

"Ah, none of that!" Markus took Beatrice's hand and kissed it. "Only my eldest brother uses the title. I'm just Markus. And I agree with Eddie. You *do* look beautiful."

Edris gave Markus a smoldering expression he hoped would convey the intensity of his displeasure, but Markus was too busy pulling out a chair to notice.

"Please…join us," he told Beatrice.

"Let me go get us some drinks," Beatrice said. "Yours look low."

Markus snatched her arm before she could leave. "Let the barmaids do that. They'll be around in a moment."

Beatrice laughed. "I work here on occasion. If I make them bring me a drink, there'll be spit floating in the foam, if not worse. I'll be right back."

Markus ogled her as she wove her way through the crowd.

Edris stepped in front of him. "No."

"No what?" Markus chuckled. "Let me guess you two have something going."

"Something like that."

"Is it serious? Are you going to put a ring on her finger?"

"Maybe."

"Really?" Markus replied, stunned.

"We've known each other since we were children."

"And you love her?"

The words caught briefly in his throat, but Edris forced them out. "I do."

Markus straightened. "Very well, then." He adjusted his surcoat, smoothing out its wrinkles. "She's off the menu."

"Promise?"

"Of course! You have my word."

Edris stared at him doubtfully, attempting to discern whether he was being forthcoming.

A throng enveloped them.

"Excuse me," one patron said. "You're the king's son—the one who adventures—Markus."

Markus bowed and announced loudly enough for everybody to hear, "Correct on both accounts, I'm afraid!"

A cacophony of greetings and accolades filled the tavern as more people pressed closer. Some congratulated him on his last win. Others inquired about the king's health. Scores of hands reached out, trying to shake his. When Markus ordered drinks for everybody, the crowd cheered.

Beatrice edged her way through the mass of bodies with three steins, brown suds dripping to the dirty floor. With an effort, she managed to get to Edris's table.

"So," she said, setting a beer in front of him, "tell me what happened. What adventures have you been having while the rest of us are stuck in dreary Bend?"

For a moment, Edris watched as his cousin went about the room, talking to everybody. He paused whenever he came to an attractive woman.

"Fortunately, nothing happened," he said, sitting next to her. He took her hand. "And the only adventure I need is right here with you."

Twenty-Five

"I remember that!" Markus said as their horses tromped along.

Around them, chickadees and sparrows sang in the trees as autumn leaves rustled in the cool breeze. They'd been riding to Strombath for nearly a fortnight and were ascending the forested foothills of the Green Mountains, laughing and telling stories the entire way. It was probably the happiest time Edris had ever known.

"Well, I'll tell you a secret," he said sheepishly, "if you promise you won't get angry."

"I promise."

"It wasn't Edros who pissed in your waterskin that night."

"It was *you!*" Markus cried. "Edros and I went to blows over that!"

"I remember." Edris added, "He pounded you good."

"He what? You take that back!"

"Never!"

"With all due respect, your esteemed and learned brother, he couldn't beat a corpse in a fair fight."

"Why do you think my father constantly pushes me to train? I have to protect him."

At the mention of Lord Elros, their robust laughter died to fitful chuckles, then to an uneasy silence. They rode side by side, through streaks of bright sunlight slipping between the trees' dwindling canopies.

Turning a bend, they came to a forest-filled gorge cut between the rocky hills by the Dean River. The road they had been following descended the southern slope, winding this way and that, often diminishing to nothing more than a thin ledge hardly wide enough for their horses. They dismounted. Stretching, Markus cracked his spine.

"Since we're telling secrets, dear cousin, I have one I'd like to reveal."

"Do tell," Edris said, hoping they'd regain the mirth they'd been sharing.

They led their horses along the ridge high above the colorful valley.

"Remember that saucy tart from the tavern you took me to in Bend?" Markus asked.

"Which one? Practically every woman in the village was hanging on you all night."

"The one you knew. She had a tight green dress and the nicest hind end I've ever seen."

Edris's heart lurched. "Beatrice?"

"Exactly. Boy, what a looker she was. Nice tits. Firm and petite. Just how I like them."

Edris stopped, attempting to breathe. "You're joking."

"Not at all. I know you had said the two of you were involved, but she indicated otherwise."

"She did?" Edris prayed that at any second, Markus would say he was only kidding.

"She said you've never stated your intentions with her one way or another."

This was true. While Beatrice had made her feelings evident every chance she could, Edris had never reciprocated—at least, not overtly.

"I had to offer her twenty gold." Markus continued along the path. "But by the gods, she was worth it. She was nearly fresh."

Edris remained riveted where he stood, seething. He tried to offer a light chuckle but couldn't exhale. "Bea would never—"

"Never?" Markus's laugh cut into Edris's soul. "All women have their price, Eddie. Your Beatrice, at least, was a skilled negotiator. She'd make a fortune in a bigger town. Whores like her are hard to come by."

Snarling, he reached for his sword.

"What's the matter?" Markus asked. "Why aren't you following? Afraid of heights?"

"I wanted to give you room," Edris said bitterly. "I'd hate to accidentally bump into you and knock you off."

Markus peered over the edge of the path. It was eight hundred feet straight down to a boulder-strewn river.

"Good idea." Then he said over his shoulder, "What were we discussing?"

Eyes narrowing, Edris proceeded along the ledge, leading his horse at a pace that would overtake his cousin.

"That's right…your friend!" Markus called. "What a looker. I tell you; she was worth every—"

Markus's horse suddenly whinnied in terror.

"Shit! Hold up, Eddie. There's a snake."

Snorting, Markus's horse reared, its great hooves punching the air.

"It's okay." Markus stroked his mare's neck. "It's gone. Everything is—"

The horse bolted forward, bashing Markus aside. Thrown, he tumbled along the path, coming to a stop along the edge of the cliff. Then the ground beneath him gave way. He slid over the brink, hands clawing frantically at the crumbling rock.

Grabbing at anything he could reach, he shrieked, "Eddie!"

"Markus!" Edris raced along the ledge.

Markus slid another foot. His legs and waist dangled high above the valley. Displaced stones tumbled past him, falling into the surging water far below.

"Hurry!"

"Hold on!" Ripping off his cloak, Edris dove to where his cousin lay.

Markus slipped a few more inches, his fingernails digging into the dirt.

"Here!" Edris threw him the end of his cloak.

White hands latched onto it.

"What are you doing?" his father's voice said in his head. *"Do it now! Do it now! Let go!"*

"No!" he cried, straining under Markus's weight.

He pulled.

The cloak stretched, its fabric threatening to tear.

Trying to find purchase against the cliff face, Markus's feet flailed. More rocks tumbled to the river.

Edris heaved.

Markus's arms appeared above the ledge.

"Kill him!" he father's voice said. *"That's what kingsmen do! They kill your father's enemies!"*

Edris pulled again.

"You have one last chance! Let go!"

Markus's head appeared. Then his shoulders. Edris grabbed Markus's belt and hauled him up. Markus flung himself sprawling onto the stone.

"You're a worthless sack of shit. Don't bother coming home. You're not my son. You're dead to me."

"You all right?" Edris asked, panting as hard as Markus.

"Great gods," Markus said, sweating. "I owe you one. Honestly, I thought…I thought I was going to feed the fish."

"Let's get to firmer ground."

"Right!" Markus fought his way to his feet and then hugged Edris, his entire body trembling. "I owe you, Eddie. Thanks!"

"I'll add it to the five hundred gold."

"Do that!" Markus laughed, but it appeared he was on the verge of tears. "With interest!" He peered nervously over the ridge. "Boy! Had I hit the river; they never would've found my body!"

Edris retrieved his horse. "Don't think about it."

"Don't think about it?" He wiped his eyes. "I nearly died!"

"But you didn't."

Markus slapped him on the back. "Thanks to you! Honestly, Ed. I'm in your debt."

"Let's go find your mare."

"Indeed. Lead on."

They followed the path further down the slope, Markus keeping as close to the cliff face as possible.

"Why did you shout 'no'?" he asked.

"What?"

"When you were pulling me up, you shouted 'no.'"

Markus's horse came into view, galloping along the valley below.

"I meant…no, you weren't going to die."

Markus laughed again. "Well, I'm certainly glad you didn't shout 'Yes!' When we get to town, the first and second rounds are on me. Hell…I'll buy you anything you want!"

Twenty-Six

Edris eased himself into one of the hot springs for which Strombath was famous. Compared to the cool evening air, the swirling water was nearly scorching; however, once his body adjusted to the temperature, it felt fantastic on his injured leg. He sat on the stone bench at the bottom of the pool and leaned back, attempting to immerse himself as much as possible.

Sighing, he closed his eyes and thought about Markus.

Should he have let him fall?

No, of course not. Markus was his cousin, and there wasn't anything more important than family. He was also the king's son. Had he died, questions would've been asked, and he might have been blamed. Yet a nagging doubt crept into Edris's mind. So many of his problems would've gone away had the bastard died.

He thought about Beatrice. Anger boiled within him again. He'd promised he wouldn't touch her.

Edris imagined Markus plunging to his death, his arms and legs flaying as his body hit the river.

He inhaled deeply, trying to calm himself, but the smell of the cedar trees filling the valley did little to lessen his mounting anxiety.

"Ed!"

Cracking open an eye, Edris found Markus standing on one of the surrounding hills.

During the week they'd been at Strombath, Markus had rarely left their room for fear other adventurers might learn of his whereabouts. If they did, they'd descend upon the tiny village like hungry locusts.

Closing his eyes, Edris ignored him. He sunk lower into the steaming water.

"Ed!" Markus called again. He hurried down the long wooden stairways connecting the town on the hilltop with the hot springs. He had a book in his hand.

"What?" Edris called back, annoyed.

"Are we alone?" Markus asked, peering about the neighboring pools.

"I paid extra to have the water to myself." Hoping his cousin would take the hint, he added, "I was tired of making conversation."

"I don't blame you. There's nothing worse than getting stuck next to a chatterbox while you're trying to relax." Markus knelt by the poolside and showed him a page from Raaf's diary. He lowered his voice. "I think I know where it is."

"Really?" Edris said, trying not to let his ire slip away. "Where?"

Markus tapped the page. "Raaf came to Strombath frequently."

"I know. Whenever he'd get into a fight with his father, his stomach would bother him. So, he'd come here. At first, it was to get away from the king, but then he began to believe the water gave him some relief. I've read the diary, remember?"

"Is something wrong?"

"I'm fine," Edris lied. "Where do you think the sword is?"

Markus tapped the page again. "He wrote here about riding among the pines. He liked the smell."

Edris played with a bubble floating in the water, not showing his interest.

"I've checked," Markus whispered. "There's only one pine grove within a day's ride of here." His eyebrows bounced merrily. "Let's go get a sword!"

Edris continued playing with the bubbles.

"What's wrong with you? Didn't you hear what I said? That sword is as good as ours!"

Unable to contain his temper any longer, Edris stood, his wet, naked body looming over his cousin. "You promised!"

"Promised what?"

"To leave Beatrice alone."

Markus retreated a step, then quickly put on a smile. "Ed! I was only kidding about that! Honest. Do you actually believe I'd sleep with somebody you have a mind for? Is that how you see me? After all we've been through?"

Markus's tone was irritated, but Edris wondered whether it was contrived. He wouldn't put it past his cousin to sleep with anybody he wanted, despite what he'd promised.

"Let me ask you this," Markus continued. "You think Beatrice is the type of woman who would've slept with me? And if she is, don't you deserve better?"

He was right. Beatrice wouldn't have slept with Markus. She wasn't a whore. And if she needed the money, she would've come to him.

Edris relaxed slightly.

"See!" Markus said, relieved. "I was just joking. And I apologize for the crack I made about her being able to make money in Upper Angle. I shouldn't have said that. I got carried away." He offered his hand. "Everything good?"

Doubt still lingering, Edris took his hand. "We're good." Then he added coldly, "However, if I find out you slept with her—I'm going to kill you."

Twenty-Seven

Edris hiked up another hill north of Strombath, grumbling to himself despite the agreeable aroma of the towering pines. His leg, while functional, still throbbed, and the hours of hiking had given him plenty of time to consider his problems.

He'd serve as a kingsman, he'd decided. Yes, Kriton would make his life beyond miserable, but he could take it. He needed to learn self-restraint anyway. Perhaps dealing with the captain's abuse for five years would make his father proud.

Then there was Markus and Beatrice.

Did he sleep with her?

On one hand, Markus was right. Bea wouldn't have slept with him—certainly not for money. She wasn't like that. On the other hand, Markus was definitely nervous. Ever since they'd hiked out of town, he'd been chittering away, unable to look in Edris's direction. He was afraid of something; Edris could see it in his worried, calculating eyes.

They reached the hill's summit.

"Now what?" Edris asked, rubbing his leg.

"Now," Markus replied gleefully, "we think."

"I'm not exactly the thinking type."

"You will be before I'm done with you, I can promise you that. You're turning into quite the adventurer. Perhaps after your stint as a kingsman, you can journey with me more regularly."

Edris didn't say anything. Spending more time with his cousin was the last thing he wanted to do.

Next to him, Markus inhaled deeply. "Ah!" he said with satisfaction. "Do you smell that?"

Through a break in the trees, Edris surveyed the endless line of rolling hills. It was beautiful this way. He could see why Raaf would want to ride around here. It was remarkably peaceful. He nodded. "I love pines."

"Not that. There are plenty of pine trees around Upper Angle. I'm talking about the smell of pending success. Victory is at hand!"

Peering about, Edris shrugged. "So where is it?"

"The question, my dear cousin, is—where *isn't* it?"

"Where isn't it?"

"Let's assume the attack occurred somewhere around here. If you killed your brother and didn't want anybody to find the body, what would you do?"

Edris shrugged again. "I'd stampede his horse to make sure it wasn't found nearby."

"Good. What would you do with the body?"

"I'd carry it off the path, trying not to spill a trail of blood, and then bury it somewhere isolated."

"Good. Except there's one problem."

"And what's that?"

"Ever try to dig in a forest?"

"I don't believe I've ever had the opportunity."

"Look at these trees." Markus patted one of the sap-speckled trunks. "They're hundreds of years old. Their roots are probably as big as your arms, and they're everywhere. You wouldn't be able to bury a cat here, let alone a man."

Edris examined the ground. Under a carpet of brown pine needles, thick tree roots crisscrossed the hard ground. He'd been tripping over them all morning.

"Plus," Markus went on as if teaching a schoolboy, "look at these hills." He stomped a boot. "They're made mainly of stone. You could dig a foot or two, but after that…you'd need an army of men with picks to carve out a big enough grave. So what does that leave us?"

Edris thought for a moment. "A cave?"

"Exactly!"

"How do we find the cave?"

"We're going to split up and systematically search these hills. What I want you to do is take the left side of the path. Walk down the slope in a straight line. When you get to the bottom, go ten paces that way." He pointed eastward. "Then come back up. Keep doing that around the hill. I'll do the same to the right of the path."

"What am I looking for?"

"Any opening large enough to stuff a body."

"All right."

"Also, look for any rock formations that don't seem natural."

"Rock formations?"

"Oh, you know. Any pile of rocks that might hide a cave opening or be heaped over a body. Understand?"

"Fine."

"Great. Meet you later." He headed to the right side of the hill, then stopped. "And Ed? Thanks for helping me with this."

"You can thank me when we find that damned sword."

"Right! One thousand gold!" Markus winked at him. "Holler if you find anything."

For the better part of two hours, Edris marched up and down the hillside, often slipping on the dry pine needles covering the otherwise rocky ground. He was tired and hungry and his back hurt from constantly ducking under low branches. He would've given his entire inheritance for a pint of beer.

From the other side of the hill, Markus shouted.

"Did you find something?" Edris called as he made his way through the woods.

He found Markus kneeling in the dirt, peering into a narrow crevice nestled behind a dead pine tree. He grinned at Edris. "Ready to find your first quest item?"

"Me?"

Markus stood and wiped the dirt from his hands. "Of course, you. Look, if I go in there and get stuck, you won't be able to come in to get me. Right? You won't fit if I don't. But if you go in and get stuck, I can help."

Something about this logic bothered Edris, but he was anxious to see what was in the cave.

Markus lit a torch. "Keep this well in front of you. Push it along the ground. Don't get burnt."

Unslinging his pack, Edris took the torch.

"And Ed?"

"Yeah?"

Markus pointed to his sword. "Best leave behind anything that'll get snagged."

"Oh, right." Edris undid his weapon belt and handed it to Markus. Then, for good measure, he took off his cloak. "Be back in a second."

"Hopefully with the Sword of Betrayal."

Edris entered the hole, banging his head in the process. At first, the tunnel was wide enough for him to clamber forward on his elbows. But as the ceiling lowered, he was forced to slither on his stomach in the cool mud. In front of him, his torch blazed, spitting and sputtering as he slid it along. Occasionally, the oily black smoke wafted into his face, making him cough and his eyes water. After thirty yards, the passage dwindled to the point he couldn't continue.

"See anything?" Markus shouted from outside.

"No," Edris yelled back. "It's too small."

"What?"

"It's too small!" he said, the echoes distorting his voice. "Hold on!"

"What? Did you find it? Is it the sword?"

Edris shimmied backward. He could feel fresh air. Then he could see the sunlight.

Markus called excitedly into the tunnel. "Find it?"

"No. The tunnel's too small. There's no way they could've pushed a body any further than I went." He wiggled out of the tunnel, covered in mud. "Sorry."

"Don't worry. I'm sure it's somewhere nearby. And Fatty Eddie?"

Prone on his dirty knees, Edris looked up at Markus. He raised his hand to shield his eyes from the sun. "What?"

A rock the size of a grapefruit smashed into Edris's temple. Pain exploded throughout his head as he collapsed to the ground.

"Don't you *ever* threaten me." Markus hit him with the rock again. "Especially over some slutty, two-bit, whore!"

Edris tried to get to his feet, but another blow knocked him down, blood pouring from a gash over his left eye.

"And do you know what?" Markus asked, pounding Edris mercilessly. The rock broke, showering stone everywhere. "I'm the son of the king. I can bed any woman I god-damned well want!" He hit Edris with his fist.

His vision going grey, Edris crumpled into a salty puddle of his own blood.

"By the way—" Markus laughed. "Your father is a no-good drunk. Your mother was lucky to have died when she did."

Another blow made everything go black.

Twenty-Eight

Moaning, Edris awoke, his head hammering. He'd never been in such agony. His skull actually felt as though it were splitting open. He fought his way to his knees and then decided to lie back down. Not moving, he squinted at the sky.

Dim light trickled through the branches of the pine trees. It was either early evening or early morning. He touched his head. Judging from the dried blood on his temple and the stained ground, he guessed it was morning.

A dozen bumps and gashes throbbed under his matted hair.

He tasted salty dirt.

Looking around, he found his weapon belt, but the scabbard was empty.

Markus…

Next time he saw him, he was going to kill the bastard.

Edris attempted to roll over, then retched.

He lay on the ground, wondering whether he was going to die.

Was that Markus's intent?

Probably not. He could've slit his throat while he lay unconscious. Hell, he could've sealed him in the tunnel, having him slowly starve to death in a stone coffin. Nobody would ever have found his body.

No. Markus was simply sending a message—a very painful message as to what would happen if Edris ever crossed him again.

Would he really kill Markus the next time he saw him?

Absolutely—if he had the advantage and he could get away with it. Killing the king's son would have repercussions, but he'd kill him, nonetheless.

Someday…

For now, he had to get help.

Forcing himself to all fours, Edris attempted to stand. His vision went in and out of focus. The ground pitched under him. He lowered himself to his knees. It was no use. He'd have to crawl the three miles to town. Taking a deep breath, he turned toward the streams of smoke rising above the green hills, then vomited.

Twenty-Nine

The sun was setting over the western hills when Edris dragged himself into Strombath. With the assistance of several townsfolk, he immediately sought out a doctor who cleaned his wounds and bound his battered head.

"You'll survive," the doctor told him. "Although, you'll have to rest several weeks. A man doesn't recover overnight from a beating like this. Thankfully, you're in the right place to recuperate. Do you have a room?"

"At the Healing Stone," Edris groaned.

"Ah! Very good. Get something to eat—if you can keep it inside of you—then rest. No alcohol. No need blurring your vision even more than it is."

"Thank you, doctor." Edris gave the elderly man a gold piece.

"I'll be in to check on you tomorrow. Remember, you need lots of rest."

Getting rest was exactly what Edris had in mind. He was going to sleep the sleep of the dead. Then he'd sleep some more.

Stumbling toward the inn, he came across two knights and their squires standing in front of a tavern, consulting a map.

"You adventurers?" Edris asked, almost inaudibly. Even whispering hurt his head.

"Beg your pardon?" one said. "Adventurers? Why, yes, we are. I am Sir Geoff. And this is Sir Maurice."

"Are you all right, sir?" a freckle-faced squire asked. "You look the devil."

Edris waved the comment away. "Raaf…" he said, fighting off the waves of pain crashing against the backs of his eyes.

The men froze as if attempting to determine whether they'd heard him correctly.

"What about Raaf?" Sir Maurice asked excitedly. "Do you have information? We have gold!"

Edris hushed them.

"Do you know where the sword is?" Sir Geoff persisted. "Are there other adventurers in town?"

With a shaking hand, Edris pointed vaguely at the pine-wooded hills north of town. "Markus…"

"Markus. Yes? What of him? Is he here? Is he looking for the sword?"

"Raaf liked riding in the pinewoods. Markus is searching caves." Feeling dizzy, Edris clutched the knight's arm. "Beat the crap out of him."

"Did Markus do this to you?" Sir Geoff asked. "Did you have information he needed?"

Edris pulled Raaf's diary from his pack and handed it to the adventurers. Their eyes practically doubled in size.

"Is this the original?" they asked, astonished.

"Raaf," Edris said again. "He liked to ride in the pinewoods."

"Thank you, sir!"

Sir Maurice attempted to give Edris a pouch of coins, but Edris refused.

"Get the sword," he whispered.

"Not to worry. You shall be avenged. Wesley, help this gentleman to wherever he needs to go. John, get the gear. We'll be camping in the hills tonight. Victory will be ours!"

With the help of the young squire, Edris reached his quarters and found Markus's belongings gone.

Had his cousin found the sword?

It didn't matter. The winner wasn't the one who found the sword, but the person who brought it to their king—and the other adventurers would make sure that wasn't Markus.

Pushing his bed up against the door in case Markus returned, Edris collapsed onto the down-filled mattress, allowing blessed sleep to overtake him.

Thirty

For days, the village's doctor tended Edris—bringing him food and water and changing his bandages. After a week, some of his strength had returned and he could eat without retching. When he was able to walk a straight line and see clearly, he staggered around Strombath, now swarming with adventurers.

From what he was told, Markus had an altercation with Sir Geoff and Sir Maurice. Out-numbered, King Michael's son was last seen riding out of town at a fast gallop. That was the day after Edris met the knights. Nobody had seen hide nor hair of him since.

After twenty days of inactivity, Edris was ready to leave. The problem was—he had no place to go. Although he longed to see Beatrice, he had no wish to see his father. Returning home was out of the question. He could go to Upper Angle; however, he was still suffering from headaches and had no desire to run into Markus until he'd fully recovered. Besides, he'd have to report to His Majesty soon enough. Spring was only four months away. He could roam about until his money ran out. But what was the point?

Somebody knocked.

"Who is it?" he asked.

"Your physician," an elderly voice replied.

Edris moved his bed from the door, then unlocked it.

"How are you feeling today?" the doctor inquired.

"Well enough to leave."

"Excellent. Though I should hope you will take things easy for a while. No physical exertion, you understand. Not for another few weeks—at least."

"I'll be riding a horse. Nothing more than a trot."

"Fine."

The doctor removed the bandages around Edris's head and grimaced.

"How do I look?"

"Like a man who got into a fight with a mule and lost."

Edris peered into a mirror above the chest of drawers.

He looked horrid. In addition to his hair being matted with dried blood, he had a jagged laceration above his left eye that was sewn shut with black thread. He also had brown bumps the size of a baby's fists along his hairline. He winced when he touched them.

"You'd best leave those be," the doctor advised. "They'll go away in time."

"How long before I appear normal?"

"You'll have a mighty big scar across your forehead until the end of your days, I'm afraid. But the lumps and discoloration will be gone in a month. Again, I'd recommend you rest as much as you can until they do."

"Thank you, sir."

"No need to *sir* me. I'm not one of those knights racing around the hills." The doctor produced a small pair of scissors. "Let me remove those stitches. Sit. I don't want to have to fetch a ladder to do my work."

Edris sat. "Nobody's found the sword?"

The doctor cut the thread. "Not that I've heard. Of course, I'm guessing they're looking in the wrong spot."

Edris stayed the doctor's hand. "Why? What do you know about Raaf?"

"About the murdered prince?" The doctor resumed cutting. "Nothing more than the fireside tales, I can assure you. However, what I do know is that two hundred years ago, when the prince disappeared, those pinewoods weren't there."

"What? What do you mean?"

"Hold still, young man, or I'll have to add stitches to where I stab you with these scissors."

"Those woods weren't there?"

"When Strombath was first settled some two hundred and fifty years ago, there were pines across these hills. Of course, people need lumber to build houses and all, so they used the trees on the northern hills first. When Raaf allegedly took his last ride, those woods weren't much more than seedlings, replanted by people who had the wisdom to realize that they'd need more lumber someday should the town continue to grow." The doctor tugged free the last of the stitches. "There you go. As I said, you'll have a memento to show the women."

"So," Edris said, trying to think, "where would you look? If you were searching for the sword, that is?"

The doctor put his scissors away. "Well, if I were big and strong like yourself, I'd look in the western hills."

"Why there? Those aren't pine."

"Right you are. They're mainly maple and oak, planted there after all the pine trees were harvested about a hundred years ago."

"So back when Raaf disappeared…"

"The only pinewoods we had would've been over that way. Not to the north where everybody's rushing about."

"I don't suppose," Edris said, hiding his excitement, "you'd be willing to keep this to yourself."

"You going to look for the betrayed prince?"

"I might."

"Tell you what. If you win the quest, send me some of that reward money, and we'll call it even."

Edris shook the doctor's hand. "Deal." He grabbed his pack and hurried out of the room.

"Young man," the doctor called after him.

"Yes, sir?"

"I meant what I said about taking it easy. Not many people could've survived a beating like you did. Best not press your luck more than you need. Hear me? I'd abstain even from sex for a while if I were you. At least until the bumps go away."

"I will. Thank you, sir. And thanks for the information about the trees."

"Hope it helps."

"I think it will. I can smell victory!"

Thirty-One

Edris rode along the hills west of Strombath. As his doctor had indicated, they were wooded mainly with maples and oaks. They were also oriented in long bluffs, rather than the tall, rolling hills where he and Markus had searched. However, Edris could see the appeal of riding along them. They offered a spectacular view of the valley, especially in the autumn with all the leaves turning brilliant shades of yellow, and orange, and red.

He came to a path plunging into a ravine to his left but decided not to follow it. If he were an ailing prince, out for a leisurely ride, the last thing he'd want to do is go headlong down a steep slope. He'd rather take the easier trails and enjoy the afternoon sun.

Edris continued along the ridge, almost forgetting his purpose for being there. For the first time in three weeks, his head was clear and relatively free from pain.

A warm breeze shifted through the woods, rustling the colorful leaves tumbling across his path. His horse plodded along at its own pace.

Then the trail turned abruptly, swinging perilously close to the edge of a cliff. Edris peered over the ledge, thinking what a precipitous drop it would be should a rider take the bend too swiftly.

He halted.

This was a perfect place for an ambush. Assassins could easily lurk in the trees, or behind some of the larger boulders, and shoot a rider slowed by the curve. In fact, it wouldn't take much to panic a horse into going straight over the lip of the ridge.

Edris considered the fall into the valley again. It wasn't a vertical drop, not like the one that nearly did in Markus. Yet, with all the trees and rocks, few people could survive a tumble that way. And those who did would likely be incapacitated, leaving them at the mercy of their attackers.

What then?

With the prince killed, where would the attackers stash the body?

Edris studied the woods to his right. The ground rose sharply, rising another couple hundred feet above the path. It wasn't an insurmountable climb, but with the weight of a corpse over one's shoulder, it would take a great deal of effort.

He considered the drop to his left again.

Throwing a body downhill would be less cumbersome. The question was—was there someplace near at hand where a body could be hidden?

Edris got off his horse and tethered it to a tree. Taking care, he left the path—part hiking, part sliding down the hillside. Coming to a stop, he kicked at the dirt.

Markus was right. The ground was too rocky and the trees too dense. It would take axes and picks to create a deep enough grave in which to hide a body, and the killers probably didn't have that kind of time. They'd want to finish their task and then get the hell out of there before being seen.

Edris steadied himself against a tree trunk. He'd slid a good thirty or forty strides and could no longer see his horse above him. Killers could have come down the slope, a body in their arms, and been completely out of view of anybody who might come along. A quick attack. And an even quicker escape…

But what to do with the body?

Below him, the slope continued for a quarter mile or so before bottoming out into the ravine. Edris didn't see much that way that would suggest a suitable burial site. He scanned the woods around him.

To the left, there were merely more trees and rocks. To the right, a creek tumbled along the hillside, eventually joining the river in the valley.

Edris's hopes rose. He didn't recall any stream crossing the path. And if that was the case...

Clutching branches and boulders, he fought his way to his right and then peered up.

It was difficult to tell, but the stream appeared to issue from a crack in the rock. It wasn't big, but...maybe.

Going on all fours, Edris clawed up the hill. Just as he thought, the trickle of water emerged from a small fissure; however, what got him excited was that the fissure was blocked by a pile of stones—as if somebody was trying to hide its opening.

Carefully, Edris pulled aside the moss-covered rocks. Beyond was a tunnel big enough to stash a body.

Thirty-Two

Splashing through the cold water, Edris slithered deeper into the tunnel. At first, all that he could do was inch forward on his hands and knees. Soon, though, he was able to lift his head without fear of cracking it on the jagged ceiling. Eventually, he could stand upright with a bent back. After a hundred feet, the tunnel opened into a small chamber. He held aloft his lantern.

There, huddled along the damp walls, were two bodies reduced by time to nothing more than heaps of grey bones covered with dirt and dust and worm-eaten rags. In the middle of the chamber, lay a third skeleton— its hands folded over its ribcage, the rotting remains of what might have been a cloak or blanket folded into a makeshift pillow under its skull. Next to the body lay a sword.

Its blade was tarnished and broken above the hilt, but even in the wavering lantern light, diamonds glittered on its finely wrought handguard. The emblem of Hillshire, a shining crown above three hills, adorned its pummel.

Edris smiled. For hundreds of years, people had hunted for the Sword of Betrayal, and here it was in his muddy hands. His father might actually be proud of him.

What should he do now?

If he were an adventurer, he'd bring the sword to his king and collect the thousand gold piece reward. However, seeing that he had initially set out with Markus, King Michael might wonder whether Edris used his son to further his own reputation. Stoking the king's ire certainly wouldn't improve his life any. Then there was Markus…

"Markus…"

Edris's growl echoed in the darkness around him.

He didn't know what he was going to do with Raaf's sword, but he'd be damned if Markus got ahold of it. The bastard would probably take credit for finding it, then Edris would have neither the money he needed to start a new life, nor the prestige he deserved.

Behind him, water splashed. Edris turned quickly, his vision blurring with the sudden movement.

Nobody was there.

He held his aching forehead.

Normally, he'd be willing to fight to keep what was his, but he was still too weak, and Markus was too skilled a fighter.

"What to do?"

If he couldn't keep the sword by force, he'd have to use deception. He needed to hide it. But where?

He could strap it to a leg, but that would be too obvious. It would also make it difficult for him to walk.

He could put it in his pack, but that would be the first place anybody looked.

"Where…?"

Then the answer came to him. He slid the broken blade into his empty scabbard. Unless somebody had him tip the scabbard over, it'd appear as though he were weaponless. That only left the bejeweled hilt. He thought about putting it in his boot, but it would undoubtedly create a noticeable bulge. In the end, he settled for tucking it under his belt behind his back. It'd have to do.

Silently bidding the three skeletons to rest in peace, Edris crawled through the tunnel and into the brilliant afternoon sun.

Thirty-Three

Dripping wet and covered in mud, Edris scrambled to the ridge along which he'd been riding. The first thing he noticed when he turned the blind corner was that there were two horses waiting, not one. The second was Markus pointing a sword at his chest.

"Fatty Eddie!" Markus drew closer. "How's your head?"

"Still ringing."

"Yes, well, sorry about that, little cousin. But you needed to learn a valuable lesson. Did you learn it?"

Edris gritted his teeth. He wanted to say something biting, but he was at a disadvantage and the gleam in Markus's eye warned him not to be cheeky. He nodded.

"Good. Now—" Markus noted Edris's muddy clothes. "What are you doing here?"

Edris decided not to lie, but not to tell the complete truth either. "I found Raaf."

"Where?" Markus demanded eagerly.

Edris inclined his head down the hill. "There's a stream that leads to a cave. He's in there with his two bodyguards."

"And the sword?"

"It's gone."

Markus smiled knowingly. "Of course, it is."

He signaled for Edris to part his cloak. Edris showed him his empty scabbard.

"Bend your legs," Markus said.

Edris brought his knees up and patted his pant legs.

"Where's your pack?"

"It's on my horse."

Markus rifled through it, chucking clothes and books to the leaf-strewn ground.

"Damn it!" he said. "It wasn't with the body?"

"No. Another adventurer must've gotten there first."

"Another adventurer," Markus repeated angrily.

"There were tracks in the mud," Edris went on, trying to add plausible details. "So, it must have been recently."

Markus's lips twitched. "Show me."

"I've already told you where it is. I'm not crawling in a cave with you. And I sure as hell am not going to crawl into one with you standing outside."

"You catch on quickly."

"You nearly killed me. I'm serious, I still can't see straight at times."

"You had to learn, Eddie. You don't put women before blood."

Keeping his back away from Markus, Edris began picking up his clothes and shoving them into his pack. "I'm taking my horse and leaving."

"Where you are going?"

"I honestly don't know."

"It's by a stream?" Markus surveyed the hillside.

"The stream comes out of a fissure. You'll find the bodies about fifty yards inside. Raaf is laid out as if for burial. Hands folded over his chest. Pillow under his head. There's no sword." Edris added sarcastically, "Do you want me to wait outside the cave while you crawl in?"

"That won't be necessary. Take your horse and ride away, Eddie. Go wherever you want. But if I find you skulking around these hills again…"

"Understood." Edris mounted his horse, praying that the hidden hilt wouldn't fall free.

"And Fatty Eddie," Markus said cheerfully.

"What?"

"See you in the spring."

Thirty-Four

For the better part of a month, Edris rode with no destination in mind. He took random paths and stayed at whatever villages or towns he came across, keeping to himself as much as possible. Eventually, he knew he had to make a decision.

"See you in the spring," Markus had said, gloating.

Edris didn't know what he was going to do in the spring, but he knew what he wasn't going to do. If he became a kingsman, he'd be at the mercy of both Kriton and Markus. It would be five years of absolute living hell. He couldn't let that happen.

Then there was the issue of his father.

Would his father disown him for not killing Markus?

Maybe…

Probably…

He'd be out on his own. True, he could turn the sword in for a thousand gold pieces; but even that would be eventually spent. He needed a career. Something that could provide him with a decent living. Something that he would be good at.

That left only one option…

Thirty-Five

Edris paced outside King Michael's receiving hall, the corridor once again crowded with waiting petitioners. As he roamed about, he went over his plan, reflecting on each word he'd say and how he'd respond if the king knew of his altercation with his son.

The gilded double doors swung open.

"Edris, son of Lord Elros," the door warden announced regally.

Edris entered the hall teeming with government officials and bodyguards.

"Eddie!" the king said, looking up from his massive oak desk. He resumed reading a paper, made a comment to a secretary standing next to him, and then motioned for the secretary to leave. The king stood and offered a hand. Edris shook it. "How are you? If I remember correctly, you're a couple months early for your enlistment. Here to borrow more books?"

"No, sir. I was wondering if I might be able to speak with you alone. It'll only take two minutes."

"Two minutes?" The king laughed. "It never takes only two minutes."

"It's concerning Markus and the latest quest."

"Yes, I've heard." The king sighed. "Sounds like the Sword of Betrayal will never be found. Shame. I know Markus really wanted to win that one."

Edris leaned closer and said quietly, "I can make sure he does."

Puzzled, the king waved for the men around him to stop talking.

"Are you implying something, Eddie?" The brightness in his eyes showed that he thought he understood what Edris was offering.

Edris held the king's gaze. "Just that I might be able to help Markus. For certain…compensation."

"Everybody out!" His Majesty shouted. "Give me two minutes with Lord Elros's son. Out!" People filed from the hall. "And somebody go fetch Markus. I want him here, too."

The thought of seeing Markus again didn't please Edris, but he thought he knew how Markus would view his offer.

The king studied him.

"Do you know where the sword is?" he asked.

"Yes, sir."

"Are you sure? I don't want there to be any ambiguity on this point. Did you actually see it?"

"Yes, sir."

"And you are sure—absolutely *sure*—it's Raaf's sword?"

"It has a gem-encrusted hilt."

"What kind of stones?"

"Diamonds. Small white diamonds all along the handguard."

The king sat in his chair, not sure how to proceed.

"There's the emblem of Hillshire on the pommel," Edris went on. "Three hills with the middle one crowned. Little lines radiate out from the crown like it was the sun."

"I always thought that was a rather pretentious touch."

"Yes, sir."

The king regarded him. "You have the sword?"

"I can get it."

The king nodded, as if realizing the large man in front of him was no longer a naïve child. "You want the thousand gold in exchange for the sword?"

"No, sir."

The door to the receiving hall popped opened. In strode Markus.

"Did you send for me, Father?" He saw Edris and stopped, his expression turning gleeful. "Well, Fatty Eddie! What are you doing here? Is it spring already? I believe there's some horse shit that needs to be carried out of the stable yard and you're the dreg to—"

Edris tipped his scabbard over. A broken blade clattered onto the king's desk. The king and Markus stared at it.

"If you look closely at the blood gutter," Edris said, pointing to the divot along the blade's middle, "you'll see runes. They name everybody who has ever borne this sword, starting with Rolf the Third and ending with Raaf."

"Where did you find it?" Markus cried.

"In the cave."

Markus cursed. "Damn! I knew I should've searched you."

"What about the hilt?" the king asked. "There can't be two winners."

"I can get the hilt, sir," Edris answered.

"You have that as well?"

"Yes, sir."

"But you didn't bring it here?"

"No, sir," Edris said, attempting to sound respectful. "I thought it would be best if I didn't."

"I'll give you a thousand gold, Eddie!" Markus said. "Think of what you could do with all that money!"

"He says he doesn't want the reward," the king replied skeptically.

"Two thousand," Markus said, louder. "I want that sword. You're not turning it in and getting credit for the win. The victory is mine!"

"I don't want credit, either," Edris said.

"Then what exactly do you want?" the king asked.

"I want to be knighted."

"Knighted?" the king scoffed. "You're fifteen!"

"Soon to be sixteen."

"Eddie," the king said politely. "You're too young. Select some other form of compensation. I believe we could go as high as two-thousand, five hundred gold."

"I don't want the money," Edris said. "And I won't be a kingsman. I want to be a knight."

His Majesty shifted uncomfortably in his seat. "Is this about what happened between you and Kriton? Trust me, I can smooth that over. Do your time with distinction and I promise—"

"I *won't* be a kingsman," Edris repeated firmer. He adjusted his tone. "Sir."

The king tossed his hands into the air. "Then take the money. We can give you three thousand gold coins. Take it and go be whatever you like."

"I want to be a knight."

"So, I can see! But this isn't the way to do it. Only people who have performed extraordinary service become knighted. Now, after a few years in the company, I can guarantee you—"

"He saved my life," Markus said. "I almost fell off a cliff."

The king turned to his son. "You told me you saved him."

Markus flashed a childish grin.

"I see." The king took a deep breath. "The sword for a knighthood? Is that's what we're talking about here?"

"I believe I've earned it," Edris said.

"He has, Father. I'm not exaggerating when I said he saved my life. I was dangling hundreds of feet over the Dean River. If it weren't for him, you'd be wondering when I'd return home."

The king rapped his knuckles on the table, thinking.

"You realize, Ed, you will become the youngest knight in the kingdom. Possibly in all the kingdoms. In fact, I can't recall there ever being a fifteen-year-old knight in all of history."

"Yes, sir."

The king raised an eyebrow. "Trying to make your father proud?"

"And my mother."

This hit the king as Edris had intended.

"Yes, well," he said awkwardly. "She would've been proud of you regardless. My sister was an exceptional woman." He considered Edris again. "The sword for a knighthood?"

"And everybody believes Markus found it."

"Father—" Markus said.

The king held up a hand, then nodded. "Bring us the hilt, and you shall have your knighthood."

This brought Edris to the tricky part of the negotiation. "I would prefer," he said as graciously as he could, "to have the declaration first."

The corner of the king's mouth lifted slightly. "Don't trust me?"

Edris thought for a long moment, trying to find a better way of answering. In the end, he simply said, "No."

If he took this as a personal slight, His Majesty didn't show it.

"As you wish. The official reason will be because you saved my son's life in a remarkably valiant manner, risking all to save him. I expect you will not divulge your role in the completion of this quest."

"I won't, sir."

"Nobody knows you found the sword?"

"Nobody, sir." Edris slid a glance at Markus. "I wasn't in the position to retain the sword should I've been challenged."

"Very well," the king said. "We'll have the ceremony this evening, if that suits your schedule."

"Yes, sir. Thank you, sir."

His Majesty gestured for Edris to leave. Edris bowed and retreated toward the door.

"Edris," the king called. Edris stopped. "How did you find the sword, by the way?"

Not wanting the king to know he had been actively searching, Edris hesitated. "You wouldn't believe me if I told you, sir."

"Try me."

"I got off my horse to relieve myself," Edris lied. "The slope was rather steep, and I slipped. I slid down the hill, stopping a few feet from a small cave." He shrugged, embarrassed. "I checked inside."

The king and Markus howled with laughter.

"That's how you found it?" Markus asked. "You're kidding me!"

"It was beginner's luck."

"Evidently!"

Edris bowed and made for the door.

"One more thing, Sir Edris," His Majesty said. "Out of curiosity, what do you plan on doing with your life now that you're a knight?"

Edris smiled and opened the door. "I plan on adventuring." He winked at Markus.

"Go ahead!" Markus laughed. "You won't always be so lucky. Falling down a slope while urinating? I wish I could tell everybody. Good luck on the next quest, Fatty Eddie. You're going to need it!"

"That's Sir Edris, Markus. And good luck to you."

Thirty-Six

Edris sat in his father's private office, staring at the mound of documents waiting for the lord's consideration. He wondered how his father was going to react to what he had to say. Then he realized it didn't matter. He'd made his decision—nothing could change it now.

The door flew open as the Lord of Bend stomped in. Sitting at his desk, he tore open an envelope, extracted the enclosed letter, and began reading.

"Father."

Lord Elros looked up abruptly. "Edris." He regarded the closed door, then his son. He leaned forward. "Have you…completed your mission?"

"Yes."

The lord gaped. "To my satisfaction?"

"To mine."

"What the hell does that mean?"

Edris didn't answer.

His father slammed the letter onto a pile. "Couldn't bring yourself to do it, could you? Couldn't do one simple thing? I knew you were weak. I knew you'd disappoint me. Honestly, I have gardeners with more loyalty than you. You're nothing but a miserable pile of—"

Edris slid the king's decree across the cluttered desk.

"What's this?" Lord Elros asked, disgusted.

Edris watched his father's eyes dart indignantly across the page. Then they stopped.

"He knighted you?" his father said, stunned. "Why would he knight you?"

"The official reason was that I saved Markus's life."

"And the real reason?"

"I found the sword."

"And you gave it to Markus?" Lord Elros flung the king's degree back at him. "For what? A lousy scrap of paper? Damn it, boy, you should've—!"

"For being the youngest knight in history," Edris replied sharply.

Lord Elros's fury wavered, whether because of his uncharacteristic insolence or because he'd achieved some degree of notoriety, Edris couldn't tell.

"You found the sword?" his father asked doubtfully. "How?"

"I told the king it was luck."

"But?"

There was a knock on the study door.

"Go away!" Lord Elros shouted. "I'm busy!"

Footsteps scurried away.

"How?" Lord Elros repeated forcefully.

"I found a clue in Raaf's diary. He liked to ride in the pinewoods near Strombath. I realized the pinewoods were no longer there."

"Nonsense! I've been to Strombath. I've seen those pinewoods. I've ridden there many times."

"They weren't there in Raaf's day. And the original woods were harvested for lumber."

His father seemed to understand. "So, everybody else was looking in the wrong place."

The room fell quiet for a long moment—the Lord of Bend rereading the king's proclamation, a contemplative expression growing on his face, Edris peering blankly at a portrait of his mother.

"I should've listened to you," he said.

"How so?"

"I should've killed him." Edris's voice cracked. "I had the perfect opportunity. Hell, I had hundreds of them. I could've slit his throat while he slept, and nobody would ever have found his body, or suspected me."

Lord Elros pointed to the jagged scar over his son's left eye. "What happened?"

"He beat me with a rock. Then left me for dead."

The corner of his father's lips trembled. Getting up, he came to the front of his desk. "You listen to me," he said. "You were smart not to tell the king how you found the sword. They'll think you're lucky and underestimate what you can do. Use that against them. Lull Markus into a false sense of security. Make him think you're afraid of him because he's the king's son. Then, when you have an opportunity—show him no mercy. You understand me? Make him suffer."

"That's exactly what I'm going to do. And I'll bury his body somewhere nobody will ever find it."

"Good." Lord Elros patted his son's knee. "You're learning."

Edris stood, towering over his father. "With your permission, sir, I'm going to fell some trees."

"You do that. Then maybe this evening, we could practice your sword work. I'm not as skilled as Markus, but I might be able to teach you a few things."

"Yes, sir."

Edris made for the door.

"Edris," his father said. "I'm proud of you."

PART TWO

Thirty-Seven

Edris sat naked on the edge of Beatrice's bed, sulking at the crumpled heap of clothes at his feet. Beatrice sat behind him, massaging his neck.

"It happens to everybody," she said.

"Don't say that," Edris replied. "I'm not like everybody."

She kissed his shoulder. "That…you are certainly not, Sir Edris."

"I'm really sorry, Bea. I don't know what's wrong with me."

"Nothing's wrong. You simply have a lot on your mind." She added tenderly, "Do you want to talk about it?"

"No." Then Edris said, "I'm going to kill him for what he did to you. I promise. On my honor."

"I told you, he didn't do anything. Not really. He just got a bit handsy. I've had worse working at the Golden Trout, believe me."

"What kind of man tries to force himself on a woman like that? He's noble!"

"Ed," she said, rubbing his muscles, "apart from you, that's what nobles are like. An unmarried woman is fair game, whether she says no or not. Besides, he was drunk."

Edris wrung his calloused hands. "I'm going to kill him."

Beatrice scooched closer so that her bare breasts pressed against his back. She wrapped her arms around him. "He's the king's son."

"Kings' sons die all the time. Look what happened to Raaf."

Beatrice hugged him tighter, her head resting on his shoulder blade. She could feel the pounding of his heart.

"What if—?" he began, then stopped.

"What if what?"

"What if…" he said, fear and anxiety building within him. "What if he took my—my manhood? When he beat me. Maybe there's something wrong with my head and I'll never—"

"Hey." Sitting next to him, she touched his cheek. "There's absolutely nothing wrong with you. You're the youngest knight in all the realms. You're the youngest knight in all of history! And you're the man I love. You just have a lot on your mind."

"I'm going to kill him."

"Ed. Look at me."

He looked at her, tears of frustration and embarrassment in his eyes.

"I won't lie to you," Beatrice said. "I wouldn't lose a moment's sleep if Markus were to die. But—don't confront him for me. And don't let emotions guide your actions. Always think things through and act with a clear mind."

"You sound like my brother."

"Which one?"

"Edros. He's given me these exercises for my mind."

"Exercises for your mind?" she asked. "You mean like reading books?"

"No, though he does that as well. You see, he lights a candle and I have to look at it, thinking of nothing but the flame."

She kissed him. "Sounds very helpful."

"It is, actually." Edris resumed staring at the floor. "But I can't stop thinking about him. I can't stop picturing…" He took a deep breath. "When I was crawling out of the cave, and he was standing over me with that rock in his hand…he had this grin on his face, like…like he was really going to enjoy beating me to death."

"Try not to think about him. Okay?"

"Easier said than done."

"I know what we can do, if you're willing," Beatrice said sensually.

"What?"

She lay on the bed. "Read me some poetry."

"You're not…you're not upset about me not being able to, you know…"

"Nope."

"You sure? You're not just saying that to make me feel better."

"You need to understand, Ed. While sex is wonderful, for me, being next to you like this, talking about your hopes and dreams—that's making love."

He traced his fingers along the curves of her breasts.

"Make love to me, Ed."

Edris kissed her, then bowed. "As you wish, my lady."

He retrieved the book of poems she'd given him. After months of being crammed in the bottom of his pack, it was battered and torn. Beatrice stayed his hand.

"I want to hear *your* poems," she said.

"You sure? They aren't good."

"They're marvelous." She reclined on the bed as though ready to be ravaged. "Now, please me, sir knight."

Drawing forth scraps of paper from his pants pockets, Edris started to read.

Thirty-Eight

"You'll have a reach advantage on most of your adversaries," Lord Elros told Edris as they strode through the pastures behind the manor.

In the distance, Edris could make out several men standing around what appeared to be a large boxing ring. Inwardly, he groaned. The last thing he wanted to do was to knock the snot out of one of the guards. He'd already beaten them all. Fighting them again wouldn't help him improve.

"And you'll probably be stronger," his father said. "But the most important thing about fighting with weapons is footwork."

Edris trudged alongside his father. He knew all of this. He'd been sparring with swords since he was five.

"You need balance," his father went on. "You need to be able to strike swiftly and move."

"Yes, sir."

"That's why I had this constructed."

They came to four tree trunks connected by thick ropes.

"What is it?" Edris asked.

"Part of your training. Climb up."

Knowing not to ask too many questions, Edris climbed up onto one of the tree trunks.

"Now," the Lord of Bend said, "cross to the other side."

Edris surveyed the twenty-foot expanse with some trepidation. "All right."

Carefully, he put his lead foot on the rope, followed by the other. The rope wavered, then flipped out from under his feet. With a strangled cry, he fell sprawling to the trampled grass, his face inches from a reeking pile of horse manure. The men around the ring snickered.

Lord Elros gritted his teeth. "Try again."

Again, Edris scrambled up onto the tree trunk and stepped out onto the rope. This time he teetered for a few seconds before thudding to the ground.

"Edris!" his father cried.

"I can do it."

Edris clamored out onto the rope a third time. It wiggled and shifted under his feet. But with his arms outstretched, he kept his balance.

"Good. Now take these." His father handed him two wooden swords, one long, the other short. "Go to the next post."

Edris swayed as he fought to keep his balance, but slowly, he made it to the other side.

"Keep going," his father said. "Go all the way around."

Sliding his right foot, followed by his left, Edris inched along.

"Faster!" his father shouted.

Edris quickened his pace.

"Good!" his father said, watching him intently. "Notice what you're doing. You're making yourself a narrow target. You're also protecting your vitals. If you get stabbed, it'll be in your shoulder, not your heart. Now switch feet. Put your left in front. You'll need to learn how to fight with both hands if you're going to be the best."

Edris attempted to switch his footing but immediately fell on his ass. Before his father could finish rolling his eyes, he'd scrambled back on the rope with his left foot forward.

"You can do this, Ed," Cedric shouted. "Concentrate!"

The others clapped.

"That's right." Lord Elros followed Edris as he wobbled about the ring. "It's all about focus and concentration. Right now, you are focusing on where to put your feet and when to shift your hips. You need to be able to move without thinking. You need to be able to move instinctively, freeing your complete attention for your foe. Understand?"

"Yes, sir."

"Do you? Or are you placating me? Saying 'yes, sir' all the time isn't going to keep you from getting killed."

Edris tottered on the rope. He'd never realized how shitty his balance was. His ankles and calves were already sore.

"This is helping. Let's do more."

"Fine." Lord Elros signaled to one of the men standing nearby. The guard climbed onto the post in front of Edris. He, too, had a wooden sword. "I want you to spar. Remember, use your reach to your advantage."

Edris fell again.

"Balance!" his father yelled. "Keep your blasted balance!"

"Yes, sir. It's becoming easier."

"It better. You'll be fighting men with far more experience than you. You have to take your training seriously."

"Yes, sir." Edris heaved himself onto the rope and inched toward his opponent. For several moments, they traded blows, their wooden swords slapping each other.

"Use your left to parry!" Lord Elros hollered. "Your left! You have two god-damned swords—use them! On your toes. Don't be so flat-footed."

The guard jabbed at Edris's lead leg, forcing Edris to spring back. He missed the rope and fell at his father's feet. To his surprise, his father didn't scream.

"Tell me," Lord Elros said, "where are you trying to strike your opponent?"

Breathing hard, Edris was unsure how to respond. "Anywhere I can, I suppose."

The lord shook his head. "Think when you fight. Be strategic. Why strike if your blow isn't going to do any damage? Look, you can kill your opponent by stabbing him in the heart or in the head or in the neck, but you can also kill him if you get to his wrist."

"His wrist, sir?"

"Ever see a man get his wrist cut? He may not die immediately, but trust me, he won't be in any condition to continue fighting. Same thing with stabbing his knee. The idea is not to always go for the killing blow, but the blow that leads to it."

Edris nodded, catching his breath. Sunlight glistened off his sweaty face.

"If you're always trying to stab somebody in the chest, you're giving up your reach advantage. Go for the hand. Go for the forearm. If they lunge toward you, parry, then counter to their lead knee. Make them protect every part of their body."

"Yes, sir."

"All right. Practice until dark, then come see me. And remember, learn to fight with your left. A man who can fight with two swords is dangerous."

"Yes, sir."

Trying to keep his balance, Edris climbed onto the rope. Brushing sweaty hair out of his eyes, he gestured for his opponent to ready himself.

"Let's go again."

Thirty-Nine

Edris knocked on the door to his father's study.

"Enter," his father called from inside.

Edris found his father by the fireplace, reading a book—something he'd rarely seen him do. "You wanted to see me?"

"Ah, Edris!" Lord Elros said, setting the book aside. "Yes. Come in. Come in. Have a seat."

This made Edris nervous. Nothing good ever came from his father wanting to speak with him. He took a seat.

"Finished with your training?" his father asked.

"Yes, sir."

"Splendid." Lord Elros pulled his chair closer to his son. "I wanted to speak with you about something. Something very important. You see, part of your training as an adventurer involves learning how to defend yourself. But there's so much more you need to master."

"Sir?"

"The trustiest weapon a man can wield is not a sword or a mace or a dagger, but his reputation."

Edris made sure his spine was straight. His father hated for him to slouch. "Yes, sir."

"Finding quest items and bringing them to the king is one thing. But what I'm talking about is survival. More than survival. I'm talking about legacy."

"Legacy?" Edris repeated.

"Yes, exactly. I've done some checking." The lord leaned forward, delighted. "You were correct. You're not only the youngest knight in The Angle, but also the youngest knight in *every* kingdom on the continent. In fact, you're the youngest knight in history. Now, that's something to be proud of."

His father was happy? Somehow, this was even more unsettling than when he was furious.

Seeing his father waiting, Edris managed to say, "Thank you, sir."

"As impressive as this feat is—" Lord Elros steeped his fingers thoughtfully. "—it doesn't mean much in the grand scheme of things. After all, someday some child will be knighted just so he can be the youngest. Your distinction will not last long."

"I understand."

"I don't believe you do," his father said. "Tell me, what do you know about Sir Theodore of West Haven?"

Edris opened his mouth, then closed it, then shrugged. "Nothing, actually. He was an adventurer, but that's all I know."

"Exactly! Even though Sir Theodore won the second most quests of all time, he has been lost to history. Few people know who he is or what he's done."

"You're saying nobody remembers the second best."

"No. Listen." Lord Elros thought for a moment. "Do you know anything about Sir Barton?"

"Barton the Black? Of course. He's one of my favorites."

"And why is he one of your favorites? He only won, what—? Five quests, if that. Maybe six?"

"I don't know." Edris mulled over the question. "I suppose it was because he was colorful. He was unpredictable. He—"

"People feared him," Lord Elros interjected. "Look, Edris, you remember Sir Barton not because of how many quests he won, but because he struck fear into everybody he met. If somebody looked at him the wrong way, Barton hauled them into the street and beat the crap of them. If somebody bumped into him, he broke their god-damned arm. You see what I'm saying? Everybody knew that if you crossed him, you were in for a hell of a fight. So, people left him alone."

"Yes, sir."

"Have you heard the story of Sir Barton fighting an entire tavern full of knights?"

"Yes, sir. Somebody spilled a drink on him, and he went crazy. Edran used to tell that story when we were children."

Lord Edros spread his hands as if his point were made. "It never happened. The story is apocryphal. See, he lived his life in such a way that he developed a reputation. It didn't matter what he did. What mattered was what people thought he'd do. His reputation not only kept him alive by warding off potential rivals, but it enabled him to live on for centuries after his death."

Edris shifted uncomfortably in his chair. "You want me to kill the next man I face?"

"I'm not saying you should be a murderer or even a lunatic like Barton. What I'm saying is that if somebody gives you cause, you should inflict as much damage as you can. You make sure they're never a threat to you again. You need to be brutal in this world. Hard and calculating. Ruthless. Because being ruthless once, will save you from having to be ruthless countless other times. Understand?"

"I believe so, sir. If people fear me, they won't fight me."

"Exactly."

Taking a drink of wine, Lord Edros inspected his son over the rim of his glass.

"I know you've become enamored with that so-called 'Code of Honor' the knights are supposed to follow. You have been since you were a boy.

But let me tell you, all those stories of knights acting chivalrously are just like the story of Barton killing thirteen knights because somebody spilled a drink on him. In the real world, nobody plays by a set of rules. They do whatever they have to do to win—Code of Honor be damned."

Edris didn't say anything. Despite all the yelling while he was falling from the rope, he'd actually had a very pleasant afternoon with his father. It was the first time he'd enjoyed being with him. He didn't want to ruin it by disagreeing.

"Let me ask you this." Lord Elros flicked his chin at Edris's scar. "Did Markus follow the Code of Honor?"

Edris touched his forehead. "No."

"Damned right he didn't. And he's the king's god-damned son. He's supposed to be all high and mighty. He's supposed to epitomize the Code and act in the name of his prissy father."

Lord Elros drained his glass and set it aside by a nearly empty bottle.

"I'm going to ask you one more question," he said, eyes gleaming in the candlelight. "You don't have to answer now, but I want you to reflect on it every day. Your life will depend upon it."

"Okay, sir. What is it?"

Lord Elros reclined comfortably in his chair and crossed his legs. "In a fight between two equally matched opponents, who would win? The one who fights by a predictable set of rules? Or the one who does whatever he has to in order to beat his foe?"

Forty

"Master Edris!" a servant called.

Edris checked his horse to a walk and lowered his bow. The human-shaped straw target he'd been shooting at had five arrows sticking out of it; however, thirty more were scattered about the field beyond.

"What is it?"

"Your father requires your presence."

Edris examined the spring sky. There were still several hours of daylight left and he wanted to continue practicing. He could fight well with his fists. He could even hold his own with a sword. But he couldn't hit a sleeping troll with his bow. "How urgently?"

The servant's terrified expression told him all that he needed to know.

"Damn it!" Edris leapt from the saddle and handed him the reins. "Any idea what this is about?"

"No, sir. But he sounded angry."

"He *always* sounds angry."

Edris trudged through the fields to the manor house and found his father waiting for him on the doorstep, a wadded-up letter in hand.

"Edris!" he shouted. "About blasted time. Hurry up. We're behind."

We're behind? What the hell did that mean?

"What's wrong?" Edris asked.

"Follow me." The Lord of Bend seized the arm of a passing guard. "When Edros arrives, bring him to the library."

"As you wish, sir."

Following his father, Edris hurried up a flight of stairs and along a dark corridor to a room filled with stacks of books and papers and overflowing shelves that hadn't been dusted in years. The only piece of furniture was a rickety desk partially covered by wooden crates.

"What's wrong?" Edris asked again. "Is everything okay?"

His father shook the letter. "This! This is what's wrong. The bastard just sent it to me. I'm sure he'd deny it, but I'd wager your mother's life he did it on purpose. The arrogant son of a bitch."

Edris unfolded the crumpled paper.

It was a royal proclamation announcing that the next quest was to find the Sacred Scarab. The competition started two weeks earlier.

"Bollocks!"

"Exactly!" Lord Elros snatched the proclamation and throttled it. "You see, Edris? This is what you're up against. Petty assholes who will do everything in their power to prevent you from winning." He threw the letter across the room.

"Let's not waste time lamenting our fortune," Edris said, sounding much like his older brother. "Let's get to work."

His father smiled at him. "Good. That's exactly the attitude I want you to have. What do you know about the Sacred Scarab?"

"Nothing. Other than the fact that scarabs are bugs, I believe."

His father searched through a crate of musty tomes. "Alas, then you know as much as I." He selected a large leather-bound book and rifled through its pages. He stopped and turned the book in his son's direction. There was an illustration of black beetle with a thick, round body and long, jagged legs.

"It says they live in the desert," Edris said, reading the text under the picture.

"The desert..." Lord Elros mused. "That's a long way away. Maybe that's why the king needed to give Markus a head start."

"Trust me, Markus has had more than a two-week head start on this. He's probably been searching for this scarab for a month or more."

The Lord of Bend paced the cluttered room. "The Sacred Scarab...The Sacred Scarab... I've never heard of it."

"I bet it's a statue of some sort."

"Why do you say that?"

"It can't be an actual bug. There are loads of them. And if it's sacred...well, what do people pray to? Statues."

For the second time, Lord Elros smiled. He patted Edris on his muscular shoulder. "Those are my thoughts as well."

The door opened. Edros hurried into the library, heaps of books under each arm.

"Find anything?" Elros asked.

Panting, Edros piled everything onto the desk. He opened to a page showing a rendering of the same type of beetle they'd examined.

"So, it *is* a bug?" Edris asked.

"It's a statue," Edros said, trying to catch his breath. "It's shaped like a bug. Evidently, it was about the size of an apple and made of solid gold." He consulted the passage. "It had jade for eyes and was considered to be a holy relic by the Hamumomi people of the Arid Waste. It was over four thousand years old."

"Poppycock," Lord Elros said. "Nothing is that old."

"I'm reading what the book says."

"Does it say anything about what happened to it?" Edris asked.

"Not this one." Edros consulted another text he'd brought. "However, I did find this." He perused several pages. "Here it is. Apparently, the Sacred Scarab disappeared some three hundred years ago. Two hundred and seventy-eight years, to be exact. Let's see. The Hamumomi were more or less nomadic. They roamed from realm to realm, establishing temples to their gods."

He scanned the passage.

"Okay. This is what's important…two hundred and seventy-eight years ago, a band of marauders came down from The Step, raiding what is now the kingdom of Green Hill, burning and pillaging as they went. They took everything they could find, including the scarab."

He closed the book.

"And that's all you know?" Edris asked in dismay. "How can anybody find the blasted thing? No wonder it has been lost for three hundred years."

"Giving up should not come so easily to one of my sons," Elros said coldly.

"Yes, sir." Edris sighed. "So, what happened to the bandits? Know anything about them?"

"If I remember correctly—" Edros flipped through a third book. "—the Step raiders were led by…" He tapped his finger on a page. "Yes. His name was Gubli-gan."

"I recall reading about him." Lord Elros went from crate to crate, inspecting several large volumes. "He was a military genius for his time."

"He was," Edros agreed. "His men rode small horses. They weren't fast, but they were tough and capable of a long day's work."

Lord Elros referred to one of his books. "He used to send his younger forces into a town, set everything ablaze, steal what they could, then flee. The pursuing cavalry would chase after them only to run into a more rested veteran force."

"It says here," Edros said, reading, "their riders were skilled marksmen and would shoot the horses out from under their opponents. Then, they'd circle their grounded foes and pick them off one by one."

"What happened to this Gubli-gan?" Edris asked.

"He was finally brought to justice by King Pembroke," Lord Elros said. "Pembroke's cavalry pursued the raiders for months. Eventually, Gubli-gan turned homeward and tried to reach The Step."

"But Pembroke had stationed a company of lancers and archers at the pass," Edros said. "When Gubli-gan's men rode up, they were ambushed and forced to retire the way they came."

"By that time," Lord Elros cut in, "Pembroke caught up with them. There was a terrific battle, all on horseback. Pembroke's men were the victors, though at heavy cost."

"Then," Edris said hopefully, "it's likely that Pembroke reacquired all the treasure the raiders had taken."

"If Pembroke had acquired the Sacred Scarab," Lord Elros said, sitting on the edge of his desk, "there wouldn't be much of a quest. His descendant, King Pendergast, would have it."

"Perhaps one of Pembroke's men acquired the statue," Edros said. "It was small enough to pilfer without much chance of getting caught."

"Very possible," Lord Elros replied. "Though his men wouldn't have to worry about getting caught; soldiers were allowed to loot opposing armies. It was how most of them were paid."

"One of the soldiers must've acquired it. Probably one of Pembroke's officers."

"Why do you believe that?"

"Well," Edris said nervously, trying to determine whether his father was being sarcastic. "I'm sure there was some sort of pecking order. Right? I mean, it wouldn't stand well with the officers if the new recruits were acquiring more wealth than they did."

"Logical." Lord Elros searched through his mountain of books. "I might have a list of Pembroke's captains, though I'm not sure if they were all present at the battle before The Step."

"There is another option," Edros said. "Like the Hamumomi, the people of The Step are largely nomadic, and both peoples tend to bury their valuables—the Hamumomi in the desert sands, the people of The Step in the treeless grasslands."

"The raiders might have buried what they'd taken?" Edris asked.

"It beats getting caught with it."

"And their acquisitions would slow them considerably," Lord Elros said, still shuffling through wooden crates. "If they were being pursued, they'd likely lighten their loads so they could get away. Treasure doesn't buy dead men anything. Both of you should remember that."

"Yes, sir," Lord Elros's sons said reflexively.

Edris attempted to wave away the great clouds of dust his father's searching kicked up; however, his efforts only made matters worse. He coughed.

"So," he said with an effort, "the raiders ride into town, setting fire and pillaging, then ride away. They can't carry all of their loot home, so they bury it with the intention of returning once the pursuing cavalry withdraws. The question is—where would they bury it?"

Lord Elros gave up his hunt for whatever he was looking for and sat in the chair behind his desk. "I believe," he said, drumming his fingers on the table, "your summation is adequate."

"Then again," Edris replied, following his train of thought, "if one of Pembroke's men acquired the Scarab, he may have sold it. There's no sense in a military man keeping a gold statue. If he melted it down first, the quest is meaningless. If he didn't, somebody would have the statue in their collection, and we'd hear about it. So we can rule that possibility out."

Edros leaned against a bookshelf. "It could be that somebody has it but doesn't realize it's *the* Sacred Scarab."

"How many gold bugs are there?" Edris retorted.

"Good point."

"I believe you're on the right track, Edris," his father said. "It would seem most likely that Gubli-gan hid their treasure prior to his demise."

"Yes, but where? They roamed hundreds of miles, ransacking every town and farmhouse they came across. Would they bury all of their treasure in one spot? Or would they bury portions of it in different locations in order to minimize loss, should somebody find one of their burial sites?"

"All excellent questions, dear brother," Edros said. "Unfortunately, I don't have any answers for you."

Outside, the bells tolled the dinner hour. None of them moved.

"The raiders were heading home," Lord Elros said, thinking aloud. "They would've buried their ill-gotten booty someplace that was easy to identify and accessible from The Step. Someplace where they could sneak in unnoticed and then quickly return to safer territory. It wouldn't be some random place."

"Someplace close to The Step that was identifiable," Edris said, resuming his pacing. "That region is basically pasture, isn't it?"

"Indeed," his father said. "The villagers there raise mainly sheep and goats. It's where most of Green Hill's wool comes from. Even now there aren't many settlements, so it would've been easy for the raiders to return undetected."

"But how would a place be identifiable? One field would look like every other."

Uncharacteristically, his father didn't respond.

"If you want my advice," Edros said, "I'd suggest starting where the story begins. Go to where Pembroke fought Gubli-gan. Then—see what happens."

"You mean, mill around and pray to stumble across something," Edris grumbled.

"That's ninety percent of being an adventurer. If the answers were always in books, there wouldn't be many quests and librarians would have greater honor."

"I don't know. Sounds like a colossal waste of time. What do you think, Father?"

Lord Elros rubbed his neck. "I think Edros is correct. Start at the site of the battle, then work your way to the Hamumomi temple where the bug was stolen."

"It's a shot in the dark," Edris admitted.

"Even shots in the dark can hit their target," his father said. "But I don't want you going alone. Now you're a knight, you need a squire."

"A squire?"

"Somebody to tend to your gear and keep an eye open while you sleep. You don't want to wake up with Markus standing over you, do you?"

"No."

"Then take somebody you can trust. That's the key. There's enough treachery afoot," his father said. "And watch out for Markus. He won't let you win two quests in a row."

Forty-One

Edris stood in his father's stables, trying to determine which horse to select. He didn't take the decision lightly. Horses were like people; each had their strengths and weaknesses. Big Red, for example, was a reliable beast. Large and strong, and not quick to startle. That was important. In a fight, he needed to know his steed wouldn't spook and gallop away. But Big Red didn't have the speed of, say, Breeze—or the endurance of White Foot. The wrong horse might mean the difference between winning the quest and having to walk home empty-handed.

"Which one?" he asked himself.

"Which one—what?" an aggravated voice asked.

A boy's head appeared above a stall wall, straw in his shaggy black hair.

"Brago!" Edris said, astounded. "What are you doing here?"

Brago stretched and stepped leisurely out of the stall. "If you recall, you told me to come here and ask for a job."

"My father agreed to hire you? That's terrific! He's changed, but I didn't think he'd changed that much."

"It is my assumption he doesn't know." Brago knocked off bits of straw clinging to his patched and faded clothes. "Herschel hired me. He lets me stay in the stables and gives me a few coins here and there for various tasks somebody of my ilk can do satisfactorily."

"He's skimming."

"Beg your pardon?"

"My father gives him a fixed amount to hire workers," Edris explained. "He's paying you less than what he'd normally pay somebody and pocketing the remainder."

"And you're surprised? That's how the world works. You can't trust anybody."

"Can't trust anybody..." Edris repeated, an idea taking root in his mind. He studied the stablehand.

Brago was short and slight and couldn't fight a lick. But he was crafty and intelligent and had been living on the streets ever since his mother died several years before. He was also a skilled thief. Such skills could come in handy.

Brago stepped warily away. "Why are you looking at me like that?"

"How'd you like another job?"

"That's mighty kind of you, Ed," Brago said, perhaps sarcastically. "What kind of animal excrement would you like me to shovel? I am well-versed in a wide variety of shit."

"I'm not talking about manual labor. You see, I'm competing in the Kings' Quest and I need a squire."

"A squire?" Brago replied, offended. His dark eyes narrowed defiantly. "I will *not* be a servant."

"You won't be!"

Brago didn't appear too convinced.

"Look," Edris said. "You're good with horses. And I can trust you."

The phrase *I can trust you* seemed to hit some sort of mark. Brago bowed slightly.

"Thank you, Ed. You've always been kind to me. But what is it, precisely, you trust me to do?"

"There are going to be adventurers who will do anything to stop me from winning the quest. I need you to protect my back."

Brago snorted bitterly. "Regrettably, I'm not exactly the fighting type. And I doubt you need protecting. What your size won't do, your father's well-deserved social status will."

Edris ignored the dig at the noble class. "I don't need a fighter...I need somebody who can keep his eyes and ears open, and maybe collect information or spy on the other adventurers. I need somebody who will make sure I won't get my throat slit while I'm sleeping."

"Sounds dangerous," Brago mused, as if calculating how much he could earn for such a position.

"It may be," Edris said. "But come with me and I'll make sure you never have to sleep in horse shit again."

Forty-Two

That night, Edris and Brago rode to Bend—Edris on Big Red, Brago on a smaller, faster horse named Grey. There, Edris bought Brago everything he'd need in order to appear to be a newly minted squire, including a long knife that would serve as a short sword, and fine clothes that fit his diminutive frame. He also wanted to see Beatrice.

He tapped on Beatrice's door. She and her family lived in a small shack on the outskirts of town, and Edris always had to be careful not to batter the wobbly door down when he knocked.

It creaked open.

"Ed!" Beatrice said, delighted. Then she noted the elegant dresses he had draped over one arm. "What are you—?"

"I want you to have these." He shoved them at her.

Beatrice fought to see over the mound of fabric. "Why?"

"I want you to have this as well." He placed a bulging pouch on top of the pile. "I want you to move your parents into town. Find someplace safe and respectable."

"Ed, what's this all about?"

"After what Markus—"

"Let's not talk about him."

Edris kicked the ground. "Very well. I thought…I wanted to make sure you're okay. You see, I'm leaving in the morning. Before dawn, in fact."

Beatrice's eyes showed her disappointment. "Where're you going? And when will you be home?"

"They've issued another quest."

"I thought they only issued quests in the fall."

Edris shook his head. "Usually spring or fall. But they could do it at any time. Anyway, we're looking for the Sacred Scarab. I'm not sure where we'll end up or how long it will take. But I'll send word as often as I can."

"We?"

"Brago is coming with me."

"Brago?" Her mood lightened. "That's really kind of you to take him under your wing. He's been alone for so long."

"I need him as much as he needs me. I only hope I can trust him."

"Oh," she said dismissively, "you shouldn't believe all the stories you hear about him. He's sweet and resourceful."

"I know. And smart. That's why I want him to come along."

He slipped a glance at her bedroom door.

She raised an eyebrow, knowing what he was thinking. "My parents are home."

"Are they asleep?"

"Ed!"

"Okay. Okay. I just thought—"

"I'm well aware of what you thought, Sir Edris. And I was thinking it as well. But, as I said, my parents are here, and I have to be at work early in the morning." She gave him a stern look. "That's not the only reason you came, is it?"

"What? No. On my honor. I wanted to see you before I left and to give you the dresses."

"Thank you. They're very becoming. And thanks for the money." She peered up at him. "But you don't have to do this. I'm managing fine. I have been working regularly at the Hen and Duck. They pay me well enough and let me bring home scraps of food that would otherwise go to waste. So, you don't need to worry about me."

"I want you to be better than fine, Bea. I want…" he trailed off, gazing at the twinkling stars.

"What do you want?" she asked affectionately.

He dithered. "I want to make sure you're safe when I'm not here."

"Unfortunately, I'm a single woman from the lower class. Beautiful dresses and your money aren't going to protect me from men like…" She shuddered.

"We're not all like him, you know. Nobles, I mean. We're not all like—"

"I know. But I don't think you truly understand what it's like to be a common woman."

"I understand!" Edris exclaimed. Then he nodded in concession before taking her hand. "No…actually, you're right. I *don't* understand."

"If a nobleman wants a girl from the lower classes," she said, "well, woe be for us to refuse. Now, if I were married…"

Edris frowned. He and Beatrice had been romantically involved for years. They'd discussed marriage, of course, but only in a casual, half-joking way; however, there was no joking in her tone. Now it was colored with a hint of desperation.

"Bea…" Edris said.

She repositioned the heaps of expensive clothes in her arms. "It's fine. I understand."

"Do you?"

"I do."

But to Edris, she seemed to harden.

"I've always known who and what you were." She sighed. "I could imagine what your father would say if you brought somebody like me home…"

"Hey." Edris touched her chin. "There is nobody like you."

She stood on her tiptoes and kissed him. "Thanks, Ed."

"I need you to know I mean it. You're the only person in this world I care about."

An uneasy silence enveloped them as they stared at the ground.

"Are you and your father still getting along?" Beatrice asked eventually.

"We are. For the first time, he's taking an interest in me."

"That must be rather disconcerting."

Edris laughed. "It is! Sometimes I wish he'd go back to not knowing my name." His laughter died away. He touched her face again and saw tears building in her eyes. "I have to get going. But I'll return in—well, I don't know when."

"I'll be here." She stood on her toes once more and pulled Edris's head toward her. "I'm always here."

Forty-Three

Riding as fast as they could, Edris and Brago reached the battle site between King Pembroke's army and Gubli-gan's raiders in a fortnight. What they found didn't please them.

Green Hill was a small bucolic kingdom populated mainly by cattle and sheep ranchers spread throughout the gently rolling countryside. Towns and villages rarely exceeded a score of permanent buildings. Yet as Edris and Brago peered into the valley separating the rolling grasslands from the colossal stone cliffs of The Step, they could see hundreds of figures milling about.

"Who are all these people?" Brago asked.

Edris groaned as he watched men digging here and there. The valley was pocked with their labors. "They're adventurers."

"Does everybody know where the golden bug is buried?"

"I'm not sure any of us knows anything of the sort. We're simply guessing."

They sat on their restless horses, watching the once peaceful valley.

"I have to say," Brago said, "burying your valuables is probably the stupidest thing somebody could do. Especially here. However, as history shows us, people are indeed idiots."

"Why would burying valuables here be stupid?"

"Finding them again would be problematic. You could draw a map, but what landmarks would remain constant over time? Trees up and die. Boulders roll downhill or are broken into dust. Even rivers change course. There's not a single feature here that could be used as a reliable guide."

A group of adventurers plowing the trampled grass plodded along the eastern part of the valley. At their oxen's current pace, it'd take them a year to till the entire meadow.

"I doubt the raiders meant to leave the treasure buried for long," Edris said. "But you raise an interesting point."

"Did I? Do tell."

"A map. If you're going to bury something, you'd make a map so you can find it again."

"You think there might be a map somewhere?"

"Maybe. The trouble will be finding it."

Shading their eyes from the late afternoon sun, they watched the horde of adventurers scouring the countryside, poking their swords into the ground, overturning the occasional rock. An adventurer who'd dug a hole big enough to be a grave gave a cry. Immediately, dozens of men converged on him, weapons drawn.

"Think he's found something?" Brago asked.

"If he did, he won't keep it."

The adventurer in the hole held up a skull. Most of the other adventurers drifted back to where they'd been searching.

"This is pointless," Edris said. "Blast it! We can't excavate this entire area. And if we could, we couldn't hide the fact we found something."

"What do you want to do?"

Edris's horse thrashed its tail at the buzzing flies.

"Let's head to the town we saw. Maybe there's a librarian or loremaster there who knows some ancient stories that might point us in the right direction."

Edris and Brago rode to the closest settlement they could find—a little hamlet called Tiny Dribbling. Surrounded by rolling fields dotted with thousands of grazing sheep, it was nothing more than a cluster of brick buildings situated around a dirt road intersecting a muddy stream.

"I don't suppose," Edris said to the elderly innkeeper, "you have a couple of rooms available for weary travelers."

"I don't have a couple, but I do have one," the innkeeper said in a tone suggesting he knew he had the only inn in town and that he was about to make a small fortune. "Became available not more than a few minutes ago."

"Wonderful. We'll take it."

"That'll be ten silver a night."

"Ten silver!" Brago grumbled. "And *I* get called a thief."

Edris quieted him. "That'll be fine, sir. Thank you."

"Very good. Let me get you situated."

They followed the old man to a table, behind which were several pegs; only one held a key.

"You're awfully busy," Edris said, attempting to get information without being too obvious. "I had no idea this place was so well visited."

The innkeeper gave him a smug look. "I'm quite sure you're here for the same reasons as everybody else." He handed him the key. "Your room is upstairs and to the left."

"Has anybody…"

"Found the golden dung beetle? Son, if I knew that, I'd be making more than ten silver. Every adventurer in town has offered sacks of gold for information about its whereabouts."

"Upstairs to the left?"

"Correct, young man. And good luck hunting."

They climbed the stairs and found their room. It was barely big enough for Edris, let alone the much smaller Brago.

"Charming man," Brago said, throwing his pack onto a chair. "We should burn his place to the ground before we leave."

"He's only trying to make a living."

"As is any thief. Funny what is considered legal and illegal."

"Never mind that." Edris peered out the dingy window to the street below. Adventurers went about in a great hurry. "This is what I want you to do. Stroll around and see what you can learn. Here. You may need some money to help loosen people's tongues. Let's keep a low profile. I don't want anybody noticing us."

"What are you going to do?"

"I'm going to see if Markus is in town."

Still wearing his weather-stained traveling clothes, Edris roamed Tiny Dribbling, trying to blend in. Wherever he went, groups of heavily armed men stood talking to townsfolk about the Sacred Scarab. Meanwhile, more and more adventurers galloped into the village, swelling the already clogged streets. Markus was nowhere to be found.

Feeling hungry, Edris stepped inside the first eatery he could find that wasn't overflowing with people. After telling the fellow behind the counter what he wanted, he sat at the far end of the bar. All around him, adventurers chatted, pored over maps, or read various age-worn documents. Nobody paid him any mind.

At a table by the front windows, a rotund man with a fleshy face grumbled loudly.

"There too many of these damned runt kingdoms," he said, his speech slurred from alcohol. "Too many. Too many blasted kingdoms. Every blasted farmer with an outhouse is declaring himself king."

One of his tablemates got up and left, leaving behind a plate of half-eaten mutton.

"I tell you," he went on to nobody in particular, "they should all be taken over by somebody. Every single one of them. Make one big kingdom worth something. Not all these, good for nothing, damned runt kingdoms."

The din throughout the common room faltered. Talk of war was never something people liked to hear—especially by those who might be commanded to fight it.

"Too many worthless kings..." the drunk said as the second of his companions moved to the other end of the bar. "Too many bastards of bastards. Assholes. The entire lot of them."

The drunk's final tablemate left. He kept talking, nonetheless.

"King Amrose. King Hamfast." He spilled some of his beer. "Worthless pissants. King Michael..."

This got Edris's attention. He glanced around the packed room. There were many knights there, but none appeared to be from the kingdoms being mentioned. He was the only one.

"Nothing but worthless pissants..." the drunk continued. "All of them."

Edris fidgeted. He didn't particularly care for King Michael, not after what his son had done. But he was family, and he did knight him.

"King Christopher..." The man by the window chortled. "He isn't fit to wipe the shit from my boots. None of them are."

Edris strode over to his table.

The inebriated adventurer looked up with blurry eyes. "What do you—?"

Edris backhanded him across the face, flinging him to the floor.

Every conversation stopped.

The drunk felt his cheek. A large white welt was rapidly turning purple. He fought his way to his feet. He wasn't tall, but he was thick of build and had a sizable belly. He easily weighed as much as Edris, if not more.

"You bastard!"

Edris slapped him again, knocking him into another table.

"I'm Sir Edris of The Angle," Edris said proudly. "King Michael is my sovereign and kin."

"Bully for—"

Edris slapped the drunk a third time, sending him reeling against annoyed diners attempting to eat their food.

The drunk stabbed a finger at Edris's chest. "I don't give a damn whose bastard you are!"

Edris shoved him out the door. "We'll finish this outside."

Chairs squealed as everybody leapt from their seats and followed them into the road.

An adventurer stepped in front of Edris. "He's drunk."

"I won't let his comments stand."

"Very well. But don't overdo it."

Staggering, the drunk drew a sleeve across his bleeding mouth. He blinked at the smear of blood, then at Edris. "Bastard! I'll kill you. You and your pissant king."

Fists raised, he charged. Edris threw a right uppercut to the drunk's jaw. The drunk fell backward, landing hard in the dirt. He didn't move.

"That's enough," said the adventurer who'd followed Edris out of the eatery. "You've maintained your honor and the honor of your king."

"Not yet." Edris unbuckled the unconscious man's weapon belt. "Who is he? Does anybody know?"

"That's Sir Rodney," somebody in the murmuring crowd said.

"Lord Ronald's son?" Edris knew the family, though he hadn't seen them in years.

"Aye," a short, balding man next to him answered. "And he won't be pleased by you taking his son's possessions."

"Don't worry. I know Lord Ronald. We're on good terms."

Edris held aloft Sir Rodney's sheathed sword. It glinted in the failing evening light.

"I am Sir Edris," he hollered over the commotion. "And any man who disparages my king gets his sword sent to his father."

Several knights chuckled in approval.

"You. Boy!" he called to one of the squires in the crowd. "Find out where this ass is quartered and carry him there. I don't want any more of his belongings disappearing. When he comes to, tell him what I did with his sword."

"Yes, sir!"

The squire and some of his comrades hoisted the lifeless knight onto their shoulders and headed to the inn.

Edris pushed his way inside and found the three steaks he'd ordered waiting for him. Famished, he began wolfing them down, Sir Rodney's sword across his lap.

"Well done," a young knight said, offering his hand. Edris shook it. "I'm Sir Kaye." He indicated the knight next to him. "This is Sir Donald."

Edris shook his hand as well.

"May we join you?" Sir Donald asked.

Mouth full, Edris motioned to the empty stools on either side of him, then swallowed. "Please. Buy you a drink?"

"I think we'll buy you one." Sir Kaye caught the serving girl's eye. "Three beers, lass. The good stuff."

"Ale," Sir Donald told her. "If it isn't watered."

Other patrons patted Edris on the shoulder. Annoyed, Edris thanked them as he tried to finish his dinner.

"How long have you been a knight?" Sir Kaye asked when everybody had returned to their tables. "Forgive me, but I've never heard of you before."

"I was knighted five months ago."

"You don't say. Congratulations on that as well."

Edris shoveled more food into his mouth. "Thank you."

"And," Sir Kaye said, as if trying to broach a sensitive subject, "how old are you, if you don't mind the inquiry?"

Edris winked at him as he chewed. "Old enough to be knighted."

They laughed.

Somebody else came by and shook his hand. Looking up, he found it was Markus.

"Well done, cousin!" he said loudly. "I greatly appreciate you defending our family's honor. I only wish I was here to do it myself!"

Forty-Four

"Markus!" Sir Donald shook Markus's hand, as did Sir Kaye. "Good to see you!"

"Good to be seen." Markus pulled up a stool.

People began gathering around them.

"You and Sir Edris are kinsmen?" Sir Kaye asked.

"We are indeed," Markus replied. "He's the youngest child of my father's sister. The baby of the family, you might say." He grinned. "And to answer your question, Sir Donald, Eddie here is fifteen years old."

Amazed, everybody faced Edris.

"Fifteen!" Sir Donald gasped in disbelief. "I knew you were young, but I had no idea."

"Actually," Edris said, aggravated, "I'm sixteen."

"Even so. How the devil were you knighted?"

The serving girl set three pints of dark ale on the bar.

"Oh, you know how it is," Markus said, reaching for one of the glasses. "Of all my cousins, Eddie is my father's favorite."

Edris grabbed his arm.

"It's Edris." Markus tried to pull his arm back, but Edris wouldn't let it go. "Perhaps you should tell them how I got knighted—Markie."

Markus blanched. Then relaxed. Edris let go and placed one of the beers in front of him.

"I jest with him because we practically grew up together," Markus told the other knights. He took a drink. "Edris was knighted because he saved my life."

A buzz of interest swept among the listeners.

"Oh?" Sir Kaye said, impressed. "How?"

"Do you know the hillside path by Strombath? The one approaching from the south and flanking the Dean River?"

"Surely. Go on."

"A rattlesnake spooked my horse."

Edris waited for Markus to finish the story, but he took another long pull from his pint as though the tale had reached its conclusion.

"What my dear cousin failed to mention is that he was unable to master his steed and found himself dangling over the edge of the cliff, screaming."

"You're kidding!"

"I wasn't screaming," Markus said.

Edris laughed. "The valley still echoes with his terror."

"That's not true!"

"Strombath?" Sir Donald thought for a moment. "Isn't that where you found the Sword of Betrayal?"

"Indeed," Markus replied proudly. "It was my most challenging win to date."

"Why don't you tell them how you found it," Edris said, chewing his second steak. "About how you fell down the hillside while taking a piss."

Everybody erupted with laughter.

"Now! Now!" Markus cried, shooting an angry glance at Edris. "That's not true. Ed is the one who fell!"

"Me? You're the one who found the sword—aren't you, Markus? Or am I mistaken?"

They locked smoldering gazes. Markus turned away first, his face red.

"Let's talk about other matters," he said. "I say we shave Rodney's head and leave him to awaken in a pigsty. That should teach the scoundrel not to speak ill of his betters!"

Forty-Five

"So, he spent the entire evening slipping these snide comments into the conversation," Edris said indignantly.

He and Brago were in their room at the inn—Edris stretched out across the lone bed, his feet dangling off its end, Brago lying on the thread-worn rug. Midnight had passed several hours before, but neither was tired.

"You should've hit him," Brago said, "like you did the other one."

"I wanted to. The problem was, he never said anything overtly hostile. It was always something like: *'Eddie used to be such a fat little boy. Now look at him. If he grows any more, people will mistake him for a troll!'"*

"That doesn't sound too bad."

"Believe me, it's bad. He's going to keep referring to me as *Eddie* and *Fatty* until one of the names sticks. Soon everybody will be calling me Sir Fatty Eddie."

"Or Sir Eddie the Fatty."

"Exactly!"

Stretching, Brago put his hands behind his head. "It seems your beloved cousin isn't the type to let things go."

"He isn't. He's always been like that. He'll keep needling me until something happens. When we were kids, we often came to blows."

"Who won?"

"We were children," Edris said. "It was mainly a lot of hair pulling and scratching. However, once I did bloody his lip."

"And how'd he react?"

"He called his father."

In the hall outside their room, the floorboards creaked as somebody passed their door.

Brago yawned. "Are you worried?"

"About Markus?"

Edris stared at the ceiling.

Was he?

His cousin was a braggart who always had to have all the attention. He also had a temper, but he usually kept that hidden behind a big smile and a quick joke.

The question lingered.

Searching the jumble of anxiety churning his gut, the answer came to him.

"No," Edris lied. "All of this will blow over eventually."

"Are you ever going to repay him for what he did to your head?"

Edris had been thinking about that a great deal. He told his father he was going to slit the son of a bitch's throat. But could he? If it came to a fight, he'd defend himself. But could he kill somebody in cold blood? Could he kill a family member?

"I don't know."

"Look, Ed," Brago said. "Men like your cousin are basically mean dogs. They'll keep biting people until somebody gives them a hard-enough rap across their muzzle."

"You want me to knock him around a bit? You're forgetting, he's the king's son. I'd need a damned good reason."

"All I'm saying is that, sooner or later, Markus will have you at a disadvantage; then he'll teach you a lesson."

"That's what he said he did last time."

"My point exactly. He tried to show you he was your superior, and you mouthed off to him in front of his friends. Mark my words, Ed. He'll come after you again."

Edris groaned. He knew Brago was right. Sooner or later, Markus would catch him in a vulnerable spot, and he might not settle for merely beating him with a rock.

"What do you think I should do?"

Brago rolled over onto his side, facing Edris in the darkness. "There are only two things you can do. Put him in his place. Or get out of his way."

Get out of his way…

Edris now realized it was stupid of him to become an adventurer with Markus in the same profession. His cousin would never let him succeed.

"Want me to poison him?" Brago asked.

"Poison! What do you know about poison?"

"You'd be surprised how many ordinary things can kill a man—or at least make him severely ill. Mushrooms, mosses, hemlock…" Brago's black eyes glinted in the moonlight. "Say the word, and I'll take care of it."

Edris laughed, then saw Brago was serious.

Guilt welled up inside him. Here he was, a foot and a half taller and twice Brago's weight, and Brago was braver than he was. He needed to grow up. He needed to become tougher. He needed to stand up to Markus.

"No," Edris said faintly. "I'll figure something out. Besides, there's no honor in poisoning somebody."

"There's no honor in dying, period."

Edris held his tongue. The last thing he wanted was to start a debate.

Outside, somebody strolled along the empty street, singing.

"Let me ask you this," Brago said, as though he'd been puzzling over something for a while. "When you beat Sir Rodney senseless for disparaging our illustrious king—where was the king's dutiful offspring?"

The question startled Edris. "I don't know. I think I would've noticed him if he were in the tavern."

"But he appeared after the fight?"

"Yeah. Right after I sat down."

"Sounds to me like he was hiding. I don't think your cousin is as brave as you give him credit for. Then again—" Brago yawned again. "—it's the cowards you have to look out for. They're the ones who'll stick a knife in your kidney when your head is turned."

Forty-Six

For the better part of a week, Edris ambled about Tiny Dribbling and the surrounding sheep-filled pastures. For the first few days, all people could talk about was his pummeling of Sir Rodney. Adventurers from kingdoms he'd never heard of stopped and congratulated him or offered to buy him a beer. Soon, however, everybody's thoughts returned to the quest at hand.

Nobody knew where the statue was. Most adventurers either waited outside of town to ambush anybody who found it or poked aimlessly around the pass to The Step. Edris stayed mainly in Little Dribbling's only tavern—thinking.

He didn't know which was worse: having to sit through an evening of Markus's gloating and subtle jibes, or not knowing where his cousin was. Even the resourceful Brago couldn't find word of him.

Eventually, Edris couldn't take it anymore. He burst into their room at the inn.

"Get our gear," he told Brago. "We're leaving."

"Finally!" Brago replied, springing out of the chair he'd been sitting in. "Little Dribbling loses its charm moments after one enters it. Where are we headed?"

"I don't know. I'm at a loss. I think this quest is going to be impossible to complete."

"If it helps, other adventurers are saying the same."

"Are they?"

Brago gathered their belongings. "Everybody seems to assume the raiders buried it before they were attacked by King Pembroke. But nobody has an inkling where. To me, it seems rather pointless to dig blindly in the fields."

"To me as well. The problem is, we don't have any other theory." Edris sighed in frustration. "Well, my brother has an expression: *always return to the point where you weren't lost.*"

"And where is that, pray tell?"

"Let's go to where the tale begins. The statue was originally taken from a temple in a town called Cornibbling."

Brago hoisted his pack. "Sounds delightful. Another pile of dung in the middle of nowhere, I warrant."

"Probably. But it beats sitting here. Go ready the horses. I'll replenish our supplies."

As Brago had predicted, Cornibbling was nothing more than a dreary farming village of thirty buildings—most with ill-kept roofs of brown turf. As soon as they entered town, a swarm of grubby children greeted them.

"Want information, mister?" one of them said, shielding his eyes from the afternoon sun as he gazed up at Edris. "We can provide it! But it'll cost you."

"Information about what?" Edris replied.

"You're an adventurer," another boy said. "Don't try to deny it. We can tell."

"Are there other adventurers in town?" Edris asked, looking about the desolate street. There were a few people in view, but they all appeared to be locals.

The boys held out a hand.

"One silver piece...each."

Brago whipped out his knife. "How about I stick you with this for free?"

They retreated a step.

"Don't mind him." Edris counted the children. "Seven silver it is. Though I'll give you much more if you tell me something useful." He tossed them each a coin.

"Well, for starters," the first child said, eyeing Brago, "we don't really have an inn. Just a few boarding houses. Most are full, but Lady Elizabeth is renting her rooms, and one's available." He indicated a two-story house that was once painted a bright yellow but had since faded into a more muted color.

"Lady Elizabeth?" Edris repeated. "She's noble?"

"She claims she is—very distantly, from what anybody can figure out. If you ask her about it, she'll give you an earful. So be warned!"

"Thanks for the tip. You mentioned other adventurers. Who's in town?"

"Sir Frank of Overshire," the second boy said, as if ticking off names he'd memorized. "Sir Duncan of Dardenello."

"Sir Hampton of Hillshire," another boy added.

"I don't think he's from Hillshire," a third opined.

"Is so."

"You're thinking of Sir Harold."

"Am not!"

"Sir Harold's here?" Edris asked, breaking up the argument.

"He was," the first boy told him, "but he left two days ago."

"Did he find anything?"

"No. Nobody has. Leastways, if they had, we'd be demanding a gold piece to keep it quiet!"

Edris laughed, his horse shifting impatiently under him. "No doubt. What about Markus of Upper Angle?"

The boys exchanged glances, each shaking their heads.

"Haven't seen him," the lead boy said.

"Where's this temple?" Edris asked, surveying the town. "The one built by the Hamumomi?"

The boys pointed to a squat dome-like structure constructed of mud brick and thatch.

"It's over there."

"It's not the original."

"The raiders burnt down the entire town," the lead boy said. "Nothing remains from those days." He cocked his head. "Want to hear how they did it?"

"Sure," Edris said.

The boy thrust a thumb northward. "They came from that direction, roughly eighty of them. All on horseback. They broke into three groups. One group rode around the outskirts of town that way." He waved his arm clockwise around the town. "Another group rode around the other direction." He waved his arm counterclockwise.

"The third came in to loot?" Edris asked.

"Right," the boy said. "Anyway, nobody escaped the ring of riders. They shot everybody who tried to flee."

"Did anybody survive the attack?"

"Uh-huh. But it depends upon who you talk to. Some people say only five people survived, hiding or playing dead as the riders looted. Others say it was six or seven. I don't know which is correct. But they're all dead now."

"Of course, they're dead, you little bastard!" Brago snapped. "They'd be three hundred years old if they weren't."

"Right. Sorry." The boy edged away from Brago. "Want to know anything else, sir?"

Edris dug into a pouch. The boys' eyes grew expectantly.

"The first person who tells me when Markus arrives gets this." He held up a shiny gold piece. "You understand? The moment he arrives, I want to know. I don't care how late or early it is. Come find me. In fact—" Edris dug out another seven silver pieces and handed one to each boy. "—if any other adventurers come to town, come get me."

"Yes, sir!" they said.

"Beg your pardon," the lead boy said. "But what's your name?"

Edris stood in his stirrups and gave a half-bow. "I'm Sir Edris of Bend."

"Never heard of you. No offense or anything."

Edris chuckled. "Not yet. But you will!"

"Confidence, eh? Good for you. I hope you win, sir."

"Thanks, young man." Edris dismounted. "Now…you all run along. But if you hear anything, let me know."

"Yes, sir. We will. Thank you!"

The boys ran off, each clutching their two silver pieces.

"You shouldn't have told them your name," Brago said, watching them disappear into a tavern. "I bet they're telling somebody you're here right now."

"Let them." Edris stretched his legs. "Everybody would find out sooner or later. You can't keep a secret in a place like this."

They inspected the village.

"Perhaps some barbarians will come along and burn it down again," Brago grumbled. "It'd be an improvement."

Edris had been thinking the same thing. There wasn't a nice building or flower garden in sight.

"What now?" Brago asked.

"Stable the horses and go find this Lady Elizabeth. Tell her we need the rooms for two weeks."

"Two weeks? They better have good wine here, and plenty of it."

Edris ignored him. "Then snoop around and see what you can find out."

Brago imitated Edris bowing to the children. "As you wish."

"And Brago…" Edris studied the round mud temple up the road. "Thanks for coming with me. I feel much better having you nearby."

"Thank you for having me, Ed. Questing assuredly beats sleeping in horse shit and begging for scraps."

"You'll never have to do either again, if I can help it. See you tonight."

"Very well." Brago subtly inclined his ear toward the tavern into which the boys had run. Several grim faces were squinting at them through the dingy windows. "But watch yourself. None of those men appear particularly happy to see us."

Forty-Seven

Edris stood in the middle of the dirt road, examining the Hamumomi temple. It had no door, only a low archway covered by a soiled red blanket swaying in the breeze. It appeared as though a prolonged rainstorm would wash the entire structure away.

Down the street, many of the boys he'd given money to were watching him. A few women were also out and about, but they appeared to be looking at him for a different reason. Wanting to get out of view, Edris pushed passed the blanket.

Beyond was a single chamber in which maybe twenty people could fit comfortably, though anybody above average height would have to walk hunched over. If Edris straightened, his head would've popped through the ceiling.

An old man with bronzed and leathery skin sat on a mat of woven grass. He gave Edris a broad, toothless smile. "Here to pray?" he asked in a high-pitched, heavily accented voice. "Or for information?"

Edris inched forward, trying not to crack his skull on the wooden beams crisscrossing the ceiling. Other than a low pedestal at the other side of the round room, the temple was completely empty.

"Maybe both."

As a rule, Edris wasn't religious. The only god he respected was Havnär, the God of Fortune. Followers of Havnär believed people were born with whatever skills they needed to fulfill their destiny; it was simply up to them to achieve it. According to scripture, there wasn't any need to pray, since Havnär wouldn't help them anyway.

The old man patted the flagstone floor in front of him. "Sit. Sit. Easier for you and for me!"

Edris sat.

"You look for Sarababi?" the man asked.

"Beg your pardon?"

The old man gestured to the empty altar. "The golden bug?"

Edris tried not to laugh but failed. "I don't suppose you know where it is."

"No. But I know where it *isn't*. That's often a good place to start!"

"Indeed." Edris folded his legs, attempting to get comfortable. "Can you tell me anything about this…Sara—babi?"

"Yes. It was made of solid gold."

That didn't help.

"About how big was it?" Edris asked.

"Oh, about—" The old man clenched a fist. "Like so."

"That small, eh? There are a lot of places it could be."

"And many places it couldn't."

Edris ignored this. He was beginning to think he'd never find the statue—nobody could. It was either melted down or buried somewhere. Without a map, the quest was pointless.

He rubbed his scarred forehead.

"If I may, young man," the cleric said, "your spirit seems troubled."

Edris sighed. "I need to find that statue."

"*Need*?" the old man repeated doubtfully.

"Want," Edris corrected himself. "It'd mean a great deal to me and my family."

"And to us as well!"

"Then help me. What am I missing?"

The old man shrugged. "Maybe nothing. Maybe a lot. Who can say?"

That didn't help either.

Edris glanced about the dimly lit chamber, trying to find some source of inspiration.

"Is that where Sarababi would've been displayed?" he asked, indicating the empty altar.

"Yes, indeed. There for all to see."

"Why a golden bug?" Edris thought aloud.

"Sarababi is our god," the man replied pleasantly.

"I'm sorry. I shouldn't have said…"

"Not at all. All questions good. Why a bug? Why anything? But where my people come from, few things survive. The scarab, or as you say…bug, teaches us much. It burrows under the sand to hide from the sun or enemies. It finds food where it can. It even works with others."

"It's a survivor."

"Precisely so. It was in the desert before we arrived. And it will be there after we are no more." The old man regarded Edris sitting in front of him. "What else is on your mind?"

Edris peered at the blanket covering the archway. "Why don't you have a door that locks? Aren't you worried about people coming in and stealing things?"

The man spread his hands. "What's to steal?"

"That's true."

The man went on. "If people worry too much about their possessions, they begin to forget what's truly important. The truly important things— kindness, integrity, love—can never be taken from us. Not even by bandits…or other adventurers."

Edris's stomach rumbled. It was well past dinner, and he was looking forward to a meal that hadn't been burnt over a campfire.

He stood, banging his head against the low roof. He cursed.

"I'm terribly sorry for my language."

"Not to worry," the old man said, standing. "You will hit your head much in life. If saying something helps you deal with it…say what you like."

Edris gave him a gold coin. "For your troubles."

"I have no troubles, young man. But thank you." He put his hands together and bowed.

Edris returned the bow and backed out of the temple, trying not to crack his head again. Frustrated and hungry, he went in search for Brago.

Forty-Eight

"I don't understand men of the cloth," Edris said to Brago as they ate. "I understand money isn't everything, but not caring if a solid gold statue of your god gets stolen seems insane to me."

Brago pulled the meat from a roasted chicken leg. "It is insane. And believe me, men of the cloth are liars like everybody else. If they didn't care about their bug being stolen, they wouldn't be asking the kings to find it for them."

"But they didn't even have a door on their temple."

"Since when do doors stop thieves?" Brago asked, chewing. "Even castles get robbed."

"Good point." Edris cut into his lamb. "But they had this golden bug sitting out for anybody to take. It makes no sense."

"I'm sure they put it away when nobody was around to watch it."

"But that's just it! There was no other place to put it."

"There are always places to hide valuables. The fact you didn't see any only means theirs is a particularly good one."

"You think?"

"Describe the room."

Edris took a drink of red wine. "Round. Probably thirty feet in diameter. An arched doorway about five feet high…"

"What's holding the ceiling up? Any posts?"

"No, but there are wooden beams crossing from wall to wall, like a wagon wheel."

Brago jabbed a chicken bone at Edris. "There you go. They could easily hide their valuables in a secret compartment in the beams."

"Maybe."

"Ed, this priest isn't going to carry around the gold coin you gave him. He's going to put it somewhere safe. Just like he would a golden statue."

Edris chewed thoughtfully. "I suppose you're right."

"Trust me," Brago said, tearing into a chicken wing, "any man who says money isn't important is a liar."

Forty-Nine

The next day, Edris returned to the temple and found the same old man sitting on his grass mat.

"Ah," the cleric said merrily. "Did you find our golden bug?"

"No, sir."

"You have more questions?"

"Yes, sir—if you don't mind."

"Not at all! Not at all!" The old man patted the flagstone floor in front of him. "Sit!"

Edris sat, crossing his legs. He thought about what he wanted to ask.

"I'm curious about something," he said after a moment. "It is my understanding that the Sarababi was moved from temple to temple fairly often."

"That is correct."

"Why? Why not keep it in one spot?"

"Ah! Many temples. Only one statue."

"So, moving it around wasn't a way of protecting it? To make sure thieves didn't know where it was?"

"No. Thieves always know things. Otherwise, they starve."

"And how long was it at this temple?"

"It was never at this temple."

"I'm sorry?"

The old man waved at the mud walls and ceiling. "This temple was built after the fire."

"Yes, of course. I understand," Edris said. "How long was it at the temple the raiders burnt down?"

"Days? Months? Years?" The old man lifted his brown hands. "Who can say?"

Edris frowned, trying to think of another question.

"Did the original temple have a door?" he asked.

"A door?"

"Yes, something other than the curtain. Something you could lock?"

The old man shook his head. "No doors in desert. No wood."

That made sense.

"What's troubling you?" the old man asked. "Is your quest about doors?"

Edris shifted his weight. His rear end and legs were falling asleep. He wondered whether the temple had a stone floor to make sure people didn't stay long.

"No," he said, casually inspecting the wooden beams. None of them were thick enough to have hidden compartments. "I suppose I'm having difficulty understanding how your people would have a solid gold statue and not protect it. And how it didn't get stolen earlier."

The old man gave his same toothless smile. "Possessions aren't everything. Keep that in mind, young man."

"What did you do with the gold piece I gave you?"

Startled, the man rocked back. "Would you like it returned?"

"No, not at all. I'm merely curious as to what a holy man does with money."

The man chuckled. "I buy food and pay the debts I sometimes incur when souls less generous than yourself come in."

Edris frowned doubtfully.

"Is it so difficult for you to believe," the old man asked, "that somebody might not be bound to material things?"

"Actually," Edris said, considering the question, "it is. You see, I grew up in a noble family. I've always had everything I've ever wanted. And now I'm setting out on my own and I'm worried…"

"You're trying to find your own path?"

"Something like that."

"And you're worried that you might not have enough—things?"

The old man's knowing expression made Edris feel ridiculous.

"Yes," he admitted. "I suppose so."

Edris sighed, wondering why he was telling all of this to a stranger. But it felt good.

"For most of my life, I've lived in fear of my father disowning me. Now that I'm older, I suppose, I'm still living in fear."

"Fear is no good. Not for you. Not for your father."

"Very true."

"Tell me, young man," the cleric asked, a quizzical expression settling on his deeply wrinkled face. "What is the source of your fear? What worries you most? That your father will not be happy with you?"

"No. He's never been happy—with me or anybody else."

"Then what's the source of this fear?"

Edris shrugged. "I suppose I'm worried he might take everything away. My home, my family—everything. Since I was a boy, he's threatened to kick me out of the house with nothing but the clothes on my back. I used to cry myself to sleep worried that I might wake up on the street, alone."

"Nobody can take away what is truly important. The trick is looking within and learning what is truly important to you." His dark eyes twinkled. "You might be surprised what you find. It won't be a golden bug!"

"I suppose." Edris sighed. "Thanks for talking."

"I hope you find what you're searching for."

Edris stood, careful not to bang his head again. "I wish I knew what that was."

Fifty

Edris stomped through town, a newly purchased ax in hand. He'd been in Cornibbling for three weeks and was becoming increasingly exasperated, not only by his lack of progress at finding the Sacred Scarab, but his lack of direction in life—or perhaps his *current* direction in life.

He couldn't explain it, but something was bothering him. He'd chosen to become an adventurer because he thought it was an easy way to avoid becoming a kingsman. He also thought it would be exciting traveling about the lands, solving riddles, finding lost relics. But over the last two months, he'd done little more than sit in squalid taverns and stew.

Then there was the issue with his father. For the first time in his life, his father seemed genuinely interested in what he was doing. More than interested, he was actively participating, sending Edris lengthy letters every few days, suggesting that he do this or that, offering encouragement. The Lord of Bend even sent Edris a list of all the men in Pembroke's army that hunted the Step Raiders and their last known living heirs.

There were over five hundred names. Did his father actually expect him to go to all five hundred relatives? And what then? Ask: "Excuse me, but did your distant ancestor happen to find a golden bug after defeating the legendary Gubli-gan?"

He could almost hear their laughter.

Yet it was his only actual lead. The statue was either buried, destroyed, or in the hands of some relative of one of Pembroke's soldiers. There were no other options.

Edris selected a tree to fell, a dying oak that was probably a seedling when the statue disappeared. Stripping off his shirt, he stretched his back and arms, then swung the ax—lodging it deeply into the tree's trunk. He jerked it free.

If the statue was buried, he'd never find it. Not without a map, at any rate.

A map…

If the raiders made a map of where they buried their loot, how could he find it? It would've been captured along with Gubli-gan.

Trying to remember everything his brother had told him about Gubli-gan and the raiders, Edris drove the ax head into the tree again.

Gubli-gan was taken alive and paraded through each of the towns he'd destroyed. Then he was disemboweled and beheaded. Children kicked his skull around the streets.

He was taken alive…

If he had a map on him, someone would've found it and explored what it was hiding. Nobody could resist a treasure map.

He swung again, wood chips flying.

Unless, of course, they didn't realize it led to a treasure. Maybe it wasn't even a map. Maybe it was a description of a location subtly included in a letter or diary entry.

He swung again.

Perhaps he should go to see if he could nose around King Pendergast's library. The clue he needed might've gotten mixed with his other stuff.

Stuff…

He swung again, his thoughts turning to the withered old man in the mud temple.

Living without possessions…

It didn't make any sense. Sure, he could see not letting gold get too strong of a hold on one's life, but to not have a door that locked? They had a solid gold statue, for crying out loud. And if they really didn't care about it getting stolen, then why ask the kings to search for it—like Brago said?

Something wasn't right.

He started to swing the ax, but something caught his eye.

Four people were hiking through the tall grass toward him and, judging by the heraldry worn by the two in the lead, they weren't townsfolk. Edris planted his ax in the ground and used his shirt to towel away the sweat prickling his forehead and armpits.

"Trying to earn some extra money?" the first figure asked cheerily as they approached. He wore a fine cloak over a polished chainmail shirt and had a long sword hanging from his leather belt.

"Something like that," Edris replied, self-conscious of his dirt-smudged body and sweat-soaked clothes.

"I am Sir Tudor." The man gestured to his shorter companion. "This is the honorable Sir Howard the Third." Sir Howard nodded. "And our capable squires, Rowan and Oliver."

Behind them, two teenage boys bowed.

Edris shook the knights' hands, wondering why two highly acclaimed adventurers would be bothering him while he worked.

"Pleasure." Then remembering he was a knight as well, he added, "Sir Edris, at your service and your family's."

"Sir Edris?" Sir Tudor replied thoughtfully, though it appeared as though he already knew his name. "I believe we've heard about you."

"Have you?"

Edris hated these kinds of games. Plainly these knights had something to say. Why didn't they come out and say it and then let him return to his thinking?

"Did you really send Sir Rodney's sword to his father?" Sir Tudor asked.

"Oh, that," Edris said, relieved. He'd half-expected to hear that Markus was spreading stories about how he'd wet the bed when he was three. "I did. Boys who can't handle their liquor shouldn't play with sharp objects."

Clapping, the knights howled with laughter. Even their squires standing a respectable distance away snickered.

Sir Tudor gasped for breath. "I tell you…I tell you, that's—that's the funniest damned thing I've heard. Good for you!"

"Somebody needed to teach Rod a lesson!" Sir Howard said. "The drunken oaf!"

"And what a lesson!" Sir Tudor dried his tears with the edge of his cloak. "He'll never live it down. Never in a million years."

"It was either sending his sword home," Edris said, "or giving him a pounding, he wouldn't forget."

"He would've preferred a pounding, to be sure!"

Their laughter died, leaving an uncomfortable silence. The two knights examined Edris's handiwork.

"Another few blows and I think you'll topple it," Sir Howard said, studying the dead tree.

"I say seven," Sir Tudor said. "Care to have a bet, Howard?"

"No," Sir Howard replied. "I do believe you're correct. Seven is the number I would've chosen."

The summer breeze picked up, making Edris's sweaty body feel chilled.

"So, what can I do for you two gentlemen?" he asked. "I'm guessing you're not here to count the swings of my ax."

"Ah! The direct approach. I can appreciate that," Sir Tudor said. "To be honest, we were curious as to what you were doing out here. I'm guessing the tree hasn't caused you any offense."

"No. I'm simply burning off some frustration."

The knights appeared to be evaluating whether this was true.

"Let me ask you something," Edris said, deciding to seize the initiative in the conversation. "Are all quests this confounding?"

"So!" Sir Tudor said, as if they'd scored a point. "You *are* questing! We weren't sure. This your first go?"

"It is." Edris quickly corrected himself. "Well, it's my first official one. I tagged along on one other."

"Then to answer your question—yes, they are always this tedious. Makes me wish I'd become a carpenter like my mother wanted."

"Oh, they're not always this bad," Sir Howard said before conceding, "But this one is particularly challenging. Usually there's more information upon which to make decisions. And since we're asking questions…what brought you to Cornibbling?"

Edris jerked his ax out of the ground and hefted it to his shoulder. "Nowhere else to go, really. I didn't want to stand around, digging holes randomly in every field the riders might have crossed."

"You've been to Little Dribbling, eh?" Sir Howard asked. "It certainly got crowded quickly. Nearly every adventurer known to the gods was there, shovel in hand."

"Good luck to them," Sir Tudor said, inspecting the dead tree again. "I can't imagine any of them finding it there. And if they do, it'll be a hell of a melee trying to get it out of the valley. It'll be one for the storybooks."

"Why are you here?" Edris asked, hoping to get some information that might help him find the statue.

But the knights smiled. "We're relaxing."

Edris offered them his ax. "There are plenty of trees."

They laughed.

"We prefer alcohol for our relaxation."

"And women."

Another awkward silence fell about them.

"Well," Sir Tudor said, "we'll be letting you return to your swinging and thinking."

They shook hands again.

"When your task is complete, come to the tavern. We'll buy the first round."

"The first round is on me," Edris said, happy to have something to do that evening. "Just let me finish up here. I won't take long."

Fifty-One

Edris stumbled into his room at Lady Elizabeth's boarding house and lobbed his key at a small table next to the door. The key missed and bounced, clattering along the floor. He giggled. "Oops!"

Reclining in a chair by the window, Brago peered up from a book. "You're out late. Everything all right?"

"I'm fine." Edris sat on the edge of the bed and attempted to pull off one of his boots. He squinted at what Brago was reading. "Hey, I have that same book!"

"It is *your* book. You left it out." Brago resumed reading. "I never knew we had the same taste in poetry. Balen is one of my favorites, though I also enjoy Lord Thomas."

Edris finally managed to remove his boot. "Oh, I love Thomas!" He put a finger to his lips. "But don't tell anybody."

"Assuredly." Brago turned a page. "What were you doing all night?"

"Drinking with Sir Tudor and Sir Howard."

"Are you sure that's wise? After all, they're your competitors."

Edris waved a wobbly hand. "They're good guys. None of us even knows where the blasted bug is anyway." He lowered himself to the floor and sprawled out, still wearing one boot. "You take the bed tonight. The floor doesn't move as much."

"As you wish."

Edris put his hands behind his head. "Hey, Brago? What do you think it's all about?"

Brago turned another page. "To what *it* are you referring?"

"Life and everything. I don't know. What do you want to do with it all?"

"Survive."

Edris made a dismissive sound. "You don't need to worry about that. I take care of my friends. And you're a good friend. A very good friend. I'll make sure you're never homeless again."

Brago closed the book of poems and set it aside.

"That's kind, Ed. However, we'll both be homeless if we don't start winning some quests. And we can't do that by sitting around these crappy villages, drinking all night."

"I know. I know. It's just…" Edris fought to keep the liquid contents of his stomach from rising. "I don't know what I'm doing. I'm a failure!"

"Got another letter from your father, I presume."

Edris groaned. "Don't mention him. He's going to be pissed if I don't win. Pissed. I don't have a clue what to do. Maybe I should've become a monk, like my brother. I could live in a mud hut and not worry about anything."

"I have some news on that score," Brago said. "It might cheer you up."

"What?"

"I went in to see your selfless monk and gave him a silver piece. I then spied on him. Know what he did with the money?"

"Spent it on a whore?" Edris snickered.

"He put it under one of the stones forming the floor."

"And? What does that prove?"

"It proves he was full of shit when he said he didn't care about material possessions. Why would he hide the coin if he truly didn't care whether it was stolen? He probably has a king's treasury under there."

Edris propped himself on his elbows. "Yeah! He lied."

"Everybody lies, Ed. And everybody cares about material things, especially those who have them."

"The bastard. I say we go beat the crap out of him."

"How about we leave him alone and focus on the quest?"

"Right." Edris watched Brago withdraw another book from his pack. "What are you reading now?"

"A treatise on herbalism."

"Eh?"

Brago exhaled wearily. "I'm trying to learn how to make more effective poisons."

"You're...you're serious? I thought you were only kidding about that."

"When you're big and strong like you, the world is easy. Ne'er-do-wells stay clear of you. People like me, however, need an equalizer, and poisons help immensely."

"Remind me never to piss you off."

"You're the only one who doesn't need to fear." Brago found the page he wanted. "Of course, herbalism isn't always nefarious. In fact, it's exceedingly stimulating and practical."

"How so?"

"For instance, there're directions here to create a salve to repel mosquitos."

"Anything for hangovers?"

"I shall check. However, in the meanwhile, self-restraint might serve you better."

"Self-restraint. Winners have self-restraint. Do you know Sir Howard has won eight quests? Sir Tutor has won five. I've won zero."

"Self-pity doesn't become you, Ed," Brago said, reading. "You simply need to start focusing."

"Focusing…right!" Edris closed his eyes again, wishing the room would stop spinning. He yawned and asked dreamily, "How did you learn how to read, anyway? I didn't think poor people could read."

"My mother was your teacher," Brago said resentfully. "Or have you forgotten what your father did to her?"

"Oh, yeah," Edris said, his voice drifting off. "I liked her. I liked her a lot." He started to snore.

"As did I."

Fifty-Two

Edris awoke the next day well after noon. His head hurt and his tongue felt fuzzy. Even his eyes felt as though they were throbbing. Had the other knights got him drunk on purpose? Probably. He'd have to be smarter next time. In fact, he didn't plan on drinking anytime soon.

Lumbering along the street looking for a place to eat, Edris beheld the monk's mud hut. His stride faltered as he recalled bits and pieces of the conversation he had with Brago the night before. Something churned in his mind.

"Still here, mister?" a young voice said.

Turning, Edris found one of the young boys who'd greeted him when he'd first arrived. "Still here," he replied. "What about everybody else?"

"Nope. Most are gone. Left weeks ago. Only you and a couple others remain. Not sure why any of you even came, to tell you the truth. There's nothing here to help you find the statue. Hell, if you think about it, we have nothing to do with the statue or the raiders."

"What do you mean?"

"The raiders burnt everything down. These buildings are new. Not new-new, but you know what I mean. The original town wasn't even here."

217

"This isn't the original town site?" Edris asked, not sure why that bothered him.

"No. It was over there." The boy pointed to where Edris had cut down the tree.

"Why'd they move it?"

"Build where an entire town was destroyed? People slaughtered? Talk about bad luck. It's like living on top of a grave."

"I suppose."

Edris stared at the field where the original town had stood.

"Need anything else, sir?" the boy asked.

"No." He gave the boy a silver piece. "I'm fine, thanks."

"Thank you, sir!"

Edris called to him as he walked away. "Lad."

"Yes, sir?"

"Was this town built in the same configuration as the old town?"

"Excuse me, sir?"

"Were all the houses and building in the same spots? The courthouse at the center of town? The stables on the east side?"

"I have no idea, sir. Why do you ask?"

Edris resumed staring at the field. There was nothing there except for a tangle of trees and bushes and a few foundations of former houses. Yet something about it seemed to beckon to him.

"I don't know. Just a hunch."

"Any other questions?"

"No. Thank you," Edris said. "But if you come across my friend, please send him my way."

"The scary fellow with the black hair?"

"That's him. I'll give you another silver piece if you can find him."

Fifty-Three

"Are you sure you've found the right place?" Edris asked Brago as they approached the overgrown fields where the original village of Cornibbling was reputed to have been located.

"I believe so." Brago pushed through the tall weeds, hooded lantern in hand. It was a cloudy night. Rain was on the way. "There're flagstones."

"That could be from any building."

"Perhaps. But if you notice, many of the other buildings had stone cellars or were built with timber." He pointed to the ruined foundations they were passing. "You can still see the holes where they secured the wood beams."

"And the temple was made mainly of mud brick…"

"And had stones for the floor." Brago stopped. "Much like these."

He uncovered his lantern and shone it over a series of flat grey stones, partially covered with dirt and grass. Saplings grew in between their cracks.

"It's roughly circular in shape," Edris admitted.

"Exactly. Now, will you please tell me what we're doing here in the middle of the night?"

Edris poked at the ground with the tip of his sword, trying to find the edges of a stone. "I have a hunch."

"A hunch?"

Kneeling in the knee-high grass, Edris turned over a flagstone. Underneath, fat worms wiggled in the yellow light.

"Let me ask you this." He drew a dagger and traced it around the edges of another stone. "Suppose you were a monk and in charge of a golden statue of your god."

"Improbable but go on."

"Raiders are circling the town, shooting anybody who tries to flee. Others are setting buildings on fire. They're coming in your direction and will be on you in minutes. What would you do?"

"Smear blood all over my face and play dead."

"Sensible." Clawing at the dirt, Edris turned over another stone. Black beetles skittered in every direction. "But what would you do with the statue?"

"You think they hid it like the monk did with the coin?"

"I don't know. But I simply cannot believe that they'd leave the statue out for somebody to steal. Even if they didn't care about the gold, they would've cared because it represented their god."

"What do you want me to do?"

"Start at the other end and turn them over. We don't have much time. Soon, somebody is going to notice us out here."

Hacking at the grass, Brago cleared a spot and began digging his knife under an exposed flagstone.

A half mile away, lights twinkled in the village.

Thunder rolled in from the west.

Edris turned over another flagstone, but he found nothing except packed dirt.

A light mist fell.

Brago flung another flat stone off into the darkness, then slashed at the grass a few feet over from where he'd been digging.

The mist turned into a heavy drizzle, soaking them to the skin. Approaching thunder warned of harder showers to come.

One by one, they dug up the stones until two rows of exposed soil ran through the weeds.

Edris stood, arching his aching back. Wiping the rain from his face, he surveyed the vague outline of where the temple used to be. They were about a quarter of the way done. It'd take another hour to look under all of them.

He stared at the black sky, fat raindrops pelting him.

They were probably wasting their time. He had no basis for believing the monks had hidden the statue. Still, what else could he do? His father wouldn't tolerate a loser.

"Ed?"

Edris turned just in time to catch what he thought was a black oval rock covered in clay. He brushed away the grime. Two green gems stared at him like eyes.

Fifty-Four

Edris scrubbed the mud from the Sacred Scarab, its tarnished gold glinting slightly in the lantern light.

"Congratulations on your first win, Ed," Brago said. "I'm sure your father will be delighted."

"For a day or two."

Edris held the statue in cupped hands, allowing the rain to wash away centuries of dirt. Despite being nearly completely black, it was unmistakably Sarababi.

"All right," he said finally. "We have a decision to make. If we grab our horses now and ride off in this weather, people will hear about it in the morning and undoubtedly come after us. If we return to our room, covered in mud, some kid is going to see what we've done here, put two and two together, and then tell everybody."

"Either way," Brago said, "we'll be found out in the morning. Best to ride now and get a few hours' head start, don't you think? Moreover, the rain might help hide our trail."

"Maybe."

"It's your decision."

Edris inspected the dark sky, heavy raindrops bombarding him. He was wet and muddy and hungry, and the last thing he wanted to do was get on a horse and ride at breakneck speeds for hours on end. But they couldn't stay where they were—not for long, at least.

"Ed?" Brago prodded.

"I know. Morning's coming," he said, unable to decide. He flipped a mental coin. "All right. We'll ride immediately. We'll need the lead."

"Very good. I'll fetch the horses. You gather our belongings."

His decision finally made, Edris felt a burden lifted from his spirit. He tightened his grip on the statue. "Quickly now. We're wasting time!"

They broke into a jog, their boots crunching the wet grass as they headed toward the handful of lights shining from the windows of Cornibbling.

In the darkness in front of them, four figures leapt up, swords in hand.

"Excellent," a voice said. "Now give us the statue."

Edris put the statue in his pocket and drew his two swords. "I'm not giving it to you, Tudor."

Sir Tudor and Sir Howard closed in, one from the right, the other from the left.

"You'd rather die?" Sir Howard asked.

Edris moved to his left, making sure they didn't flank him. "Absolutely."

"Come, come," Sir Tudor said. "You don't mean that. It's too soon in your young career. Give us the statue. We'll tell everybody you put up a valiant fight."

"It's my first win," Edris said, finding a place with firm footing. "Wouldn't you die for your first win?"

The knights faltered. Evidently, they remembered all too well what their first win felt like.

Rain pounded around them.

"Stay your hand!" Sir Tudor called to Brago, who had drawn a throwing knife from his belt. "This is for knights only. Our squires will not intervene either."

"Then why do they have their weapons?" Brago asked dryly.

"Put them away, lads," Sir Howard told their squires. "And stay clear."

The squires sheathed their swords and retreated a few paces.

"It's still two against one," Brago said. "So much for your so-called Code."

"I can handle two against one," Edris said.

Sir Howard smirked. "Think so?"

Spitting rain that ran into his mouth, Edris readied his weapons—one to parry, the other to counter. He had to strike the first person quickly, then move to the second. He couldn't afford to duel both at the same time. He stepped forward, careful not to trip over the debris littering the ruins.

"Think about what you're doing, son," Sir Tudor said. "This isn't a game."

Lightning split the western sky, revealing the doubt in the knights' eyes. They obviously didn't expect any resistance.

Thunder shook the rain-soaked ground.

"I'm sorry I'll have to kill you," Edris told them. "But you brought it on yourselves, so pardon me if I don't weep over your graves."

Bounding forward, Edris swung one sword at Sir Howard's chest, then jabbed the other at his lead leg. Sir Howard parried the first, but not the second. It bit deeply into his thigh, turning his pant leg red. He cried out. Pushing his advantage, Edris brought a sword down on his foe's outstretched parrying arm. He intended to slap the wrist with the flat side of his blade, compelling the knight to drop his weapon; however, the blade's edge sliced cleanly through the knight's bone.

For a second, everybody froze in horror as half of Sir Howard's arm fell into the wet grass. Then the screaming started.

Sir Tudor rushed to his companion's aid, but Edris held him at bay with the points of his swords.

"Do you yield?" he shouted through the driving rain.

"Yes!" Sir Tudor cried, tossing away his weapon. "I yield." He caught Sir Howard as he collapsed to the ground.

"Damn it!" Edris crouched at Sir Howard's side. "I didn't mean for this to happen."

Streams of blood spurted from the end of Sir Howard's arm.

"We need to stop the bleeding," Sir Tudor said.

Edris grabbed the end of Sir Howard's arm and squeezed as hard as he could. The blood slowed slightly.

Lightning crackled.

"Damn it!" He shouted at Sir Tudor, "Go get a doctor! Run!"

Covered in blood, Sir Tudor sprinted off into the darkness.

"You!" Edris yelled at one of the squires standing in the shadows, mortified. "Do you have a rope?"

"What?"

"Rope! Do you have a god-damned rope?"

"No, sir!"

The other squire shook his head.

Edris swore, rain pouring over him. "Give me your belt. Now! We don't have much time."

Brago leaned over Edris's shoulder. Of all them, he seemed unaffected by what was happening. "What do you require of me?"

"Get the horses and our gear," Edris answered. "Make ready to ride."

Brago tipped his dripping hat. "As you wish."

One of the squires held out his belt, trying not to get too close to the now unconscious knight.

"Come here!" Edris commanded.

"Why?"

"What's your name?"

"Rowan, sir. He's Oliver."

"Grab ahold of his arm, Rowan."

"Me? Why?"

"Because when I let go, blood is going to shoot everywhere. We need to keep him from bleeding to death."

"I can't…"

"Damn it, Rowan. Get down here and hold the bastard's arm. That's it. Use both hands. Squeeze tight. Tighter. Squeeze like you're choking somebody to death. All right. I'm going to tie the belt around his elbow. Don't let go! You understand? You let go and he dies."

His eyes closed, the squire tightened his grip. "Okay!"

Quickly, Edris let go and wrapped the belt around the knight's arm as tightly as he could. Sir Howard lay pale and motionless in a growing puddle of red water.

Shouts joined the thrashing wind.

"You!" Edris said to the other squire. "Oliver! Go meet them. Make sure they know where we are."

"Yes, sir!"

"Can I let go?" Rowan asked, eyes still squinted shut.

"Not yet." Edris tied the belt as best as he could. "All right. Let go."

Blood seeped through the wound.

"Bollocks!"

A crowd of people hurried to them, some still in their bedclothes.

"Who's the doctor?" Edris asked Sir Tudor.

A man slid to Edris's side. "I am!"

"Can you save him?" Edris asked.

The doctor touched the knight's throat. Then lifted an eyelid. "We have to get him to town. He's lost a lot of blood."

"Do what you can."

As townsfolk lifted Sir Howard onto their shoulders, Brago rode up, leading Edris's horse and holding his pack. Edris leapt onto his horse.

Lightning detonated overhead.

"Tudor!" he called through the storm. "I didn't want this. This isn't my fault. You understand? If you follow us, you'll die too!"

Fifty-Five

For twelve days, Edris and Brago rode as fast as they could, buying fresh horses each time they came to a town. When they finally reached Upper Angle, evening deepened throughout the river valley. Galloping up to King Michael's castle, Edris leapt from his horse and ran to the gate. He shouted for the gatekeepers.

"Name?" a gatekeeper asked.

"Sir Edris of Bend," Edris said, panting. Then he added, hoping it'd help, "Son of Lord Elros. I'm the king's nephew."

The gatekeeper scrutinized him more closely. "Business?"

"I need to see His Majesty."

"Is it urgent?"

"Yes. It concerns the Kings' Quest."

"Very well." The gatekeeper signaled for the portcullis to be opened, then beckoned to a row of messengers sitting on a bench by the gatehouse. Two boys ran up. He wrote a message on a piece of paper and handed it to the first boy. "Please deliver this to His Majesty's secretary."

"Yes, sir!" The first boy took the message and sprinted off to the castle.

"Bennie," the gatekeeper said to the second boy, "please bring Sir Edris to the receiving room."

"Yes, sir!" Bennie bowed to Edris. "This way, sir."

Edris followed him even though he knew the way. Turning back toward the gate, he noticed the gatekeeper handing a note to a third boy.

"Sir?" Bennie held open a door to the west wing of the castle.

"Sorry." Edris caught up to him.

"I hope you don't mind me asking," his guide asked, barely containing his excitement, "but…did you find the Sacred Scarab?"

Edris winked at him.

Bennie exhaled in disbelief. "Great gods! And this was your first quest, too!"

"I got lucky."

"My pa says there isn't no such thing."

They turned down a corridor filled with artwork.

"My father says the same thing," Edris said.

They came to the royal receiving hall. Nobody was there.

"Please wait here," Bennie said formally. "Do you require anything, sir? Something to drink, perhaps?"

"No, thank you. I'm fine."

The boy pointed Edris's belt. "I'm sorry, sir, but I've been instructed to…"

"Oh, yes." He gave him his two swords. "I'm not used to relinquishing my weapons. I was practically raised here."

"Yes, sir." The boy fumbled under their weight, trying not to drop them. He stared at the writing on one of the sword's hilts.

"Can you read?"

"Not well, sir. But I'm learning."

"Good. You'll never regret being smarter." Edris pointed to the engraving. "This is my great-grandfather's name, Lord Edward the third." He moved his finger along the hilt. "This is my grandfather—Lord Edmund. And my father—Lord Elros."

"Why isn't your name listed?"

"To be honest," Edris whispered, "it isn't my sword. It's my brother's."

"Does he know you have it?"

Edris considered making a joke, but he didn't want to start a rumor that he'd taken his brother's sword without permission. The last thing he needed was people continuing to think of him as a child.

"He knows. He lent it to me."

"Don't you have a sword of your own?"

Edris smiled wryly. "Somebody stole it."

"Bugger!"

"My thoughts exactly."

He watched the boy marvel at the polished handguard.

"Here." Edris took the swords from the boy and slid them under his belt on either side of his waist. He ruffled the boy's hair. "Go protect the castle."

The boy saluted. "Yes, sir!" He bowed. "Somebody should be along momentarily to tell you His Majesty's wishes. I will bring your swords to the gatekeeper. I'll make sure nobody touches them."

Edris sat on one of the long marble benches lining the hall. "Thank you."

"And sir?"

"Yes?"

"Congratulations!"

Edris winked at him again. "Thanks."

The boy marched out of the hall, the two longswords banging behind him. He closed the gilded doors with an unsettling thump.

Unable to remain seated, Edris got to his feet and paced the hall, the rhythmic thud of his anxious strides echoing in the frescoed ceiling high overhead.

He'd been in this chamber many times, but in the dim evening light, the shadows behind the sculpted pillars unnerved him. He pulled the Sacred Scarab out of his pocket to make sure it was still there.

His first win…

Actually, it was his second win.

Two wins…

He couldn't help but smile. Being an adventurer was frustrating as hell at times, but when he found his quarry—there wasn't a better feeling in the world.

The far door flew opened. But the figure barging in wasn't the king; it was Markus.

Edris thrust the scarab into his pocket and felt for his missing weapons.

Markus leveled his sword at him. "Give me the statue, Eddie."

"You won't kill me, Markus. Not here. You'd be hanged. In fact, drawing a sword in this chamber is a capital offense."

Markus put the sword point to Edris's chest. "I'm the son of the king, remember? Rules don't apply to me."

"You always were spoiled." Edris glanced at the still-open door, hoping somebody else would enter.

"Give me the statue right now."

"You're not getting it, Markus. Two people have already tried to take it from me and failed. It's mine."

"I'll give you a thousand gold."

"The prize is more than that."

"Two thousand."

"You're not getting it."

Markus tightened his grip around the sword's hilt. "Hand it over, Edris!"

"No."

"I need it! With that statue, I'll be closer to being one of the greatest adventurers of all time."

"Not if you buy your wins."

"Nobody will ever know."

"They will after I tell them."

Markus snarled. "I'll kill you if you do."

"Only if you catch me sleeping." Edris exhaled contemptuously. "I used to look up to you, Markus. I was so proud that we had an adventurer in the family. Then I realized you were nothing but a gutless coward."

Markus's hands shook. "You bastard. Give me the damned statue."

"Why don't you kill me, Markus? You better hurry. I hear somebody coming."

Markus glanced toward the hallway. As he did so, Edris knocked the sword away and slammed a fist into his jaw.

Markus fell sprawling to the floor, his sword clattering next to him. He immediately scrambled to grab it, but Edris stepped on the blade. He pulled up on the hilt.

"Stop it!" Markus said, blood trickling from his mouth. "You'll break it!"

The blade bent, then snapped a foot above the handguard. Edris handed the hilt to his prostrate cousin.

"That was my father's sword!" Markus said.

Edris took the gem-encrusted handguard back. "Then I'll give it to him myself."

His face burning scarlet, Markus leapt to his feet. "You wouldn't dare."

"You need to learn a lesson," Edris said, retrieving the broken blade. "Isn't that what you told me after you bashed my skull in with a rock?"

"You had that coming. Putting a whore before family."

Edris punched Markus in the stomach. Markus doubled over, spitting a spray of blood onto the polished marble floor. Edris cocked his arm, about to drive a hard uppercut into Markus's exposed face—but he shoved his cousin away in disgust instead.

"You're pathetic," Edris told him. "Look at you. You're probably about to cry!"

"I'm going to kill you," Markus said, gasping. "I'm the son of your king. Do you know how miserable I'm going to make your life?"

"As long as I don't buy my fame, I'll still consider myself a man."

Markus glowered at him.

Footsteps echoed toward them. Markus shot a terrified glance up the corridor.

"Give me that statue."

"No."

"Give me my sword."

As he'd done with the Sword of Betrayal, Edris slid the broken blade into one of his empty sheaths and tucked the bejeweled handguard under his belt behind his back. He pulled his cloak tighter around himself. "Not on your life."

The footsteps drew closer.

Markus straightened as best as he could, still clutching his stomach. "You'll regret this, Edris."

With that, he dashed to the far door, disappearing behind it right as King Michael came into view, grinning.

"Sir Edris!" he called, entering the receiving hall.

Edris bowed. "Your Majesty."

"I'm guessing you have something for me?"

"I do." With another bow, he presented the king with the Sacred Scarab.

"Is this it? It's such a small thing. I was expecting it to be much bigger. How on earth did you find it?"

"Unfortunately, there isn't much of a tale. I wouldn't want to bore you."

"Nonsense. I'm sure it took some doing. Come with me. Mariam was hoping to see you again. You can tell us all about your exploits in one telling." Edris followed the king. "And we must find Markus. He's going to be positively green with envy!"

PART THREE

Fifty-Six

Muted morning sunlight slipped between the curtains as Edris stroked Beatrice's blonde hair. Next to her bed, a beautiful new silk dress lay discarded on the floor.

"You must be really proud," she said, her finger caressing his muscular chest.

"You know," he said, "I am."

"You sound surprised."

"Growing up, I was never allowed to feel proud about anything. My father would always point out that I could've done better."

"He's proud, too."

"Maybe."

"He is!"

Edris snorted skeptically.

Beatrice propped herself on an elbow. "When word came that you won, he had heralds march through the streets announcing your victory! There were musicians playing all night. Ed…he went into all the taverns, buying people drinks. I heard there were tears in his eyes!"

Edris pulled her to him. They kissed.

"You made that up," he said.

"Only that last part."

He raised an eyebrow.

"Okay!" she admitted. "He didn't actually buy people drinks…and there weren't any bands. But he *did* send heralds through the town square! I swear!"

"Sure, he did."

She stroked his chest some more. "He's proud. You know that, right?"

Edris put his hands behind his head, enjoying being next to her.

"I'm sure he is…for now."

For several moments, they lay in silence, then Beatrice giggled.

"Two wins in a row!" she squealed. "How can you not be ecstatic?"

"Yes, well, let's keep that first one to ourselves."

"You're not going to tell anybody?"

Would he tell people? He'd already told his father and brothers, and Bea and Brago. Somehow, though, telling anybody else seemed dangerous.

"No," he said. "I don't mind taunting Markus when we're alone, but I don't want to get on the king's bad side. Our deal was a knighthood for the sword. I don't think he'd be pleased if I told people Markus didn't actually find it."

Beatrice's tone cooled. "Let's not talk about him."

Edris kissed the top of her head. "Sorry. But if it's any consolation, I'm sure he's sitting in a tavern somewhere, brooding over a pitcher of beer, wondering how the hell his fat little cousin found two quest items in a row."

"It's not any consolation. If he comes here—"

"He won't. Believe me. He's going to stay clear of me for a while."

"And then what?"

"And then we'll see."

"Ed…"

"Bea," Edris said, frustrated that the contentment he'd felt was slipping into annoyance. "He's a coward. He won't do anything. I know too much that'll hurt him."

"Exactly! Do you really think he'll let you lord that over him?"

Edris kissed her. "Don't worry."

"That's easy for you to say. What if he comes here while you're gone?"

"When I'm gone, we'll both be questing. He won't give up a quest just to come here and bother you. Questing is too important to him." Edris examined the book of poetry on her nightstand. "This new? I haven't seen this one."

"Brago got it for me. And don't change the subject." She sat up. "Ed, I'm serious. What if he comes to Bend and you're not around? Last time he was too drunk to do anything other than tear my clothes. What if he's sober next time? He's the king's son!"

Sensing his moment of peace was irretrievably gone, Edris got out of bed and searched his pile of clothes. He handed her a dagger. "I want you to keep this. Hide it under your pillow or mattress, someplace where you can get to it quickly."

"And do what with it?"

"Cut his balls off."

"Ed!"

Deep down, he knew she was right. Markus wouldn't let him be. Sooner or later, they'd have to settle scores. Like two young rams fighting over part of the mountainside, they were destined to bash heads—and only one of them was going to be left standing.

"Maybe," he said, "I should train you how to fight."

"I'm not a knight," she said, her concern growing. "I'm not a fighter. I'm a commoner—and a woman."

"Women need to know how to defend themselves."

"What could I do against a man who's been training to kill people his entire life?"

They stared at each other—desperation in Beatrice's eyes, fatigue and annoyance in Edris's.

"Bea…"

"I know, you can't be around all the time, but…" She brushed away a tear. "How much did you win for finding the statue? Two thousand gold? You could buy some land and start a life. You could be a farmer like you've always wanted. You don't have to worry about your—!"

"Bea…" he said more firmly. He started getting dressed.

"Where're you going?"

"I have to go home. Father is expecting me."

"When will I see you again?"

He kissed her forehead. "As soon as possible." He smiled and added for good measure, "Don't worry. I'll always be here to protect you. Okay? You'll never have to worry about Markus or anybody else. On my honor."

Fifty-Seven

The guards cheered as Edris rode through the gates to his father's manor.

"Congratulations, Master Edris!" one shouted.

"Well done!"

He saluted. "Thank you. Let's hope it wasn't a fluke!"

He rode along the road to the main house. The door opened and his father stepped out, wearing formal robes lined with white ermine.

"Ed!" he said, his breath appearing in the chilly morning air.

Edris dismounted and shook his father's offered hand.

His father patted him on the shoulder. "Congratulations on your first official win."

"Thank you, sir." Edris motioned to the robes. "Why are you dressed up?"

"Lord Braverton is coming today," Lord Elros said, annoyed.

"Why?"

"The gods only know. Hopefully he won't stay long. I can't stand the man."

"He *is* a bit of a blowhard."

"A bit?" Lord Elros repeated. "He's like that entire side of the family. Worthless, arrogant assholes."

"Yes, sir."

Lord Elros noted the pale blue sky. "You arrived rather early. Did you ride through the night?"

"No. I stayed in Bend last evening."

"Celebrate with your friends?"

Edris nodded, waiting for the explosion he knew would come.

"That's fine," the lord said. "You deserve to celebrate."

"Thank you, sir."

"But I don't want you resting on your laurels. No one ever made the history books by winning one measly quest."

"Yes, sir."

Lord Elros surveyed the manicured lawns, watching his gardeners hasten about the grounds, getting everything ready for his guest's arrival. "What's your plan?"

Edris had his answer ready. "I'm going to stow my things and resume my training."

"Very good! Work on what you're bad at. Work on what you already do well. That's how you keep getting better." The Lord of Bend made sure nobody was within earshot. He lowered his voice. "Any run-ins with Markus?"

"Nothing I couldn't handle."

"That's what I like to hear!" He patted his son's shoulder again. "Go store your gear. Then get to work. Your competition won't be resting. Neither should you. In fact, I want you to clear the north fields. Widen them a good dozen paces. Fell the trees and dig out their stumps before the ground freezes. There're also too many boulders lying about. We'll break plow blades if we try to till."

"I'll take care of them, sir."

"Good. And Edris…"

Edris turned.

"You did well this go-around."

Fifty-Eight

"So, tell us about your quest, Sir Edris," Lord Braverton said as they ate dinner in Lord Elros's private dining hall. "I'm dying to hear the details."

In his upper fifties, Lord Braverton was a few years older than Edris's father. He had a frail, almost elderly pall—as if what little life left in him was slowly seeping out with each wheezing breath. Edris could have easily lifted him above his head with one hand.

"There's not much to tell, sir," Edris replied, cutting into his steak. "It turned out the statue was never stolen."

"Never stolen? How can that be?"

Edris had his mouth full, so Lord Elros answered for him.

"My son deduced that the bandits never acquired the statue…" He lifted his crystal goblet to the candlelight, inspecting the wine's color. "…as everybody else assumed."

"The monks," Edris said, swallowing, "must have hidden it as the raiders set the town on fire."

"They hid it under the flagstones forming the temple's floor." Lord Elros took a sip with evident satisfaction. "Rather ingenious, if you think about it. Hidden in plain sight."

"And it had been sitting there the entire time?" Lord Braverton asked, amazed. He slurped his soup, making Lord Elros recoil. "Incredible."

"Yes," Lord Elros said, putting on a more or less pleasant expression. "They moved the town, you see. After it was destroyed. So Edris had to excavate the ruins of the original site."

"Excavation," Lord Braverton repeated. "Sounds thrilling."

"That really wasn't difficult," Edris said. "The challenging part was getting it to the king."

"I heard that you had a duel of some sort," Lord Braverton said, bits of bread falling out of his mouth as he chewed. "Two against one, if the tales are true."

Attempting not to look in his guest's direction, Lord Elros speared a baby potato with his fork. "My boy is very accomplished with a blade. He can handle two opponents."

"I can believe that." Lord Braverton laughed. "He's enormous!"

"It's not about strength," Edris said.

"It's about footwork," Lord Elros agreed.

"And quickness," Lord Braverton added. "Or so I've heard. I've never been one for such things, you understand. Better to have others do your fighting, I say. But I've always admired adventurers. Going here and there, solving problems, living off the land, competing against the best from across the realms. Speaking of which, your kingdom has been doing remarkably well as of late. Between you and Markus, King Michael has won the last four or five quests, if I'm not mistaken."

"His Majesty's son has indeed been successful—" Lord Elros smiled. "—in the past."

Lord Braverton gave a great wheezing cough. Flecks of food shot across the table as he pounded a fist against his chest.

"Understood." He took a drink. "I'd bet money on your boy if it wouldn't raise King Lionel's ire. He insists we all support his men. A bunch of ill-bred vagabonds they appear to be."

"And how is King Lionel? Well, I hope."

Lord Braverton gave Lord Elros a nauseated expression. "Let's discuss something else. Thinking about imbeciles makes me want to vomit."

Picking up his bowl, he drank from it like a cup. Mushroom soup trickled down his chin. Lord Elros cringed.

"So, tell us," Edris said, sharing his father's discomfort. "What brings you to Bend?"

"Yes," his father said hurriedly, "and how long will we have the pleasure of your company?"

Setting his soup bowl aside, Lord Braverton dragged his sleeve across his mouth. "Ah! Well, let's just say that I am on a quest of my own, though one less perilous than yours, I should hope. We'll see how it turns out."

Launching into another violent coughing fit, Lord Braverton held out his goblet and gestured for the server to refill it. He drained his glass as skillfully as he had his soup bowl.

"Speaking of quests." He belched. "When do you expect the next one to be proclaimed? Perhaps I could place a little wager while in Upper Angle. Purely as a token of my support for my host, you understand."

"The quests are usually announced in spring," Edris said, looking ruefully at his steak. Somehow, he'd lost his appetite.

"Pity." Lord Braverton motioned for more wine. "There's too few of them, I think. Not enough entertainment for the rabble. What we need is a good war."

Fifty-Nine

"Sorry I'm late," Edris said, jogging up, his breath appearing before him. He'd told his father he'd start training before dawn, but the sun was already well above the eastern mountains. "I spent the night in town."

"Beatrice?" Cedric asked knowingly.

Edris gave a begrudging nod.

The two men traipsed through the frost-covered north fields behind the manor house. Edris had felled several dozen trees along its borders over the past couple of weeks, but he had yet to cut them up or dig out their stumps.

"Things getting serious between the two of you?" the Captain of the Guards asked as they walked. "Or is it purely pleasure?"

Edris struggled with his response. If he said it was only pleasure, he'd demean Beatrice, as if she were nothing but his whore. Further, Cedric might infer that Beatrice was available. If he said it was serious, however—

"I don't know," he found himself saying. "I like her a good deal, but…" He trailed off.

"But she's a commoner?" Cedric suggested.

That was definitely an issue, but not an insurmountable one. After all, nobles often married commoners; but in such cases, the commoners usually had something to offer the noble family, such as large farms or successful businesses. Beatrice had none of that. In fact, if Edris didn't keep giving her money, she'd be homeless. Then she might have to become a harlot to survive.

"She wants more than I can give her right now," Edris said.

"I see."

They walked along for several paces.

"I'm a fighting man," Cedric said finally, "and I don't pretend to know a thing about women. But it seems to me that in order to be successful in life, whether it is as an adventurer, a guard, or a husband, you have to focus on one thing, and one thing alone. I suppose the question is—what do you want to focus on?"

Edris pulled his cloak tighter around him. Winter was coming on and the wind had an edge to it. "You sound like my father."

"Maybe. He's very pleased about your win, you know. He wants to make sure you continue winning. He's been checking in with me every day, asking what you're doing and how your training is going."

Edris grimaced. "Sorry."

"It's nothing to be sorry about. To tell you the truth, it's wonderful to see him happy again. He's actually been a delight to be around lately."

"Well, let's see what happens when I lose."

"That's what I'm here for."

They came to a section of the field where the knee-high grass had been trampled. A variety of wooden weapons were piled off to the side.

Cedric handed Edris a wooden dagger.

"What's this?" Edris asked.

"I heard about your duel."

"It wasn't a duel. Two adventurers wanted what I had. I changed their minds."

"That's going to happen. In fact, it's going to get worse. As your reputation grows, the target on your back will grow with it. Your competition will want to take you down a peg or two. And they're not going to simply stroll up to you and issue an official challenge. They're going to wait until they have you at a disadvantage."

Cedric drew a wooden longsword from the pile.

"Dagger against a sword?" Edris asked.

"Like I said—disadvantage."

Edris thought about Markus beating him with a rock and Sir Tudor and Sir Howard attempting to ambush him. "So, what do you want me to do?"

"Fight."

"All right." Edris took his defensive stance, a wooden dagger in his lead hand. "But it isn't going to be much of a fight, I'm afraid. On your guard."

Cedric leapt forward, jabbing his sword. Edris sprang back, unsuccessfully trying to parry the much longer blade.

"No. No. No," Cedric said.

"No, what?"

"Look, Ed…when did you first start learning how to fight?"

"You kidding? My father put a sword in my crib. I used it as a pacifier. Why?"

"Your fighting is technically superb."

"But?"

"But you can't always fight by the book. Think of this way…for every move you learned as a child, there's a countermove, correct?"

"I guess."

"And if I, your opponent, am similarly trained, I'll know the counter to any of your actions. I'll know your next move before you actually do it. Do you understand how dangerous that is?"

"I see what you're saying," Edris said, considering the ramifications. "So, what do I do?"

"You improvise and do the unexpected. Throw something into their eyes. You sweep their leg—"

"Bash their head in with a rock?"

"Exactly. Now, let's try again."

"I'm not going to fight like that."

"Why not?"

Edris stared at the manor house. Somehow, he could feel his father watching him from one of the arched windows.

"I don't want to be that kind of person," he said.

"Ed…"

"I'm not going to be like Markus. I want to stand for something."

Cedric frowned, then nodded. "All right. Your sword breaks. And all you have is a dagger."

"I fight with two swords."

"Humor me."

"Fine."

"What would you do? Your opponent has you at a disadvantage and he isn't going to allow you to yield. He wants you dead. Understand the situation?" Cedric took a defensive stance. "On your guard."

Reluctantly, Edris complied.

Again, Cedric bounded forward. And again, Edris sprang back, trying to parry.

Cedric stopped, frustrated.

"I'm not sure what you want me to do," Edris said.

"Here." Cedric gave Edris his wooden longsword, then took the dagger. "I'll show you what I mean. Attack me."

"All right."

Edris readied his weapon, gave two quick thrusts, then sprang forward, swinging at Cedric's head. Cedric ducked under the blow, then hurled himself at Edris's ankles. Half diving, half rolling, he barreled into the bigger man's legs, causing Edris to fall to the ground. Cedric leapt on him, throwing three hard punches to Edris's head.

Breathing hard, Cedric got to his feet.

"You have to figure out how badly you want to be the best, Ed." Casting his wooden dagger on the ground, he stalked toward the manor house. "Let me know when you want to start taking your training seriously."

Sixty

Edris reclined in his parlor, rereading the book of poetry Beatrice had given him. He hadn't spoken to her in a couple of days and missed her terribly, but he didn't want to appear needy. He also wanted time to think about where their relationship was—and where he wanted it to go.

He turned a page.

A firm knock rattled the door. It opened before he could say, "come in."

"Sir." Edris quickly put the book on the end table, its binding facing away from his father. He stood. "It's late. Is everything okay?"

Candle in hand, Lord Elros strolled about his son's quarters, almost as though he were inspecting the walls for structural damage.

"As far as I know, everything is fine." He motioned for his son to sit, then sat in a chair next to him. "Settling into the routine of being at home?" He set his candlestick on the end table.

For a heart-faltering moment, Edris thought he was going to pick up Beatrice's book.

"What?" Edris attempted to concentrate on their conversation. "Routine?" He could sense where this was going. The old routines wouldn't be permitted. He was an adventurer now and had to be training constantly. "No, sir. Actually, I'm itching to return to the hunt. Hopefully the kings will proclaim a new quest soon."

"Itching?" The Lord of Bend picked the lint from his pants. "There's always a cure for the itch."

Edris paused. His father was being pleasant enough, but he wasn't the type of man to sit and make small talk. In all his years, he couldn't recall his father ever visiting him in his quarters and chatting.

"Yes, sir." Then Edris tried to direct the conversation to more manageable waters. "Has Lord Braverton left yet?"

"Alas, no." Lord Elros groaned. "He's given no indication as to how long he'll torture us with his presence."

"Has he said what he wants?"

Lord Elros absentmindedly picked up Beatrice's book, then repositioned it so it was in the exact middle of the table. "He wants what all men his age want."

Edris attempted to tear his eyes from the book. "Sir?"

"He wants an heir."

"But I thought Lord Braverton had a child," Edris said, puzzled. "I remember his wife giving birth a few years ago."

"She did. She's given him five children. All girls."

"And he's looking for a male heir here?"

"He's desperate," Lord Elros said, giving his son a pointed expression. "And desperation makes men make poor decisions."

Edris stared about the room, trying to find a more fertile—and safer—subject. "I had an interesting training session with Cedric today," he said. "I'm glad you decided to retain him as your captain."

Lord Elros brushed the comment away. "He has his utility." He arched an eyebrow at his son. "I spoke with him earlier as well. Tell me—do you believe you've been training particularly strenuously?"

And there it was…the reason his father paid him a late-night visit.

"I can work harder, sir."

"See that you do."

Lord Elros got to his feet, then looked at his son. "You realize Markus is going to come after you, don't you? He'll try to kill you, or worse. He can't allow himself to be upstaged by a boy ten years his junior."

Markus was only seven years older than him, but Edris didn't think the correction would be appreciated. "Yes, sir."

"I'm not exaggerating, Ed. I know Markus, and I know his father. They won't tolerate you succeeding. You need to prepare yourself for a war."

"I understand."

"Do you?" His father's face betrayed his genuine concern. "Do you know what they'll do to you? First, they'll try to separate you from any potential allies. They'll spread lies about you and tarnish your reputation. They might suggest somebody else found the statue and that you bought it from them. If that doesn't work, they'll attempt to humiliate you. They'll make you out to be a laughingstock—a boy who was given a knighthood by his well-meaning and loving uncle.

"If that doesn't work, Ed—they will kill you. You need to understand that. Families don't rise to the throne without killing people who get in their way. This isn't a game. I must know that you truly understand your peril."

Edris took a deep, uneven breath. He nodded. "I'll train harder. I'll be prepared." Then he added, almost to convince himself, "And if I can, I'll kill Markus first."

"I believe," his father said slowly, "that will be in your best interest. But killing the king's son won't go unpunished. If you're caught…they'll flay you, then burn you alive." He lowered his voice. "If you find yourself in the position to remove Markus as a threat, make sure you have an alibi. That's where strong friends come in. You need allies."

"Yes, sir."

"And train. Remove any distraction that'll get in your way. Because if you don't—Markus will destroy you. Understand?"

"Yes, sir. I do."

"Splendid." Lord Elros retrieved his candlestick. "Have a good night."

"You too, sir."

"Oh, and Edris…" his father said, making for the door, "do whatever Cedric god-damn tells you to do. It may save your life."

Sixty-One

Edris sat on the end of Beatrice's sofa, her head in his lap. He stroked her hair.

"So is your father going to be mad you're here?" she asked.

"He would be, if he knew," Edris replied. "But he thinks I'm hiking in the hills. I told him I was building my legs."

Beatrice laughed, rubbing his thighs. "They're already as big as tree trunks. How much bigger does he want them?"

"I'm never going to be big enough or good enough for him. *Strong legs*," he said, mocking his father's voice, *"are the mark of a strong man!"*

"Your father said hello to me a while back."

Edris started. "He did? When?"

"It was when you were gone. He stopped by the Three Crows. He probably had no idea who I was. He said hello to all the girls."

"He didn't try to you—you know?"

"What? Ew. No!" She sat up. "Say what you will about your father, but he isn't a womanizer."

"True. I don't think he's been with a woman since my mother died."

Beatrice drew closer to him. "That's sweet."

"It is, actually." Edris put his arm around her. "Was he cordial? When he came into the tavern?"

"Perfectly."

"Really?" Edris considered this. "He's actually been civil with me as well. The other day he came into my quarters to chat."

"A chat?"

"Well, actually, he came in to tell me to train harder. But he did spend a few minutes making small talk, which isn't something he's prone to do." Edris kissed Beatrice, then pulled away. "I wonder what his game is."

"I'm sure he's trying to share in your success. Maybe feel like he's part of it."

"Perhaps. Still, he's been behaving oddly. Does he come to the tavern often?"

"Once in a while," Beatrice said. "He was there last night. He was with some obnoxious man who looked like death."

Edris laughed. "That's Lord Braverton. He and my father are distantly related. My father said he's always been sickly. That's probably why he's had difficulty producing an heir."

Beatrice snuggled closer. "Do you want a son?"

The seriousness of the question unsettled Edris. "Not in the immediate future!"

"I'm not asking about now." She kissed his neck and unbuttoned his shirt. "I mean…when you get older. Do you want a family? And children? Or are you going to roam around the rest of your life, looking for long-lost trinkets for the king?"

Ignoring her advances, Edris watched the occasional snowflake flutter by the window.

He'd often thought about having a family. He particularly liked the idea of having a son, somebody he could train to fight and ride and hunt. Most of all, he wanted to be a better father than the one he had.

"I don't know," he said. "Why can't I have all of that someday? Plenty of adventurers have families. As a matter of fact, I can't recall any who didn't. Sir Barton the Black, maybe. And Sir Drake. But they're it. Adventurers are like kings…they want somebody to carry on their legacy."

She stopped unbuttoning his shirt. "You're going to keep adventuring?"

"It's my profession."

"Yes, but…" she said, her tone less sensual than it had been a moment before. "I thought you wanted to make enough money to live comfortably somewhere as far from your father as possible."

Edris considered this. "No," he said, perhaps more to himself than to Beatrice, "I'll never be a farmer. I like questing. It's frustrating as hell. But then you find your quarry…" He smiled. "I can't explain it."

"You *really* love it, don't you?" She sounded disappointed.

"I do. I like being outside. I like the thinking. And…"

"The fighting?"

"No. I hate that. I was about to say that I liked the comradery. I like being part of a tradition, part of a group. I like—"

Somebody knocked. Beatrice and Edris exchanged glances. It was close to midnight; having a guest at that hour was unusual.

"Who is it?" Beatrice called out.

"It's me," a wry voice said. "Brago. I need to speak with Ed. His father sent me."

"My father?" Edris opened the door. "What's wrong?"

"Nothing as far as I know." Brago glanced at Beatrice, a guilty smile spreading across his thin lips. He gave her a slight bow. "Beatrice."

Beatrice straightened her clothing. "Brago. It's good to see you."

"Always a pleasure."

"What's wrong with my father?" Edris asked, interrupting the pleasantries.

"As I said, nothing as far as I can tell. He simply sent me to let you know a new quest has been issued."

"Already? There shouldn't be any quests until spring!"

"Yet, here I am."

Edris grabbed his cloak. "Let's go."

"Ed?" Beatrice pleaded. "Can't this wait? Just a couple of hours?"

"I'm sorry, Bea. I have to get a jump on the competition. I'll return as soon as I can."

Sixty-Two

Dripping with sweat and breathing hard, Edris burst into Lord Elros's darkened library. His father and brother were seated at the table, hunched over a mound of books. They looked up, a flickering candle illuminating their startled faces.

"Sorry I'm late," Edris said. "I came as soon as I got the message."

"You're not late at all," his father said. Whether he was being sarcastic or not, Edris couldn't tell. "As a matter of fact, with you hiking in the hills, I'm pleased your squire found you at all."

"Brago? He's more of a friend than a squire."

"You don't need a friend! You need a loyal servant who will do what he is told."

"Yes, sir." Edris dusted the snow from his cloak. "He said there's a new quest."

"Indeed." His father flipped him a parchment with King Michael's seal. "They want the Horn of Borin."

"The Horn of Borin?" Edris repeated, reading the royal announcement. King Michael was offering six hundred gold for it. "Didn't Sir Royce already find that?"

"Depends on whom you believe," Edros said.

A servant entered the library bearing a tray laden with three glasses and a crystal decanter of brandy. He set it on the table in front of Lord Elros, then left.

"They held a quest for the horn fourteen years ago…" Lord Elros said, filling his glass, "but nobody turned it in."

"It was a failed quest?" Edris asked doubtfully. "I could've sworn—"

"Sir Royce claimed he found the horn, but he never presented it to King Gustav."

Edris pulled up a chair across from his brother. "Who did he present it to?"

"He didn't present it to anybody," Lord Elros said crossly. "You should know these things, Ed. This is your chosen profession!"

"Yes, sir," Edris said, eyeing the brandy. "I'm just a bit confused."

Edros came to his rescue. "If the rumors are true, Sir Royce found the horn, but he refused to give it to anybody."

"Refused? Why?"

"If found, the horn would have been returned to Borin's family," Lord Elros said, as though this were explanation enough.

If Edris remembered correctly, Sir Royce was the great grandnephew of Sir Rosser, who feuded with Sir Borin. The two families had hated each other for centuries.

"He didn't want the horn being returned to the enemy," he said.

"Exactly." Lord Elros searched through a large tome, snapping its pages as he turned them. "I'm glad you're getting your wits about you."

Chuckling, Edris attempted to lighten the mood. "Strange that Royce would refuse to win a quest because of a feud he hadn't even been involved in."

"Never underestimate hatred," his father said. "It drives men more than anything else. Even love. Remember that."

"Yes, sir." Edris stifled a yawn. He'd been up since before dawn and it was already well past midnight, but he couldn't afford to have his father see him tired. "Should we assume Royce was telling the truth? Or should we pursue the horn as though it were lost?"

"Either way," Lord Elros said, "it's lost. Think!" He drained his glass and refilled it to the brim.

"If you want my opinion," Edros said, "you should first try to eliminate the possibility that Royce was telling the truth. Then—if you aren't able to do so—search for the horn where it was last seen."

"The Battle of Forest Glen," Edris said, trying to impress his father.

"Right." His brother went on, "If I had to wager, I'd bet Royce didn't find the horn and was attempting to get people to stop looking for it. It shouldn't be too difficult to determine whether he was lying."

"Sir Royce died a while ago, didn't he?" Edris asked. "About ten years?"

"Eight years," his father replied. "Do you know how he died?"

"In a duel with Sir Halfred."

His father's expression softened. "Correct."

"Clearly he didn't have the horn on him when he died," Edris said, "or else Halfred would've given it to his king."

The revulsion in Lord Elros's face returned.

"This is the horn." He turned a large book, so it faced Edris. There was an illustration of a man blowing a long, straight horn extending all the way to the ground.

"How big was it?" Edris asked, squinting at the picture.

"About eleven feet," Edros replied. "It's one of the horns of the mountain people. It was nearly five hundred years old and made of silver."

"A giant horn shouldn't be too difficult to find," Edris said.

"It won't be if you stop screwing the tavern wench and focus on the task at hand," Lord Elros said.

So, his father knew. He wasn't happy, but at least he wasn't irate. Perhaps in time, he'd allow him to court Beatrice properly.

"If Royce found the horn," Edris said, ignoring his father's outburst, "I bet scores of people must've seen it. You can't have something that big without drawing attention to yourself."

"Actually," Edros said, opening a book, "it says here hundreds of people claimed to have seen Royce with the horn. According to this, he dragged it behind his horse as he rode through Williamshire."

"Williamshire?" Edris said. "That's where Royce was from, wasn't it? That complicates matters."

"How so?" their father asked, drink in hand.

"He was their local hero. They'd want to support him, even making up lies and exaggerating his fame." He rubbed his tired face, hiding another yawn. "Maybe it won't be as easy as that after all."

"Giving up already?" Lord Elros sneered.

"No. I'm evaluating the situation." Edris got to his feet and paced the shadows. "Okay. Let's assume I'm Royce and I found the horn. I hate Borin's family enough to prevent them from regaining their precious heirloom, even though that'd mean I wouldn't officially win the quest. What would I do? Destroy it? If that's the case, this quest is pointless."

"Go on," his father said. "What else might Royce have done with the horn?"

"Well, if I really wanted to stick it to Borin's family, I would hide the damned thing, perhaps despoiling it in such a way that they'd never forget my name."

"You'd also ensure that there were enough stories and eyewitnesses to make Borin's family believe you have it," Edros said. "Otherwise, what's the point?"

Edris mulled that over. "I don't think so. If I were Royce, I wouldn't want Borin's family to be absolutely convinced I had their horn. I'd want them to suspect that I *might* have it. If they knew for sure, they'd come after me to get it."

Lord Elros slapped the table, shaking the half-empty decanter. "Yes! Exactly. That's how you need to think. Get into the minds of the people involved. Either way, Royce would sow doubt and create confusion. But if he actually had the horn, he'd despoil it like you said. He'd then stow it someplace where it would be found someday."

"Found?" Edros repeated. "Why? Assuredly, he'd bury it someplace deep where nobody could get to it. Maybe throw it into the ocean."

"No," Edris said. "Where's the fun in that? If he hid it permanently, people would eventually forget about it or assume that Royce never found it. He'd want it unearthed after he died so he could get the credit for the win."

"He'd also want to infuriate Borin's family," Lord Elros said. "I'll bet you anything that when you find it, it'll be packed with shit, or worse."

"*When* I find it…" Edris repeated, appreciating his father's confidence in him. "Brago and I will set off at once."

"Where to?" Edros asked.

"Williamshire seems the best option. I want to talk with the people who say they saw the horn. Hopefully their memories are still relatively intact. Fourteen years is a long time to forget."

"You'll need to watch for Markus," Lord Elros said, standing. The hand clutching his brandy shook slightly. "He won't want you to win two in a row."

"I can handle Markus."

"Perhaps," Lord Elros said. "But make sure that squire of yours watches your back."

"I will. I only hope this isn't a wild goose chase. Williamshire is a good three week's ride—"

The word *squire* struck a chord in Edris's mind.

"What is it?" his brother asked.

"Who was Royce's squire when he allegedly found the horn?"

Edros hunted through several books, scanning their pages. "Ah. Here it is. It was a lad named Melville."

"Melville?"

"Find this Melville," Lord Elros instructed. "But be wary. Every other adventurer will have the same idea."

Sixty-Three

Edris and Brago rode between the wooded hills five days south of Bend, the evening gloom deepening around them. Suddenly, the twang of a bowstring sliced through the stillness. Edris's horse shuddered, then reared.

"Brago!" Edris shouted as he fought to steady his screeching mare. "Ambush! Turn about! Turn about!"

Another arrow slammed into the horse's ribs. It crumpled to the snow-flecked ground as Edris vaulted from the saddle.

Behind him, Brago hesitated. "Ed!"

"Go!" Edris shouted, diving behind a tree. He drew a sword.

Pulling hard on the reins, Brago wheeled his grey rouncey.

Edris glanced around the tree's trunk.

Up the steep incline, fifty feet above the road, a cloaked and masked man loosed another arrow—this time at Brago. He missed as Brago shot off down the hill.

"Bastard!" Edris charged the figure. Slipping on the snow, he fell as an arrow glanced off the tree next to him.

Clawing his way up to a rock outcropping, Edris jerked a dagger from its sheath. Another arrow struck directly above his head, shards of stone and snow flying. Leaping to his feet before his assailant could nock another arrow, he made to heave the dagger—but the figure had already disappeared into the darkness. From the other side of the hill, the sound of galloping hooves faded off into the night. But it was the gurgling cry of his dying horse that seized Edris's attention.

"Bollocks!"

Snatching his sword, Edris allowed himself to slide down to the road. His horse, a big brown bay he'd had for years, writhed in red snow, blood spraying from its nostrils.

"It's all right, boy. It's all right."

The horse lifted its neck, its eyes rolling in terror. It attempted to stand.

"No. That's okay. Lie still." Edris put the tip of his sword to the horse's chest. "Lie still. Okay, boy? Everything is okay."

The bay did as it was told, laying its long neck and head on the bloody ground. It released one last snort.

"I'm so sorry."

Tearing up, Edris shifted his weight and drove the sword into the horse's heart, blood spurting into the air. "Bastard!" Edris hollered into the darkness. "I'm going to kill you. Hear me? I'm going to take this damned sword and shove it—"

Something moved along the road behind him. Wrenching his sword from the dead horse, he spun.

Brago crept along the road, his finger to his lips. He pointed up the hill and then lifted a hand in silent question.

Edris wiped his eyes. He felt foolish crying but decided he didn't care. He loved horses. As far as he was concerned, he'd never met a horse he didn't enjoy being around. People, on the other hand—

He wiped his bloody sword in the snow, then slid it into its scabbard. "The bastard's gone."

"Sure?"

"He rode away, the gutless coward."

Edris unsaddled his fallen horse, pulling the arrow from its side. He studied it, then handed it to Brago.

"If you ever see somebody with arrows like this, you let me know."

"Of course." Brago stowed the arrow with his gear. "Think he was aiming for the horse?"

Edris stopped unpacking his saddle. He'd assumed the figure was a bandit, but then again, bandits wouldn't be acting alone.

"It was probably one of my competitors. Damn them. We can't make for Williamshire on foot. The quest would be over by the time we'd get halfway there."

"I can ride to Bend and get another horse."

"No. That'd take another ten days at least."

"What then?"

Angry, Edris scanned the hills. Above the leaf-bare trees, winter stars glimmered in the black sky. His weary breath appeared before him as grey vapor.

"There's a farm not far from here." He pointed at a neighboring hill. "Just beyond that ridge, maybe four or five hours' ride west. Ride back along the road. Take the first path you come to heading into the valley. It should lead you right to the farm. Give them some of this and my thanks." He handed Brago a pouch heavy with coins. "I'll meet you tomorrow morning where this road fords a river about ten miles ahead."

"You're going on by yourself? Ed, that isn't—"

"I've hunted in these woods most of my life. I'll be fine. Besides," he said, "I want to see if I can pick up the asshole's trail. And the gods help him if I do."

Sixty-Four

Standing in an abandoned campsite near the top of the hill where he'd been ambushed, Edris surveyed the surrounding countryside. It was the perfect surveillance point. Even at night, he could see for miles, especially to the north toward Bend.

Who did this?

Markus was the only one who came to mind.

Markus…

He stared down the slope to where his horse lay dead in the road.

If it were Markus, the masked man's third shot wouldn't have been at Brago. It would've been at him.

Was the bowman trying to slow him by killing their horses?

Who'd do such a thing?

Somebody who is desperate to win…

Hell. That could be any adventurer—not just Markus.

Winning breeds enemies, his father often said. And Edris clearly had enemies.

He knelt and examined the campsite. Something bothered him. What was it?

There was only one horse. He could tell by the distinctive pattern one of the horseshoes made in the snow. It had a slightly bent nail.

A lone assailant…

Edris jabbed his sword at the burnt-out remains of a fire. There were far more ashes than he'd expect. And there was a small pile of dry wood stacked neatly nearby.

He sniffed. Where the fiend's horse must've been tethered, there were many piles of manure. Some had already dried.

Only hatred would make somebody wait for days in the cold.

He had to be on his guard.

Sixty-Five

The next morning, Edris sat on a boulder where the southern road from Bend forded the River Mine. He enjoyed listening to its cold-water tumble over the glistening rocks. Behind him, the steady clopping of horses came up the valley. Turning, he found Brago riding out of the woods, leading a broken-down nag.

Edris groaned. "That's what you bought?"

"This's all they were willing to sell," Brago said. "I considered killing the farmer and taking one of his plow horses, but I thought you'd be opposed to such decisive action."

"I would indeed." Edris examined the horse, pity swelling in his heart. The beast was missing patches of its mane and had a swayback. It probably only had one more winter in him before dying. "If I mount it, I'll break the poor thing's spine."

"If you prefer, I can ride to the farm and steal one of their good horses."

"No. Honor means something."

"So does winning the quest." Brago climbed from his saddle. "Any clues as to who our friend was last night?"

"He wasn't a bandit," Edris said, frowning at the elderly horse. "Whomever he was camped in these hills for days, maybe even a week."

"Waiting for you? Sounds like the work of your cousin."

"Markus would've tried to kill me, not the horse."

"Perhaps he missed."

"Twice?" Edris shook his head. "Doubtful. He's an excellent marksman. He's won the kingdom's archery title five years in a row. And from that range, he wouldn't have missed me. I, unfortunately, am a sizeable target."

"Then who?"

"My guess is that it was another adventurer attempting to make sure I didn't win two in a row."

"If we can't get to Williamshire soon," Brago said, grimly, "he's succeeded."

Edris was thinking the same thing. "We'll get there. But not with this—"

Galloping hooves echoed from the hills. Scanning the tree-lined ridge, Brago pointed. "There."

"I see them."

Two riders were descending the hills at a quick run. The lead rider, a large, middle-aged man, noted Edris and Brago standing by the ford and lifted a hand. The young man following checked his horse to a walk.

"May we approach, lads?" the lead rider called in a thick accent.

"Please," Edris called back. To Brago, he muttered, "Get a peek at the fletching of their arrows, if you can."

"Maybe we should acquire their horses while we're at it."

"That's not how I want to play this. No fighting unless needed."

The lead rider rode up.

"Sir Hans," the older gentleman said bowing. "Is this the River Mine?"

"Edris and Brago," Edris replied. "And yes, it is."

"Sir Edris?"

Edris nodded, trying to get a good view of the tracks their horses were making without being too obvious. They didn't appear to be the same prints he'd seen in the assailant's camp.

Sir Hans dismounted.

"It's an honor." He motioned to the young man on the horse behind him. "This is my son, Heinrich. He's interested in becoming an adventurer as well. I'm teaching him what I know."

"Pleasure." Edris stepped forward and extended a hand, but the tall, thin boy didn't shake it. "Have I done something to offend you?"

"No," Heinrich mumbled.

"Then shake his damned hand," Sir Hans admonished.

Reluctantly, Heinrich shook Edris's hand. He nodded to Brago holding the horses.

Brago tipped his hat. "Charmed."

"Forgive him," Sir Hans said. "He's bursting with jealousy."

"Why's that?" Edris asked.

Sir Hans chuckled. "The youngest person ever to be knighted. Not to mention the youngest adventurer to win a quest. His *first* quest, nonetheless. You've already made a name for yourself, lad. Good for you. But you know what they say: jealousy drives most men."

"My father says it's hatred."

Sir Hans laughed. "The two go hand-in-hand. At any rate, Markus taught you well."

"Markus?" Edris repeated, not showing his shock. "Have you spoken to him lately?"

"Not lately. I was in Upper Angle a couple of months ago. He and your king speak highly of you. Indeed, between you and Markus, King Michael has been doing exceedingly well of late. He's won, what—? Eight out of the last twelve?"

"Something like that."

"You two are probably the best young adventurers currently in the field."

"That's very kind, especially coming from you, Sir Hans. I believe you won four in a row at one point."

"Yes, well, that was long ago, I'm afraid."

"Yet still a worthy accomplishment. And I'd love to hear how you won the Quest of the Golden Lance. That was said to have been an epic affair."

"It was! Took nearly a year to find the accursed thing. But getting it to my king was the real ordeal. That's the trick, bringing the prize home."

"Right now, it's a trick simply getting to the prize." Seeing Sir Hans's confusion, Edris added, "We were ambushed last night. Somebody shot my horse out from under me."

"That was your beast we passed? Bastards. I love animals."

"So, adventurers will kill horses to slow the competition? That's part of the Code?"

"I'd never do such a thing." Then Sir Hans conceded, "But others certainly would. Or worse. You'd best be careful, young man. People are talking about you, and that's not always a good thing."

Edris shook his head. "I had no idea questing was like this."

"Don't take it personally. If you haven't realized it yet, we adventurers are a petty lot. Anybody who makes us look bad is a target, especially newcomers. We grizzled old veterans hate you young upstarts and will do whatever we can to put you in your place." Sir Hans turned to his son. "Keep that in mind, Heinrich. You haven't made a name for yourself until you've pissed everybody else off."

"Yes, sir," his son grumbled.

"Any other advice you could give me would be greatly appreciated," Edris said.

"Advice? I'll give you good advice, lad." Sir Hans leaned closer to the much taller Edris. "Never believe what another adventurer says!" He winked. "In addition to being petty, we're also all liars. Like fishermen." He pulled himself into his saddle. "Best of luck, young man. And be careful."

"Thank you, sir. And good luck to you."

Sir Hans stared curiously at the swaybacked horse. "Is that yours?"

"We had to buy it from a farmer."

"You're not going to actually ride it, are you?"

Edris sighed, looking at the mournful beast. "No. Though it'll likely put me more than a few days behind."

"Since you're kind to beasts," Sir Hans said, pulling on his riding gloves, "I will repay the creature's debt for him. Do you believe Royce found the horn?"

"To tell you the truth, I have no clue."

Sir Hans said in a mock whisper, "He did. I saw him with it."

"Father!" Heinrich cried.

Sir Hans said something to his son in a language Edris didn't understand. Then he added in the common tongue, "No need to make enemies when you can make friends." He saluted. "Until we meet again, Sir Edris and Brago."

"I look forward to it," Edris said.

Sir Hans clicked his heels into his horse's ribs. "The first round will be on me."

Edris and Brago watched them wade across the ford and scale the bank to the road on the other side. When they were out of earshot, Brago muttered, "The little bastard had dark-feathered arrows."

"The son? Are you sure they were the same?"

"No. But best to err on the side of caution."

"You're probably right. All right let's get to the next town. Maybe we can find a more suitable horse there."

Sixty-Six

It took six days of walking, but Edris and Brago finally made it to a small river town named Sandbank. As soon as they arrived, they raced to a horse dealer.

"If you be wanting a horse," the owner said when they ran into his stable, "I'm afraid you're going to be disappointed."

"What do you mean?" Edris looked about. All of the stalls were empty. "Where are your horses?"

"Gone."

"You don't have any horses? None at all?"

"What kind of place is this?" Brago asked.

"Over the last week or so…" the owner said, "a busy one."

Edris's gut tightened. "Somebody came here and bought all of your horses, didn't they?"

"That was the way of it, young man. Never seen anything like it. And I'm guessing you won't find an available horse for twenty miles around."

"Bollocks!" Edris shouted, a fist in the air.

The stable owner nervously retreated a step.

"I'm sorry," Edris said, calming himself. "I had a horse shot out from under me and it seems that the person who did it might've come here to stop me from acquiring a replacement."

"What did he look like?" Brago asked the owner. "The patron who purchased all of your horses?"

"He was a young man with a big bag of gold. Paid five times what I would've asked. Kept insisting I tell him about anybody else who might have a horse to sell. He must've purchased a dozen horses, all told."

Brago leaned toward the man. "I said—tell us what he looked like."

The stable owner recoiled. Strangely, he seemed more afraid of the smaller Brago than of Edris. "Young. Like the two of you. Maybe a tad older. Had a sword and a bow. Brown hair."

"That's it? Brown hair?" Brago growled. "That's all you can remember?"

"And young!" the stable owner repeated. "He was young."

Edris put a restraining hand on Brago's shoulder. "One man couldn't have ridden twelve horses out of town."

"It might not have been twelve. I was only guessing. He bought six of mine and a few others from people in town. He paid a handsome price!"

"I understand," Edris said. "But there had to be more than one man."

"Aye. From what I hear, there was another. The second led the horses out of town in a long line. Though I didn't see him. Just heard tell of him."

"This doesn't make any sense," Brago grumbled to Edris. "Whomever it was would've been slowed with that many horses."

"Not as slowed as we've been. Curse them." Edris gave one of his few remaining coins to the stable owner. "Thank you for your help."

"I'm sorry I don't recall what he looked like," the stable owner said apologetically.

"Not to worry. I'm sure you were looking at the bag of gold."

Edris and Brago left the stable. They watched a woman with two small children pass by.

"I'm beginning to get angry," Edris muttered.

"Beginning? I exceeded angry some time ago."

"Getting upset won't help us." Edris sighed. "We're never going to get to Williamshire in time. Half the adventurers on the continent are probably already there looking for the blasted horn."

"Want me to talk to the stable owner again? I'm sure I can get him to remember something other than young and brown hair."

"No. If my guess is correct, he was threatened by somebody not to reveal what the horse buyers looked like."

"So, what do you want to do?"

Edris stared off into the distant hills, considering his options. "They knew we'd be using that road. And they knew we'd be coming to this town."

"They seem to know too much."

"Exactly. We need to do something they wouldn't expect. I don't want to keep worrying about somebody jumping out of the bushes and shooting what horses we have or stealing our gear."

"What do you have in mind?"

Edris evaluated the sky. They had another five hours before the early winter evening descended on the countryside.

"Let's buy a boat."

"A boat?"

"Nothing too big," Edris said, contemplating the idea. "Something large enough for the two of us and our supplies."

"I didn't think the Mine headed to Williamshire."

"It doesn't. But the William River does. If we take the River Mine south four or five days, then carry the boat over to the William River, we can get to the city from the east."

"I suppose we can travel faster on the river than walking. Though I'm afraid I won't be much help carrying a boat."

"I'll take care of the lifting. You just make sure I don't get shot from the shadows."

Sixty-Seven

Finding a suitable boat wasn't difficult. Nearly every fisherman and trapper in Sandbank had at least one they were willing to part with. And after selling their horses to the stable owner, Edris came out ahead on the deal. However, it was winter, and the River Mine was low. For the first few days, they frequently had to get out of their boat and hoist it over the many sandbars and exposed rocks barring their way. Then the weather turned cold, making their travels less than comfortable. By the time they'd finally reached Williamshire, the quest for Borin's horn was nearly two months old.

"Remind me again why I chose adventuring as a profession," Edris muttered as they approached the town.

"I don't even know why we bothered coming," Brago replied. "Surely, somebody has found the accursed thing by now."

"At the very least, it's warmer here. We'll consider it a holiday."

"Holiday." Brago grunted. "Next time let me acquire a horse my way. I still feel sick from being pitched about in that damned boat."

They studied the forty or so buildings before them.

"Another crappy village." Brago cursed. "Why can't these quests bring us to big cities?"

"You prefer cities?"

"I prefer graveyards to shitholes like this."

At the town's entrance, they came to a larger-than-life statue of a muscular man—a fist raised victoriously to the sky as he pulled a long horn behind him.

"This him?" Brago asked.

Edris read the plaque. "This is him. Sir Royce. He was one for the ages. Look! When they listed the quests he won, they included Borin's Horn. That takes nerve."

"Let us hope your statue says the same."

Past the statue, people packed the streets of Williamshire. An irritated wagon driver shouted for everybody to get out of his way.

"Perhaps the quest isn't over," Edris said hopefully. He called to a young boy running by. "Hey!"

"What is it?" the boy asked.

"Has anybody found Borin's Horn?"

He held out a hand. "I'll tell you what I know, but it'll cost you three silver pieces."

Brago snatched the boy and put a knife to his throat. "I can think of a cheaper way to loosen your tongue, you little brat."

The boy screamed. "No! Nobody has found it. I swear!"

"Let him go, Brago. He's only trying to make some money." Edris offered him three silver pieces. "For your trouble."

"Keep it, you crazy bastards!" He ran off, lifting his middle finger as he disappeared into a group of townsfolk gathered around a merchant's cart.

Edris looked reproachfully at Brago. "You shouldn't do that. No sense creating more enemies."

"I'm cold and tired and hungry. And judging by all the musclebound imbeciles promenading about, there isn't going to be a warm room available. I'll be damned if I have to sleep out in the streets."

"I've told you, you'll never have to sleep in the streets again. Not while I'm around, at least." Edris considered the people going here and there; many of them appeared to be adventurers. "Tell you what. I smell something good cooking. Go get a hot meal and relax while I nose around."

Brago sniffed the smoky air. "It's probably pork. By the gods, I hate pork."

"It's not pork," Edris told him. "I'd guess it's fish. We're within a day's ride of the sea. They have fresh fish here the likes of which you'll never find at home."

"Wonderful. Hopefully they also have some horses in this shithole. I'm not taking a rowboat anywhere anytime soon. And I am *not* going to walk all the way back to Bend."

"I'll check on the horses while I'm at it."

"Fine." Brago stomped toward a tavern.

"Don't drink too much," Edris called after him. "Okay? The last thing we need is trouble."

Brago lifted his middle finger as he entered the tavern. He slammed the door behind him.

Sighing, Edris surveyed the town.

"Another crappy village…"

"Beg your pardon?" an elderly man asked.

"Oh, nothing. I was repeating something my friend had said." Then Edris added before the man walked away, "I'm sorry, but is there a horse dealer in town?"

"Up two blocks, and right three. The stables are on the east end of town. Can't miss it."

"Much obliged."

Edris had taken no more than two steps when somebody yelled his name. He peered about. A group of burly men was leaving a dry goods store. Judging by their gear and swagger, they were all knights.

"You Edris?" the knight in the lead asked, plainly unhappy.

Edris examined the growing crowd. Two squires looked vaguely familiar, though he couldn't recall their names or whom they served. The lead knight bore the emblem of Eryn Mas on his tabard. Only he seemed angry.

"You hear me?" the knight asked. "Or are you deaf as well as stupid?"

"It's customary to announce yourself before making demands." Edris resumed heading toward the stables. "Talk to me when you've learned some manners."

A strong hand gripped his shoulder.

Edris turned as the knight threw a right hook at his jaw. Edris easily blocked the blow and countered with a short right to the man's nose. Blood gushing from his nostrils, he fell into the arms of the people behind him.

"Now," he said, stepping forward. "What's this all about?"

The knight straightened. "I'm Sir Harlan, nephew of Sir Howard!"

Edris recalled where he'd met the squires standing among the onlookers. "Rowan?" he said, pointing to the taller of the two. "And…Owen?"

"Oliver," the boy corrected. "Good to see you, Sir Edris. Congratulations on your win."

"Thank you. How is Sir Howard? Did he survive?"

"He survived!" Sir Harlan shouted. "No thanks to you, you murdering—"

"Glad to hear it," Edris said, cutting him off. "Now, if you'd all excuse me. I have business to attend to." He tipped his hat.

"Don't turn your back on me, you coward."

"Go have somebody look at that nose," Edris said, walking away. "You're bleeding everywhere."

Somebody chuckled.

Sir Harlan hollered, "I challenge you to a duel!"

An uneasy hush settled over the busy street.

Edris faced Sir Harlan, a palm resting on the pommel of one of his swords. Sir Harlan was older than he was by at least five years, but he was still young—perhaps in his early twenties—and he didn't give off the air of somebody terribly experienced in mortal combat.

"I don't want to hurt any more of your esteemed family," Edris told him.

Sir Harlan laughed. "How sweet. Didn't I say he was a coward, mates? He's nothing more than a big, baby-faced oaf who was given his knighthood because he was the last son of some lesser nobility."

This was a dangerous thing to say. Most knights were the last sons of lesser nobility, and many men in the crowd bristled.

Sir Harlan shouted again. "Coward!"

"I didn't say I *wouldn't* fight you," Edris said. "I merely said that I didn't want to hurt any more of your family. I feel bad for what happened to your uncle. He's a good man and a credit to our profession."

There was much nodding by the older knights.

Taking a step closer, Edris gave a polite—yet threatening—smile. "But if you call me a coward again, I'll feel no remorse in killing you."

Sir Harlan tightened his grip on his sword. "You're a coward!"

Edris shook his head, then inclined his chin toward one of the knights watching them. "Am I correct in assuming that I get to determine the type of weapons since I'm the challenged?"

"You are," the knight replied. "And the time and place of the confrontation."

"Very well." Edris strode to the middle of the street, now crammed with adventurers and townsfolk alike. He took off his pack and weapon belt and laid them aside. "I choose fists, and now."

"What?" Sir Harlan snorted. "You have to pick weapons. Don't you know the Code?"

"He is well within his right to select fists," said one of the knights behind him.

Sir Harlan drew his sword and shook it. "I want satisfaction!"

"I'm not going to kill a man for defending his family's honor," Edris told him. "I maimed your uncle. I don't deny it. But it wasn't my intent to do so."

"And it was two against one," the squire named Rowan said. "I was there."

"As was I," Oliver added.

"All I know is that my uncle is a cripple because of this…boy! And I plan on making him pay."

"Let me ask you this," Edris asked. "Do you have quarters here?"

"What?"

"A room? Do you have a room at the inn?"

"I have one in somebody's house."

"Very well." Edris dragged his foot in the dirt road, marking off the ring. "We'll fight for it. Best out of three falls. If you win, you can kill me. If I win, I get your room."

"You're making a mockery of my challenge!"

"Do you want to fight or not?"

Sir Harlan cast aside his cloak and weapon belt. "Rules?"

"Simple fair fight," Edris said. "No weapons other than fists."

"Fine. You got lucky with your first shot." He wiped away the blood flowing from his nose and stepped into the makeshift ring. "You won't get lucky a second time."

"Keep clear," somebody called. "Everybody back up. Give them room."

Edris watched Sir Harlan pull off his tabard and chainmail. Like most adventurers, he was an enormous man—well-muscled with thick arms and legs. But he didn't have Edris's height or reach. Also, Edris could tell by how his opponent held his hands that he was almost entirely right-handed. He'd wade across the ring, perhaps throw a left jab, then try to land a hard right to Edris's chin, just like he had before. The question was, how fast was he? Speed meant everything in fights. Power had its advantages, but if you couldn't land a blow, it was useless.

One of the older knights got between the combatants. He looked at each man and asked, "Ready?" Both fighters indicated they were. "Best out of three falls." He stepped away. "Commence!"

As Edris anticipated, Sir Harlan charged forward, his right hand cocked, his left up to protect his face. He faked a left jab, then attempted to throw a roundhouse right—but Edris was quicker. His blow landed square on Sir Harlan's already bloody nose, snapping his head back. Sir Harlan toppled, sprawling to the dirt.

"One!" the referee said, pointing to Edris. "Return to your corner."

Edris began to ask, "Which is my—?"

Snarling, Sir Harlan got to his feet and rushed across the ring. However, instead of throwing a punch, he threw a fistful of dirt. It caught Edris full in the face. He spat and tried to wipe his eyes, but that only made matters worse.

Blinded, Edris felt Sir Harlan grab his legs as he barreled into his midsection. Edris fell, hitting his head on the ground.

"One, one," somebody called.

"What?" Edris sat up, trying to see. "Foul! Foul!"

Something hit him in the mouth. Instinctively, Edris swept his right forearm in front of him, blocking the next blow. He then punched as hard as he could with his left. He hit whatever was in front of him.

"Foul!" Edris shouted again, unable to see. He tried to get to his feet but fell to one knee.

"Two, one. It's over!"

"What?" Edris spit dirt. "I was fouled! *Fouled!*"

He managed to stand.

"It's over," somebody said. "Stop! Clear the ring! Clear the ring!"

Flailing, Edris shoved the people jostling around him.

"Stop! Stop!"

Somebody thrust what felt to be a waterskin into Edris's hand. "Here."

He poured water over his face. Through burning eyes, he could see the squires Rowan and Oliver standing next to him.

"I said a fair fight! The bastard threw dirt! How the hell can anybody say he won? This is bullshit!"

"He didn't win." Rowan handed him his cloak. "You did."

Wiping his face, Edris peered over a group of men kneeling around Sir Harlan. He was lying prone in the road, blood dribbling from his mouth, his chest caved in.

"By the gods!"

"He's dead!"

A child gasped.

The knight who refereed the fight steered Edris along the street. "Let's get you a drink."

"Dead?" Edris repeated. "I didn't mean to kill him. I gave the bastard every opportunity to—"

"I know." They pushed through the crowd to the tavern, followed by a long line of other adventurers. "And he broke the rules."

"Exactly! The bastard had it coming."

The knight called to the bartender. "Barley! Bring us beer, and keep it coming."

"What the devil happened to you?" Brago asked from a corner table.

Edris sat with him, still wiping the dirt and water from his face. He spit the grit from his mouth. "I got into a fight."

The adventurers pulled up tables and chairs.

"That was the damnedest thing I've ever seen," one of them said, shaking his head. "You really couldn't see? I'm Sir Timothy, by the way."

Dozens of other knights and squires introduced themselves. Edris struggled to remember everybody through the deluge of names. Serving girls appeared, setting pitchers of beer and empty glasses on the cluster of tables.

"So, what happened?" Brago asked.

"Remember Sir Howard?" Edris asked.

Brago sipped his wine. "I'm afraid all of you knights look the same to me."

"He was the adventurer who tried to take the Sacred Scarab from me. The one who lost his hand."

"Is he here?" Brago asked, sitting up.

"No." Edris poured himself a glass of beer. "However, his blasted nephew was—Sir Harold or somebody."

"Sir Harlan," a knight corrected him.

"Right. *Harlan*. The bastard."

"And?" Brago persisted.

Edris took a drink of warm beer. The bartender must have watered it down, but he was happy to wash away the taste of dirt. He drained half his glass. "The ass comes out of a building, shouting my name, demanding that we duel."

"Duel?" Brago said, concerned. "I'm sorry I wasn't there."

Taking another long pull, Edris waved a hand. He gasped for air.

"So, I tell him that I'd fight him with fists, there in the streets. Best out of three falls. If I won, we'd get his room. If he won, I told him he could kill me."

"You shouldn't take people so lightly, Ed. You won't win every fight."

"I could tell I could take him."

"Perhaps. But go on. What happened next?"

The group of thirty or more men leaned closer, even though most of them had seen the entire affair.

"He comes in at me," Edris said, demonstrating, "right hand reaching back."

"Feint with his left?"

"Exactly! So, I slip a jab into his nose."

"Nearly flipped him over!" somebody in the crowd said.

A chorus of agreement bubbled around the packed tavern.

"And then what happened?" Brago asked.

"I'm up one fall to none and the bastard rushes me."

"Throws dirt in your face?"

"How'd you know?"

Brago motioned to the dirt still in Edris's hair.

"Right. I can't see a blasted thing. It's in my mouth. It's in my eyes. I can't breathe. And the bastard tackles me. He starts hitting me."

"You actually blocked one of his punches," said a knight who introduced himself as Sir Audley. "How did you do that, if you couldn't see?"

"He was right-handed," Edris explained. "If his first blow was with his right, his next one was going to be with his left. When you're on top of somebody, you try to get as many punches in as fast as you can, so you use both hands."

"So after he hit you…" another knight said, "you knew another one was coming from his left."

"Definitely." Edris drained his glass. Somebody reached over and refilled it for him.

"You blocked his left," Brago prompted. "Did you knee him in the groin?"

"No," Edris said. "I told him it was going to be a fair fight with only fists."

"He punched him in the chest," said a knight named Jost. "He was literally sitting on his ass in the road, and he punched the villain in the middle of his chest. Right to the heart."

"Crushed his rib cage!"

"I could hear the crack from half a block away."

"You should've seen him," one of the younger squires said, amazed. "If there really was a ring, he would've flown over the ropes."

"I've never witnessed anything like it. You were sitting on your ass!"

"I didn't think anybody could hit that hard."

Brago drained the last of his wine and stood up. "Well done, Ed. Where did the corpse reside? I call dibs on his bed."

Many in the crowd looked him as though he were crazy.

"I can take you to his room, sir," a local boy said. "I know where it is."

"Splendid." Brago hefted his dusty pack and made for the door. "Congratulations again. Your father finally got his wish."

The door opened and Edris bounded to his feet. Everybody turned to look at the man entering the tavern. It was one of the knights who had tried to take the Sacred Scarab from him.

"I don't want any more trouble," Edris shouted. "I didn't want to maim Sir Howard. And I didn't mean to kill his nephew. But if people push me—!"

Sir Tudor calmly lifted his hands. "I understand. Harlan wasn't acting in accordance with his family's wishes. There'll be no retribution. He wanted to make a name for himself and lost. End of story. Congratulations on your first win, by the way. It was impressive."

"Are you the same Edris who sent Sir Rodney's sword home to his father?" somebody asked.

"There's only one of me," Edris said grimly.

"There looks to be three or four of you!"

Everybody laughed, except Edris.

"If people want to fight me," he declared to the crowd, "I'll fight! However, I'm here to find a damned horn."

Many adventurers lifted their drinks. "Hear! Hear!"

Edris noticed Brago watching a vaguely familiar squire slipping out of the tavern. He called to him. "What are you doing?"

Brago winked. "Hunting." He followed the squire out into the street.

Sixty-Eight

Edris lay propped up on a rickety cot in the cobweb-infested attic of one of the houses not far from the center of town. The family's cat, an old black-and-white mangy thing, sat on his lap purring as he pet it.

The door to the tiny room opened.

"Brago!" Edris said. "Good to see you. I was hoping you'd find where I was."

"It's not too difficult to track you down," Brago said, closing the door. "You cast a rather large shadow." His nose crinkled. "It stinks of rotting wood and mildew up here."

Edris examined the ceiling. "Looks like the roof leaks. Good thing it isn't raining. Do you want to try to find someplace else?"

"I'm sure there is no place else." Brago nodded to the cat. "What's with the fleabag?"

"He came in when the landlady showed me the room." Edris picked up the miffed cat and stood. "My brother, Edros, loves cats. He's always bringing strays home. I love all animals, but dogs are far more useful."

"Dogs are stupid slaves to anybody with a bone. Cats, at least, can fend for themselves."

289

Edris lay on the floor and put the cat on his chest. It turned in a circle, then curled into a furry ball.

"What are you doing?" Brago asked.

"You called the bed."

"You're paying the rent."

"You deserve a good night's sleep. The bed's too small for me, anyway. Where have you been, by the way? I was expecting you to get here first."

Brago motioned to the pack and supplies piled in the corner. "The former occupant's?"

"Yeah. I looked through it, but there's nothing that'll help us find the horn. He kept a journal. That was good for a laugh. *Sunny day. Ate wild turkey for dinner.* Who writes about that kind of crap?"

Brago rummaged through the pack and withdrew a pouch of coins. He slipped it into his pocket. "Waste not, want not."

"You shouldn't do that. I'm sure his family will be in town soon to collect his things."

"And I'm sure they wouldn't mind payment for our troubles."

"As long as they don't want retribution."

"Make no mistake, Ed. People always want retribution. It's in our nature."

"You're probably right. Noble families rarely forgive an injury. I'll have to be more careful." Edris stroked the cat. "You never said where you were. You snuck out of the tavern pretty quickly. See a woman you fancied?"

"I leave that lecherous behavior to you adventurers. But to answer your question, I was busy solving one of our other problems."

"How so?"

"As you were basking in the limelight after your bout, I recognized a friend of ours."

"Who?"

Brago took an arrow from his pack and handed it to Edris. "Look familiar?"

"Yeah. It's what I pulled out of Bay. Why?"

Brago handed him another arrow. They were identical.

Edris sat up, disturbing the cat. "You found the bowman? Here? How?"

Brago tossed his pack into the corner and reclined on the musty cot. "As everybody in the tavern was reveling in your success, I observed that one of the patrons was scowling. He got up in a hurry, as though he wanted to let somebody know what'd happened. As he passed me, I spied his quiver."

"Bastard! Did you find out where he's staying?"

"I did indeed."

"Good. Let's go pay the horse killer a visit tomorrow. I'm going to crush his chest, too."

"No need."

"Why's that?"

Brago grinned.

"You killed him?" Edris gaped. "Brago!"

"Why are you upset? You were going to kill him tomorrow. I merely saved you the aggravation. Now your day is completely free. A thank-you would be appropriate."

Edris lowered his voice. "You can't just go around killing people."

"Says the man who caved in somebody's chest."

"That was different."

"How so?"

"There's a Code. There are rules."

"Codes and rules are for men big and strong enough to defend themselves when playing by them. Trust me, Ed, those rules don't protect those of us who can't swing a sword or punch through an oak tree. Somebody shoots an arrow at me and I kill them the way I see fit—that's my code."

"By the gods, Brago."

"Not by the gods, Ed. By *me*. If there were gods looking out for my interests, my life would be different."

"And you're fine with this?"

"Perfectly. Your bay has been avenged."

Edris shook his head in dismay. "Do you even know who he was?"

"I don't know. And I don't care. I only wish I'd been able to make him suffer. Alas, I had to act swiftly."

Edris groaned and lay on the floor.

Another death. The list of his potential enemies was growing. He was going to have to start watching every shadow.

"How did you do it?" he asked, trying not to sound as though he condoned Brago's actions. "Is anybody going to be able to trace it to you?"

"Doubtful. I was very discreet. It's one of the advantages of being a weakling. Nobody ever expects you to defend yourself."

"You're not a weakling. Few people could've survived on the streets for as long as you have."

"Thank you. I'm very proud of my survival. I hope it continues."

Edris stared at the rain-stained ceiling. He always knew Brago talked tough. Being a homeless orphan, he had to—his icy glares and bitter way of talking were what kept the thugs away. But he never thought he could actually *kill* somebody.

"How did you do it?" Edris asked again.

"I followed the villain to his room at the inn. Knocked on the door. And stabbed him in the heart when he answered. I took one of his arrows, then closed the door. Which reminds me, tomorrow we should check to see if his room is available. It had two beds and didn't stink of mold. Then again, it probably reeks of blood now. Still, it's more spacious than this place."

"Forget about the room," Edris said, still amazed at what Brago had done. "You're sure he's dead?"

"Quite."

"Gods, Brago!" Edris cried. "I can't believe you'd do such a thing!" He sighed. "Well, it'll be interesting to see how this plays out."

"Interesting indeed."

They fell silent, both listening to the purring cat.

"Are you angry with me, Ed?"

Edris considered Brago's question. "No," he said begrudgingly. "Like you said, I would've killed him when I got the chance."

"Would you've?"

The doubt in Brago's tone annoyed him. "Of course! I won't let somebody shoot at me and kill my horse without suffering the consequences."

"Glad to hear you're coming to your senses. You're playing games with people who have no regard for your life. You can't have any for theirs."

Sixty-Nine

The next day, Edris woke late, flashes of the fatal fight lingering in his sleepy mind as he stretched and yawned. Taking his time, he got dressed and made his way downstairs. Apparently learning that he'd killed somebody the night before, the woman of the house greeted him fretfully, bowing repeatedly as he passed.

Not liking to be thought of as a murderer, Edris smiled reassuringly and tipped his hat as he set off to find Brago. He found him lounging in a rocking chair on the front porch, his feet perched on the railing as though he were a cat who'd eaten a fat mouse.

"Morning, Ed," he said. "Or should I say afternoon?"

"It's still morning, judging by the sun," Edris grumbled, though he knew he was wrong. He noted Brago's smirk. "Hear something?"

"I did, indeed."

"Must be good news if you're making me work for it."

"Some things are best savored."

"Speaking of savoring, I'd like to get something to eat. Can this be discussed in public?"

"It can."

Brago followed Edris along the busy street. In addition to the many townsfolk going about their business, there were also companies of heavily armed guards present, evidently intent on keeping the peace should another duel break out.

"So, what happened?" Edris asked, getting annoyed. "Somebody find the horn?"

"Alas, no. At least not that I'm aware of."

"Then what?"

A cluster of knights appeared from around a corner. Sir Hans, the adventurer they'd met coming out of the hills south of Bend, lifted his hand in greeting. Edris returned the wave.

"It seems somebody's precious squire was killed last night," Brago said softly. "Nobody knows who did it...but the knight in question is offering five hundred gold pieces for the assassin. Think I should turn myself in?"

Edris lowered his voice as the knights approached. "Whose squire was he?"

"Have a guess."

"Brago, I'm not in the mood to—"

"Lads," Sir Hans said, walking up, "this is Sir Edris. He cares for horses, so I consider him a friend."

The knights around Sir Hans shook Edris's hand.

"I'm terribly sorry for your loss," one of them said.

"Loss?" Edris frowned. "I'm sorry, Sir..."

"Sir Conrad," the knight said. "We met yesterday. But there's no need to apologize. You met an army of admirers. It's impossible to remember us all, especially when you had other things on your mind. Allow me to reintroduce ourselves." He motioned to his right. "This is Sir Langdon..."

A distinguished-looking gentleman with flecks of grey in his hair bowed. "Congratulations on your victory last evening. I'm dreadfully sorry it has been marred in such an egregious manner."

"Egregious—?" Edris repeated.

Sir Conrad continued around the circle. "And these are Sir Flannery and Sir Adair,"

Both knights saluted.

"You were the referee," Edris said to the older of the two.

"I was, indeed," Sir Flannery said. "And I'll be telling my grandchildren about it, no doubt. I've been in this bloody business for twenty-three years. Been in seven duels myself and witnessed countless others. I've never seen anything like your performance. Never."

Sir Adair laughed in amazement. "When you selected fists as your weapon, I thought you were merely going to give him the thrashing he deserved."

"That was my intent," Edris said earnestly. "I didn't mean to kill him. I was only defending myself."

Four guards strode casually by, eyeing the assembly of knights standing in the middle of the dusty street. Satisfied no trouble was brewing, they resumed their patrol.

"Not to worry," Sir Adair said. "The fiend had it coming. Nobody blames you."

"Aye! He should've been shot right then and there for breaking the Code. Throwing dirt. Who'd do such a thing?"

"He's a disgrace to his parentage," concurred a short, dark man with shaggy black hair and a long beard tucked into his gold belt.

"And you are...?" Edris asked.

"This is Sir Kelby," Sir Conrad answered. "He's from Loc Haven."

Clicking his brightly polished boots together, Sir Kelby bowed low. "Duels with fists. I never heard of such a thing. It was, how you say in your language—a moment to recall."

"Actually..." Edris groaned. "I'm hoping to forget it."

The knights chuckled.

"Finally," Sir Conrad said, "you appear to remember Sir Hans."

"How's your son?" Edris asked. "I'm sorry. I forgot his name."

"Heinrich," Sir Hans replied, "and his disposition is as sour as ever. I suppose that'll only grow worse with your success."

"The only success I want is to win quests. I'd rather leave the dueling to people who have an actual argument."

"Well put. But I don't think you need to be concerned about another duel anytime soon."

The others voiced their agreement.

Edris tried to refocus the conversation. "I'm sorry, a couple of you mentioned something about an egregious—"

Somebody shouted from up the street. "Edris! You miserable son of a bitch!"

Markus charged through the crowd.

Edris put his hand on one of his swords, though Markus didn't appear to be armed. "What's wrong?"

"You know damned well what's wrong. I should kill you right here and now!"

"Will somebody please tell me what the hell is going on?" Edris demanded.

The other knights seemed as perplexed as he was.

Markus thrust a finger into Edris's chest. "You killed Jacob!"

"What?" the knights around them cried.

"You're mistaken, Markus," Sir Flannery said. "Sir Edris was with us all night."

"We walked with him to his quarters," Sir Adair said. "That was, what—? About midnight."

"Ja," Sir Kelby said. "At least. And your squire was killed before then, no?"

"It was him," Markus growled. "I know it!"

"Why would he kill your squire?" Sir Langdon asked. "You two are countrymen."

"And kin," Sir Hans added.

"He has his reason!"

Edris returned his cousin's cold stare. "Do I, Markus? What reasons are those?"

Markus spit and sputtered, his face burning bright red. "I should kill you right now. I have every right!"

"Then perhaps—" Brago said dryly from the edge of the group. "You'd like to challenge Sir Edris to a duel?"

Markus glowered at Brago. "Who is this?"

"He's my friend," Edris said. "He's been kind enough to act as my squire for the past few months."

"You should teach your squire how to mind his manners."

"And you should've taught yours how to shoot a bow," Brago replied.

Markus stiffened. Then, with forced bewilderment, he said, "I have no idea what you're talking about."

Brago winked at him. "I'm sure."

"This isn't over, Edris!" Markus said, stalking away. "I won't let this stand. Jacob *will* be avenged!"

Seventy

Standing among the group of knights and well-wishers, Edris watched Markus stomp down the street. "Perhaps," he said to Brago, "I should start wearing my chainmail."

"That'd be most advisable," Brago replied.

"What was that all about?" Sir Conrad asked. "Aren't you two related?"

"We are," Edris said, wondering how much he should reveal. "But too many adventurers in the family can create tension."

"Ah," Sir Conrad said, "that *does* explain it. You could say the same about too many carpenters or masons, I suppose."

"I've never heard of masons accusing each other of murder," Sir Flannery said doubtfully. "If you wish, I can help mediate the situation. I can vouch for the fact you were with us all night."

"As can I."

"Absolutely."

"You can count on us."

"Thank you, gentlemen," Edris said. "But I'm not sure that will help. Markus and I have a long history. Unfortunately, he'll always see me as his little cousin."

"I can't imagine he sees you as little," Sir Adair said.

They watched Markus storm into the inn.

"At any rate—" Sir Flannery held out his hand; Edris shook it. "—it's been a pleasure. Good luck on the quest. And watch yourself."

"Thank you," Edris said, shaking their hands. "Good luck to all of you."

The crowd of knights dissipated, leaving Edris and Brago standing by themselves.

A rider rode by.

"What now?" Brago asked.

"Now we find a horn."

"Ed...he's not going to let you be. You saw him. He's going to kill you."

"I'm not so sure. He didn't even have a sword."

"That's because he didn't want you to challenge him right then and there. Make no mistake, your cousin may talk about codes, but he does not live by them."

"I suppose you're right." Several townsfolk passed. "Think you can keep an eye on him? I want to make sure we know where he is."

"I can try. But what are you going to do?"

A young girl with a satchel draped over one shoulder walked up to them. She squinted at Edris as though interrogating a prisoner. "You that knight? The one who killed the other fella last night?"

"I'm afraid I am," Edris replied wearily.

"Is your name—" She selected a letter from her pack and read, "Sir Ed...Ed...ris. Sir Edris?"

"I am. What do you have for me?"

He reached eagerly for the letter, but she didn't give it to him.

"It'll be half a silver."

Edris pulled a fist of coins from his pocket. He counted out ten bronze, then ended up giving her a silver piece. "The rest is for you."

"Thanks." She handed him the letter, then produced two more. "These are for you, too."

Edris laughed. "I suppose you weren't going to give me those if I didn't give you a little extra."

The girl shrugged. "Assholes don't get much mail, if you know what I mean."

"I do, indeed, little lady." He gave her two more silver pieces. "You must be pretty smart to have this job."

"It's my brother's. He's sick, so I'm doing it for him. I can't read as well as he can, but I can manage."

"You must know a lot about this town."

"You want information about the horn?"

Edris laughed again. "Absolutely. Do you have any?"

She held out her hand. "One gold piece."

"A gold piece!" Brago growled.

"Its fine, Brago." Edris gave her a gold piece. "What do you know?"

She tucked the coin into her pack. "I don't know anything. But you might want to talk to Melville. He knows everything there is to know about the horn, but he'll cost you more than a gold piece, I can tell you that."

"Melville?" Somebody across the street waved to him. He waved back. "I've heard that name before. Where was it?"

The girl tutted. "You must not be very good at this if you don't know who Melville is. He met with all the adventurers, weeks ago. Charged ten gold per person. Still, I wouldn't want to be him no matter how much he got."

"Where's this Melville?" Brago asked, looming over her. "And don't even think about asking for more money."

She stuck out her tongue. "I'm not afraid of you!"

"Then, darling, you aren't nearly as smart as you believe you are."

"Brago," Edris said. "Let's be pleasant."

The girl pointed to a small, ill-kept shop. Several faded boards were hanging from its eaves.

"He's in there." Her eyes narrowed at Brago. "And you better be nice to him."

"We will." Edris handed her a few more coins. "Thanks for your help. If you come across any useful information, find me. Okay?"

"Mister, if I come across any information about where the horn is, I'll get it myself and give the damned thing to King Westley."

"I don't blame you. Thanks anyway."

Inspecting her other letters, the girl headed to the inn.

"It must be nice to be so stinkin' rich you can throw coins at every street urchin who crosses your path," Brago snapped. His expression twisted into embarrassment. "And I am well aware of the hypocrisy of my indignation!"

"Adventurers use kids all the time to collect information. She seems smarter than most."

Edris studied the shop, trying to deduce what Melville sold. The dirty window contained everything from pots and pans to swords and children's toys.

"I'm going to talk to this Melville and see what he knows. Go keep an eye on Markus. I want to know everything he does. And Brago—remember, he's the king's son. If he gets a knife in the chest, people will find his killer and burn him alive."

Seventy-One

A dented cowbell clanged over the door as Edris stepped into the small, stuffy shop. He looked about the chaotic shelves. Nothing in the store was worth buying. It appeared to be a collection of junk other people might have thrown away.

A man in his early thirties hobbled out of a storage room. His left foot hung limp and he used a crutch to get around; however, what Edris noticed first was the mass of white scars covering the side of his face and hand. He'd been severely burned.

The man with the crutch stopped when he saw Edris standing by the door.

"Are you Melville?" Edris asked.

"I am," the man replied. "And if you want to discuss Borin's Horn, it'll be ten gold for ten minutes."

"Ten gold?" Edris replied, trying not to stare at the man's disfigured face. "First, tell me who you are and why you'd know anything about the horn."

"You must be new to questing."

"This is my third quest," Edris found himself saying defensively.

"Then allow me to educate you." Melville took an hourglass from the counter and turned it over. Grains of sand fell from the top chamber to the empty one at the bottom. "I was Sir Royce's squire."

"That's right! I remember. I'm sorry. I couldn't place the name."

The shopkeeper held out a hand covered in burn marks. "Ten gold for nine and a half minutes."

Edris fished in his pocket, gave him ten gold coins, then realized he didn't know what to ask.

"You really *are* new at this, aren't you?" Melville hobbled over to a stool. "Perhaps you want to know whether Sir Royce actually found the horn…"

"Yes. Yes, that would be a good place to start." Edris pulled up another stool and sat in front of him. "Thank you."

"I can assure you he did. It was a long horn, about twelve feet long. It extended all the way to the ground, like the kind the mountain people use. It was made almost entirely of silver with gold bands. Sir Royce found it in a glacier in a valley not far from the High Pass in the Haegthorn Mountains. Despite what he would've told you, he found it by beggar's luck. Some of our supplies fell off our baggage pony into the valley below. When he went to retrieve them, he saw part of the horn sticking out of the snow. It took us a good two hours to dig it out. It was frozen and weighed more than a man. What else do you want to know?"

Edris eyed the sand trickling out of the hourglass, questions coming and going through his mind. He wished he would've been more prepared.

"I don't suppose," he said, "you know where it is."

Melville laughed like a man who hadn't heard a good joke in a very long time. "No, I'm afraid I don't. Otherwise, I wouldn't be living in this sty."

"What happened?" Edris motioned to his hand and face. "Did somebody do that to you?"

"That's what you want to talk about?"

"Sure."

Melville exhaled resignedly. "It's your money." He picked up his left leg and draped it over his right. "The leg is the fault of a young horse that wasn't broken in properly. Let me give you some advice that may be worth more than ten gold—always ride sturdy, dependable steads. Young horses might have speed and spirit. But you'll never go wrong with a well-trained horse who's been around a bit."

"A horse threw you?"

"He got spooked. Reared and fell on its side, crushing my leg."

Edris winced.

"That wasn't the worst of it," Melville went on. "The worst was lying on the ground, realizing the nearest town was a two days' ride away and my horse was gone. If a rancher hadn't come by a few hours later, I'd still be lying in that field…praying I'd die quicker."

"And the burns?"

Melville looked at his hand. "Cripples can't be squires, or knights, or soldiers…or much of anything, for that matter. I needed money for food and clothes. A friend of my father's was a blacksmith and he thought he could teach me a trade. I was still young and strong and could pound molten metal…" He trailed off as though thinking of the past. "I'll give you another piece of advice. Don't go around fire when you can barely walk."

"You fell?"

He nodded. "Right into the firepot. My hand outstretched." He regarded Edris. "You sure this is what you wanted to hear?"

"It's good to know something of the people around you. Besides, I have more money."

"Don't mind wasting your money on a cripple, is that it?"

"I don't mind giving money to people who need it."

This caught the shopkeeper off guard. "What's your name?"

"Sir Edris." Edris stood up and shook Melville's hand. His palm felt like blistered leather.

"Sir Edris, eh? I believe I've heard about you. Killed a man last night."

"Let's hope that's not all I'm known for."

"It's better than being known for being crushed by a horse or for falling into a forge."

"I bet."

Edris racked his brains trying to come up with a worthy question. Meanwhile, the sand continued to fall. Eventually, he gave up.

"Look," he said, ashamed, "I don't have a clue what I'm doing. I'd be grateful if you could tell me anything you might have told the others. Anything useful would be a big help."

"I think you're as clueless as everybody else, so don't worry so much. Most of questing is luck. And it sounds like you have a good deal of it, if you can kill a man with one punch while being blinded by dirt."

"Luck will only carry a person so far. I wish I were smarter."

Melville studied Edris, then turned the hourglass onto its side. He leaned forward. "This is what you need to know. One—Royce found the horn. Don't let people convince you otherwise. And two—he wasn't about to give it to the king, no matter how much gold he was offered."

"He didn't want Borin's family to get ahold of it?"

"Exactly. Their families loathed each other. It gave Royce no greater joy knowing he had something they dearly wanted."

"Did Royce really parade the horn through town? Or is that only a story?"

Melville laughed again. "You might appreciate this. You see, after we finally dug the blasted thing out of the snow, we had a devil of a time getting it home. It was huge, as I said, and when we strapped it to Royce's saddle, its weight pulled the horse to one side. The poor creature kept going in circles. It was infuriating. Eventually, we had to drag the damn thing behind us. But that didn't work either. It snagged every rock and root and we couldn't go faster than a walking pace."

"Must've been frustrating given that other adventurers were probably looking to take it from you."

"It was! And we couldn't hide it. It was too blasted big! So we kept to every country trail and deer path we could find. It took us three months to haul the thing from the mountains to here. Three months of constantly peering over our shoulders, worried that somebody would find out we had it." Melville chuckled. "Then we realized it came apart!"

"It came apart!"

"The gold bands were like nuts, holding the silver sections together. I think there were maybe seven or eight sections in total. When Royce realized it could be dissembled, he screamed to the heavens. Then he laughed for hours. Honestly, when we were lugging it home, he must've threatened to throw it into a lake or river a hundred times. He cursed the day he found it. I came close to smashing the thing to bits. Then we were told that it came apart!"

"Who told you it came apart?"

"Royce's younger half-brother, Roderick. We hid the horn in his quarry."

"Quarry?" Edris repeated, getting excited.

"I know what you're thinking, but I doubt it's still there. Half the town knew where it was. Remember, this was when we thought it was one solid piece of metal. He paid everybody to keep his secret. Then when Roderick realized it could be dismantled…"

"I bet that opened up a lot of other hiding spots."

"Absolutely. There are only a few places where you could conceal a giant horn."

"Why not bury it? Or throw it in a lake or river, like you said? Or the sea? The sea is only a couple days' ride away. He could've dropped it over the side of a boat and watched it sink to where nobody would ever get it."

"You didn't know Royce. He was stubborn, and in his way, immensely spiteful. He didn't want to destroy it or put it out of reach. He once said he was going to chop it into little pieces and send it to Borin's family bit by bit. That was his humor. He wanted to infuriate them for generations."

"So, he wanted it found someday?"

Melville dithered. "Certainly not while he was alive. His boasts about finding the horn nearly started a war. Our king personally begged Royce to turn it in. In the end, he told His Majesty that he didn't actually find it."

Edris thought for a moment.

"How many people know all of this?" he asked. "The other adventurers…do they know about the horn coming apart and how spiteful Royce was?"

"They know about Royce wanting to stick it to Borin's family. That's no secret. As for the horn coming apart…" He lifted a scarred hand. "As far as I know, only Royce, myself, and Roderick knew about that."

"And where's this Roderick? What happened to him?"

A twinkle appeared in Melville's eyes. "Ah! Now we're getting to the important stuff. Personally, I think it's the key to the whole endeavor. Maybe a year or so after we brought the horn home, he disappeared."

"Disappeared? What do you mean?"

"He up and left. Left his business. Left his possessions. He left town and was never seen or heard from again."

Seventy-Two

Edris roamed around Williamshire, rehashing everything he'd learned. To him, there were only two reasons why somebody would ride out of town, leaving all their possessions behind—either he was afraid for his life, or he had a better life ready someplace else. It was also possible he had taken the horn and was going to hide it for Sir Royce. The question was: where?

As Edris strolled, people came and congratulated him on his fight the night before. Many offered to buy him drinks. Others wanted to hear how he managed to win. All the while, a group of children followed him. Whether they were paid by other adventurers to gather information or were merely curious about "the killer," he didn't know; but he was painfully aware that at any moment, Markus could dart out of the crowd and stab him.

He was about to ask one of the children to run to his room and fetch his chainmail when he put his hand in his pocket. In addition to several coins, he found the letters the young girl had given him. His heart sank. He already felt like a failure. The last thing he needed was a letter from his father telling him he was one.

Edris glanced at the first envelope. The writing wasn't his father's. It was neat and almost feminine. He flipped through the others. They were all written by the same person.

Opening one, he extracted a cream-colored sheet of paper. It read: "Come home—PLEASE!" It was signed, "Beatrice."

Seventy-Three

"And then Markus rode out of town?" Edris asked.

He and Brago were in their room—Brago reading by the window, Edris struggling to put on his chainmail.

"Indeed. He was leading another horse, which I can only surmise belonged to that sweet young squire of his."

"I wonder what his play is."

"If I had to guess…" Brago said, turning a page, "he's devising a plan to cut out your heart."

Edris slid the chain shirt over his head. His father had it made after he'd been knighted, but he'd grown since then and it felt tight in the shoulders.

"That's what I'm thinking as well. Honestly, your crack about teaching his squire how to shoot was a dead giveaway. He's going to want retribution."

"Yes. Regrettably, holding my tongue is not one of my many attributes. I apologize." He turned another page. "By the way, what did your father want?"

"My father?" Edris asked, flexing his arms. The chain shirt pinched around his shoulders.

"He sent you three letters. He must have had some important insights on the quest or your character."

"Oh, those weren't from my father. They were from Bea."

"Letters from Beatrice?" Brago lowered his book. "What did she say? Is she all right?"

"She was rather cryptic." Edris moved his arms as though swinging a sword. "In the first letter, she said something had come up and she needed to speak with me as soon as possible."

He twisted. The polished rings went taut under his armpits. "The second letter said that she needed to talk with me about something very important and asked when I planned on returning home." Edris beheld himself in the mirror. "This isn't going to work. It's too small. Can you help me take this off?"

"And the third?" Brago asked, pulling the chainmail over Edris's head.

Edris threw it in his pack. "She just wrote: *Come home—please!*"

"What are you going to do?"

"What do you mean, what am I going to do? What can I do? I'm in the middle of a quest. I can't ride home because she wants to see how much I care for her. Besides, I left her enough money to get through the spring. She should be fine."

Brago's expression turned cold. "And how much do you care for her, Ed?"

Edris lowered himself to the floor and stretched out. He was about to tell Brago the truth—that he loved Beatrice but had no idea how things would end up. Then he remembered his father had used Brago to go find him when the quest was announced. He might also be using Brago to spy on him and Beatrice.

"She's merely another girl," Edris lied. "My father's worried we might get married or something, but he shouldn't be."

"Merely another girl?" Brago repeated.

"Well, not another girl," Edris admitted, aware that Brago and Beatrice were friends. "What I mean is…she and I—"

A great clamor erupted in the street.

Somebody shouted, "Fire! Fire!"

Hundreds of townsfolk and adventurers rushed outside.

Edris jumped to his feet.

Brago peered out the window. "Sadly, it isn't this building. It's several blocks over, toward the edge of town."

"Come on. Let's go man the buckets."

"Let this horrid little dung heap burn."

"Brago!"

"Perhaps we can find the horn in its ashes."

Edris jerked open the door. "Let's go. You're helping."

Sighing, Brago leisurely set his book aside. "As you wish."

They exited the boarding house and found a flood of people streaming to the south side of the town where a towering pillar of black smoke rose into the evening sky. Edris started to run with them, but Brago seized his arm.

"Tell me," he said, choking on the thick grey haze enveloping them, "if you found the horn and needed a diversion to get away—what would you do?"

"You think this is a diversion?"

They both peered northward. Nobody was headed that way.

"Get our gear and the horses!" Edris told Brago. "Then come find me!"

Edris sprinted along the street, pushing past everybody racing in the opposite direction. Many people called to him, but he kept running. Then, in the deserted north side, he found what he sought.

Two figures dashed about Sir Royce's statue, tying one end of a rope to the great stone horn, the other to a large wagon. The taller of the figures clambered into the wagon and urged the horses forward. For a moment, they struggled. Then, with a loud crack and a hail of shattered rock, the stone horn behind Sir Royce's statue broke free. Amidst the wreckage was the actual Horn of Borin.

Seventy-Four

Stepping from the shadows, Edris drew his two swords. "Sir Hans!"
The figures froze.

"Congratulations on finding the horn," Edris said, approaching. "But I'm afraid I'm going to have to ask for it."

Sir Hans swore. "I thought I was going to win this one. You can put your weapons away, Sir Edris. I'm certainly not going to fight you."

"But father!" Heinrich said. "There's two of us!"

"And we are greatly outmatched, Hein. The first rule of fighting is to do so only when you have a chance of winning. Always remember that."

"And I don't wish to fight," Edris said. "I just want the horn."

"How did you know we'd found it?" Sir Hans asked as Brago thundered toward them, leading Edris's horse.

"I had a hunch," Edris told them. "How did you realize it was in the statue?"

The older knight nodded to the remainder of the statue still standing in the middle of the road leading out of town. "The body and the pedestal are carved stone—marble, to be exact. The horn was plaster."

"Indicating Royce covered the original horn to make it appear part of the statue. Ingenious. I will let everybody know of your brilliance."

"No need to embellish," Sir Hans replied. "I value honesty as well as horses."

"Ed…" Brago began, "how the hell are we going to get this monstrosity out of here? As soon as we ride away, they're going to raise the alarm and every adventurer in town will be on our heels."

Judging from the son's defiant expression—that was exactly his plan.

"I have an idea." Edris motioned to Heinrich. "Put the horn in the wagon, if you please."

Heinrich didn't move.

"Do as you're told!" his father said. "They have the prize fair as fair. There's always next quest."

Cursing under his breath, the lad heaved one end of the horn into the wagon, then shoved the rest in.

"Thank you," Edris said. "And now your weapons."

Sir Hans unfastened his weapon belt and gave it to Sir Edris. Reluctantly, Heinrich did the same.

"You aren't going to send it to my father, are you?" The knight chuckled.

"Not at all. In fact, I'll be returning them shortly." Edris climbed into his saddle. "Now drive the wagon out of town. After we've gotten away, we'll release you to do as you like. That should give us a couple hours' head start on our pursuit."

"A couple hours won't mean a thing," Brago said. "A child could outrun a wagon like this. Perhaps we should deal with this matter another way."

"No, Brago. There's a Code."

"I've seen how these knights live by their precious Code. Once it doesn't suit their needs, they cast it aside like the women they bed."

"I'm not saying we won't attempt to reacquire the horn," Sir Hans told them. "But I'll do so honorably."

"Noted," Sir Edris said. "And thank you again for—"

Brago cut in. "We're wasting time."

On the other side of town, the smoke was clearing, and the cries of the bucket brigade were dying away.

"All right." Edris smacked the lead horse's flank. The wagon lurched forward into a slow roll. "Let's get out of here."

Seventy-Five

Unfortunately, Brago was correct. Even with four stout horses pulling, the wagon rattled along the rutted road barely as fast as a man could jog. Every time it struck a rock or a root in the darkness, the precious silver horn banged as if sounding an alarm. Going up hills was even worse. Several times, Edris had to dismount and push. Gradually, though, they put the smoke and lights of Williamshire far behind them.

After they'd gone nine miles, Edris told Sir Hans to stop the wagon by a stream. There, they let the horses drink their fill while they had the chance.

"You're free to go," Edris said, tying his horse to the rear of the wagon. He handed the knight and his son their packs and weapons. "Sorry again for taking the prize."

"No need to apologize," Sir Hans said. "It's all part of the game."

"Still, I don't enjoy feeling like a thief."

"Not at all." The older knight shook Edris's hand. "You've carried yourself admirably. Good luck to you. I'm guessing the hunt will be up with the sun."

Edris considered the stars shimmering overhead. Dawn was three hours away.

"I'll do what I can with the time I have."

"That's all you can do in life." Sir Hans saluted. "After this is over, I look forward to buying you a beer."

Edris snapped the reins. The wagon pitched forward. "I'll buy the first round!"

The wagon splashed across the stream and clamored up the opposite bank.

"We'll meet again, Edris!" Heinrich shouted, his fist raised.

His father cuffed the boy across the side of his head, but Edris laughed.

"I'm sure we will, Hein!" he called. "Until we do…ride to good fortune!"

For several miles, the wagon rumbled on, Brago often doubling back to make sure the knight and his son weren't following them.

"You know," he said, riding next to Edris. "There isn't a chance in hell we're going to get this thing to Upper Angle. I'm not sure why we're even trying. We should dig a hole and bury it, then return after the pursuit has ended."

Edris bounced on his bench as the wagon hit another stone. "That's a good idea. But I think I have a better plan. Let's stop where the road passes that grove."

"Why? What will happen there?"

"I'll show you."

As they drew closer to the clump of maple trees, Edris reined the horses to a halt. He scrambled into the wagon's bed.

"Now what?" Brago asked, watching Edris wrestle with the horn. "Going to hide it in the woods?"

"Maybe." Edris pounded the horn against the wagon bed and then resumed twisting. There was a sudden snap as part of the horn gave way. "We might win this quest yet!"

"It comes apart?"

"Not only does it come apart…" Edris said, unscrewing another section, "but it looks like all the pieces can be placed inside each other."

"Making it easier to hide."

"Much!" Edris twisted off another segment of the horn. "This is what I want you to do. Go into those thickets and ride your horse around. Make it look like somebody has been camped in there. Then stampede the wagon's horses in different directions."

"Ed, you're inspired. I am sorry I ever doubted you."

Edris laughed. "We're not home yet. But I believe we might be able to kill two birds with one horn. Hurry up. We need to make everything look convincing."

Within an hour after sunrise, Edris could hear the riders coming. Then, moments later, he saw them, thundering toward him. There must have been forty adventurers in all, plus their squires. Swords drawn, they swarmed around Edris and Brago, sitting patiently on their horses.

"I hate to disappoint all of you," Edris said loudly over the pounding hooves. "But Markus got to it first." He pointed up the road. "He went that way."

Several adventurers set off immediately, galloping madly in the direction Edris had indicated. Others searched the woods, making sure the horn wasn't hidden inside.

"How come you're not in the hunt?" Sir Conrad asked.

Edris gave a well-rehearsed sigh. "We've spent the better part of the night recovering the horses he stampeded. Believe me, we plan on giving chase shortly."

Sir Hans and Heinrich rode up. Heinrich beamed with pleasure.

"Alas," Sir Hans said to Edris, "I was afraid you wouldn't make it far. How much of a head start does Markus have?"

"Two hours," Edris said. "Not more."

"Why didn't he take the wagon?" Sir Conrad asked.

"It's too slow." Then thinking quickly, he added, "He tied the horn to another horse. It was listing to one side under its weight. He won't go far like that."

Sir Hans chuckled. "He should've learned from Sir Royce!"

"He's not one for learning, I'm afraid. Now, if you gentlemen don't mind, I have a cousin to overtake."

For most of the morning, Edris and Brago rode with a group of adventurers, in hot pursuit of the imaginary Markus. Each time the road forked or intersected with other roads, the adventurers split up—some going one way, others going another. When tracks led cross-country to a distant farmhouse, a good many adventurer raced through the fields, searching for clues as to Markus's whereabouts. By sunset, Edris and Brago were by themselves.

"You're lucky they didn't check your pack," Brago said as they rode leisurely along.

To their right, a hamlet came into view through the trees, budding with new leaves. Smoke from chimneys rose into the blue sky. They could smell somebody's dinner cooking.

"I took a gamble that nobody else knew the horn came apart."

"Would you have fought them if they had?"

Edris thought about this.

"No," he said. "I would've run. Remember, they raced out of town and had been galloping for a couple hours. Our horses were well-rested and watered."

"I never thought you'd ever advocate running over fighting."

"Like Sir Hans said, only fight when you have a chance of winning. I couldn't have fought all of them at once. I'm not Barton the Black."

Their horses clomped along, the early spring breeze bringing with it the hint of growing things.

"I take it we're not headed directly to Upper Angle," Brago said.

"Not directly. I think we should pretend to search around for Markus for a few weeks, then gradually make our way northward."

"And if we come across your cousin? Will you fight or run?"

Evert

"Let's focus on one battle at a time."

Seventy-Six

Edris paced the royal receiving hall waiting for King Michael. He and Brago had taken their time returning to Upper Angle, often resting for days in whatever town they stumbled across. Here and there, they came across adventurers hunting for the horn. Some questioned Edris about how Markus took it from him. Most appeared to doubt the young knight had ever acquired it. But none suspected the Horn of Borin was hidden in his pack.

The doors to the receiving hall opened, revealing King Michael and a bodyguard.

"Sir Edris!" The joy in the king's face faded to bewilderment as he glanced about the empty hall. "I was under the impression you brought me another present."

"Your Highness." Edris bowed. "I do have something for you."

He untied the top of his pack.

"It's in there?" the king asked. "What did you do? Cut it up?"

"Not exactly, sir." Edris pulled out the disassembled horn. "It comes apart." He screwed two pieces together. "See?"

"Clever! I thought it was one long piece. I heard Sir Royce had a devil of a time getting it from the mountains to Williamshire." He leaned forward, examining how the sections fit together. He pointed to drawings scratched into the silver. "What are those?"

"It would appear Sir Royce made some alterations to the horn's original design."

The king squinted closer. "Is that…?"

"Yes," Edris said. "It's a picture of Sir Borin having sex with a goat."

The king chortled. "Who would've thought the goat would be on top like that?"

Edris fitted another section together. "You should see how he decorated the mouthpiece. I'm not sure anybody will want to blow it again."

"Two quests in a row." The king marveled. "You're a credit to the kingdom and the family. Well done!"

"Speaking of family," Edris said uneasily. "How's Markus?"

"He has yet to return; however, I'm sure he'll turn up as soon as I announce you've completed the quest."

Edris screwed together another section of the horn, this one illustrated with numerous goats having sex with Sir Borin.

"Sir," he said, wondering whether he should say what was on his mind. "I think you should know Markus and I got into a little…altercation in Williamshire."

"Look, Eddie," the king said, unconcerned. "As a father, I might be blind to some of my children's faults. But as a king, I see more clearly. I understand Markus is going to be jealous of your success. He's very proud and doesn't wish to share the adoration of our people. But I'm sure the two of you can work it out."

"Yes, sir."

A knowing expression crept over the king's face. "I also don't want you to feel as though you have to take me into consideration in these matters. You and Markus are family, but you're also competitors. The rules of the games allow you to take what the other has. Provided that you both act in accordance with the Code of Honor adventurers are sworn to uphold, you never have to worry about me. When Markus is here, in my halls, he is my son. When he straps on a sword and searches for the-gods-only-know-what, he's an adventurer. Never confuse the two."

"Yes, sir." Edris hesitated, then said, "This altercation was over his squire."

"Jacob?"

"Yes, sir. You see, somebody killed him, and Markus believes it was me. There's no truth to this. In fact, I was drinking with a tavern full of knights when it happened. They can all vouch for me."

"Did these knights vouch for you in front of Markus?"

"Yes, sir. Sir Hans, Sir Conrad…" Edris struggled to remember all of the knights' names. "They all told Markus in no uncertain terms that I was with them when Jacob was murdered."

"And Markus didn't believe them."

"No, sir."

"I see. You're worried about some sort of retribution."

"I'd want it if the tables were reversed."

The king nodded solemnly. "I'll take care of Markus. I'll host a formal inquiry and invite the knights you mentioned. We'll get this all cleared up. You two will be friends again before you know it."

"Thank you, sir."

Edris fitted together the last piece of the horn.

"Sir Royce did that?" Grimacing, the king inspected the mouthpiece. "He wasn't much of an artist, but he certainly got his point across."

Seventy-Seven

King Michael offered to throw Edris a celebratory dinner honoring the young knight's second official win, but Edris declined. He'd been away for the better part of five months and was eager to see Beatrice.

A couple weeks earlier, he'd sent her a letter from Lower Angle. But he had to keep his wording ambiguous for fear another adventurer might read it. So he simply said that he missed her and would return as soon as he found "that blasted horn." He also sent her a poem he'd written about willow trees.

Riding into Bend, Edris stopped and picked a bouquet of tulips and crocuses growing by the road. He then raced to the small brick house he'd purchased for Beatrice and her family. Jogging up to the door, he knocked a little more enthusiastically than what would've been considered polite.

The door popped opened to reveal Beatrice's elderly father.

"Eddie," he said, his annoyance changing to surprise. "Or should I say Sir Edris?" He gave as much of a bow as his age would allow.

"It's always Eddie to you, sir." Edris gazed past the old man, hoping to see his daughter in the room behind him. Instead, he noticed a bunch of new furniture and expensive wall hangings. "Is Bea home?"

The old man appeared stunned, then apprehensive. "Didn't you get her letters?"

"Yes, sir. I got them. Well, I got three of them. Why? What's wrong? Is she okay?"

"I don't know how many she sent, but there were definitely more than three." He looked up at Edris, girding himself for something unpleasant. "She's not here, Eddie. She got married a few weeks ago."

"M—married?" Edris gasped. "To whom?"

"To a very nice gentleman. I believe you know him—Lord Braverton?"

"Lord…Braverton?" Edris repeated, trying to exhale. "Bea married Lord Braverton?"

"Yes. Your father introduced them, in fact. He said you'd be happy for her."

Suddenly everything felt cold. Edris looked around for something to sit on, but ended up leaning against the door, blinking.

"His Highness courted Beatrice for a couple months," her father went on. "Then he asked my permission for her hand. I said yes, of course. A complete gentleman he was. Came here and everything. He even offered me and Beatrice's mother a house in his fiefdom. But I didn't want to travel so far, so he gave us enough money to get along here without her. She says she'll come home regularly, but with children—"

"Children!" Edris's chest grew heavy.

"Yes. They plan on having children straight away. He was particularly interested in knowing that I'm one of seven boys. Apparently, he has daughters from a previous marriage and he—"

"My father," Edris said, trying to stay upright. "When…when did he introduce Bea to Braverton? Do you remember the day?"

"Not exactly," Beatrice's father replied, confused. "It was in November. Early November, if I remember. You had just left."

"I'd just left?"

"Yes. Beatrice was all mopey and sad, and that's when Lord Elros came by."

Edris gritted his teeth. "Father!"

Not waiting to hear more, Edris sprang onto his horse and raced to his father's manor. By the time he arrived, it was well after midnight. He galloped past the guards shouting their congratulations and rode to the front door of the main house. He stormed in, searching for his father. He found him drinking brandy in his study.

"Edris!" His father got to his feet and came forward, arms outstretched. "Congratulations on—"

Edris's fist rocked his head back, blood and snot flying into the air. The Lord of Bend fell against his desk, scattering piles of papers to the floor.

Lord Elros drew a hand under his nose, looked at the blood, then his son.

"I suppose," he said evenly, "this has something to do with that woman."

"You had no right interfering!" Edris shouted.

"Why? Because you loved her?" his father asked mockingly.

"Absolutely!"

"You don't know what love is! Love is mourning your loss—even years after she's dead. Love is being with only *one* woman, no matter how many whores throw themselves at you. Love is giving up everything for the woman you want to spend the rest of your life with."

"I would've—!"

"No, you wouldn't. You had all the opportunities in the world to be with her, and you chose to be an adventurer."

"That's because of you!"

"Because of me?" his father repeated. "You're the one who went to the king and begged to be knighted. You're the one who chose questing over the military. Had you done what I told you, things would've turned out differently. The king's brat would be dead, and you would've distinguished yourself as a military hero. And yes, you might have even had a beautiful peasant for a wife."

Breathing hard, Edris was about to ask if he would've approved of the marriage, but he knew that his father would say "yes"—if only to torment him.

"Where were you when she needed you?" his father went on. "Hmm? Where were you, Ed? She needed you and you were out playing your games."

"I gave her money! I bought her a house!"

"Money and a house? Is that what you think women want?" Lord Elros found a handkerchief and pressed it to his bleeding nose. "Women want security. They want to know they'll be safe and protected and will never starve. They want to be held and loved."

"I—!"

"You did nothing but treat her like your own personal whore."

Edris sucked in air.

Lord Elros smiled. "Do you know who came to Bend a couple weeks ago?" he asked. "The king's god-damned son. And guess who he was looking for? It wasn't you."

"Markus was looking for Bea?"

"That's right," his father said, gloating. "And what do you think he was going to do to her? Who was going to protect her? Not you. Not the great Sir Edris. You were off playing adventurer. She needed you and you weren't there. I gave her somebody who would take care of her. I gave her wealth and security. By the gods, Ed. Think! She went from being one step above being a homeless harlot to a lady of standing. Her son will be a lord. You should be thanking me!"

"Thanking you?" Edris hollered. "You didn't do this to help her. You never do anything to help anybody but yourself! You did this to keep us apart, so I'd focus on winning!"

"Either way, I did what was best. Now—" He pointed at the door. "—get the hell out. You're no longer my son. You're a worthless sack of shit who will never win another quest. You're nothing without me. Do you hear me? You're nothing but a big, soft loser who won't even protect the people who matter to him."

Epilogue

Edris sat on the edge of his bed at the Crooked River, Bend's only inn.

He had his horse, his swords, a few sets of clothes, his pack, chainmail that didn't fit, and the remainder of the six hundred gold that the king had given him for finding the Horn of Borin—but that was it. He was officially disowned. He was alone.

He put his face in his hands, his father's words spinning in his tired head.

You were off playing adventurer. She needed you and you weren't there.

On the table next to his bed, the lantern flame bobbed and danced.

His father was right. He wasn't there. He had Beatrice's letters for weeks before he finally got around to replying. He got so wrapped up in the adventure, he didn't want to think about anything else.

Come home—PLEASE!

Those were the last words she ever sent him.

Could he have stopped the wedding?

Maybe Bea wanted to marry Braverton. After all, like his father said, she was now a lady of standing. And she'd never have any wants or needs that wouldn't go fulfilled. Her children would be noble.

Children…

The thought of Beatrice sleeping with Braverton made Edris want to vomit—and cry.

What was he going to do? Should he go talk to her? Should he fight for her?

Edris peered through the window at the sleeping town. A block over from the inn stood the small brick house he'd purchased for Beatrice and her family.

Maybe he should've gotten her something bigger and nicer.

No. His father was right about that as well. Bea didn't want money or dresses, or big houses. She wanted to feel safe and loved. And, for a time, she wanted him…even if he was only a poor farmer.

What had he done?

He thought about his brothers. Would they adhere to their father's wishes and shun him? Probably in public. But he couldn't imagine Edros or Edran completely abandoning him. Edran was the lord-in-waiting. He'd have to do what their father wished—or else. But even he would eventually send word once he learned what had happened. Perhaps they would intervene and convince his father—

There was a tender tapping on his door.

Edris straightened, wondering if he was hearing things.

The tapping resumed.

Edris heaved himself off the bed.

"Bea?"

Wiping away his tears, he opened the door.

A glint of steel flashed, then pain sliced across his right ribs.

Crying out, Edris staggered. "Son of a bitch!" He clutched his side. Blood seeped between his fingers.

Markus tottered into the room, reeking of alcohol. He pointed a bloody dagger at Edris. "You!"

Edris considered diving for his swords leaning against the wall but thought better of it.

"Put the dagger away, Markus."

"You killed Jacob!" he said, his watery eyes going in and out of focus.

Edris retreated, leaving a trail of blood on the floor.

"No, I didn't. And that's the truth. I have witnesses who'll—"

"Liars!" Swaying, Markus took an uneasy step forward. "They're all so enamored with the great Sir Edris. The youngest knight in history! The youngest knight to win a quest! Won his first quest!" He spit at Edris's feet. "You're not so big. You're not so tough. I could've killed you scores of times."

He stumbled toward Edris.

Edris thought about grabbing the lantern and throwing it, but that might burn the entire inn down, killing everybody else staying there.

"You're not so special," Markus went on. "I'm the son of a king. You're the son of a mean, spiteful drunk."

Edris winced as he inhaled, pain shooting through his rib cage. Perhaps if he kept Markus talking, somebody would pass by the still-open door.

"Regrettably," he said, sounding lighthearted, "my father disowned me earlier this evening."

Markus's grin turned sinister. "So, he won't put up a fuss when I gut you like a pig."

He lunged, but Edris dodged the blow. He threw a hard-right jab into Markus's face. Reeling, Markus dropped his dagger, his teeth awash in blood.

"Go home, Markus," Edris ordered. "Go sleep this off."

"Home." Markus teetered. "You know what they're talking about there? You! You fighting Kriton. You winning two quests in a row." He drooled blood. "Even my sister keeps talking about how big and handsome you are. So, help me…if you ever get near her…"

"You'll win the next quest. You'll see."

Markus smiled. With the lantern light flickering across his pale face, he looked like a drunken ghoul.

"Yes, I will. But first…" He snatched one of Edris's swords. "I have something else to do." He pulled the sword from its scabbard. "Beg for your life, Fatty Eddie."

Gasping in pain, Edris picked up Markus's dagger. "The only begging I'm going to do is for you to go to bed. Things will look better in the morning."

Markus swung the sword, missing Edris's neck by a foot.

Holding his side, Edris bounded toward the door. But Markus blocked his path.

"Will Jacob be alive in the morning?" He swung again, drawing closer to his target. "Will my father be talking about me?"

"What do you think your father will say when he learns you murdered me?"

"He liked Jacob. He'll understand."

Markus swung again. Edris ducked.

"I spoke with your father about Jacob." Edris moved to his right. He grabbed a wooden chair. "He's going to have an inquiry."

"Inquiry?" Markus snorted. "Fat lot of good that'll do. There was an inquiry after Raaf's death as well."

He brought the sword down. Using the chair as a shield, Edris blocked the blow, then drove forward, his shoulder barreling into Markus's chest.

Tangled together, they fell to the floor, Edris on top. He wrenched the sword from Markus's grasp and cast it clattering out of reach.

"Get off me!" Markus's fists flailed, but his blows were wild and without power. "Get off! I'm the king's son!"

Edris pinned his arms. "You need to let this go. I didn't kill him."

Tiring, Markus lay under Edris, breathing hard.

"I wish I would've stabbed you in your god-damned heart like you did Jacob. I should've killed you. Next time I will. Next time…next time I won't just kill your fucking horse. Next time…"

Markus closed his eyes and stopped struggling, his breaths becoming shallow and even.

Edris stood and stared at him as he lay unconscious at his feet.

He'd admitted to setting the ambush in the hills. He also admitted he was never going to let him be. Markus might sober up. He might pretend to have forgotten about their many confrontations. He might even pretend to be Edris's friend. But sooner or later, he'd do more damage than a cut across the ribs.

Quietly, Edris closed the door to his room. He regarded the bloody dagger in his hand, then set it aside. Kneeling, he cradled his cousin's head.

"I'm sorry," he whispered. "I won't let there be a next time."

With a loud crack, he snapped Markus's neck.

The End

Dear Reader,

Thank you very much for reading *The Sword of Betrayal*.

If you've enjoyed it, please tell your friends! Every e-mail, post, tweet, and review helps ensure that Edris's adventures continue. Further, if you have any comments or suggestions on how to improve these stories, I'd love to hear from you.

Thanks again for taking the time to read my work.

Ride to good fortune!

Robert Evert
Robert.Evert.Author@gmail.com

Dedication

I'd like to dedicate this book to me. That's right—me! Not to my wife. Not to my kids. Not to my dogs or my eleventh grade English teacher. My wife hates fantasy and thinks it's pointless. My kids are too busy looking at their damned cell phones to notice I'm around. My dogs are tearing up my yard and peeing on the rugs. And Ms. Heiten told me that I'd never be a writer. Screw them all. The bastards. This one was for me!